Manuel Vázquez Montalbán lives in Barcelona where he was born in 1939. He is a journalist, novelist and creator of Pepe Carvalho, a fast-living, gourmet private detective. Montalbán has won both the Spanish Planeta Prize and French Grand Prix of Detective Fiction for his thrillers, which are translated into all major languages.

OFF SIDE

Manuel Vázquez Montalbán

Translated by Ed Emery

Library of Congress Catalog, Card Number: 00–109823

A catalogue record for this book can be obtained
from the British Library on request

The right of Manuel Vázquez Montalbán to be identified
as author of this work has been asserted by him in accordance
with the Copyright, Designs and Patents Act 1988

First published in 1988 as *El Delantero centro fue
asesinado al atardecer* by Editorial Planeta, S.A.,
Barcelona

Copyright © 1988 by Manuel Vázquez Montalbán
Translation © 1996 by Ed Emery

First published in 1996 by
Serpent's Tail, 4 Blackstock Mews, London N4 2BT
www.serpentstail.com

First published in this 5-star edition in 2001

Phototypeset in ITC Century by Intype London Ltd
Printed in Great Britain by Mackays of Chatham, plc

10 9 8 7 6 5 4 3 2 1

The universal hero myth, for example, always refers to a powerful man or God-man who vanquishes evil in the form of dragons, serpents, demons and so on, and who liberates his people from destruction and death. The narration or ritual repetition of sacred texts and ceremonies, and the worship of such a figure with dances, music, hymns, prayers and sacrifices, grip the audience with numinous emotions (as with magic spells) and exalt the individual to an identification with the hero.

C. G. Jung
Man and His Symbols

The room still smelt of medicine, or whatever it was, she thought irritatedly, and her nose became a kind of mobile proboscis as she tried to identify the source of the offending aroma. I don't like my house smelling like that. A decent house doesn't smell like that. She made the bed and flicked through the sports magazines that were lying round the room. The pockets of her lodger's suits offered no enlightenment. Nor did his underwear, where it lay tidily arranged in the chest of drawers. The flashing of the neon sign of her boarding house threw into chiaroscuro the torment which was evident on Doña Concha's face. The light found her irritated and perplexed, while the dark sank her into deep suspicion. He's probably on drugs. That's all we need. There's enough shit in this barrio already. But he hadn't looked the drugs type. In fact she'd taken him for a clean-living sort of person, because he seemed to have his feet on the ground, always kept himself clean and tidy, and was always polite to her. From the room next door she had listened, worriedly, to the sound of the water drumming against his body as he took repeated showers, day after day. She thought this rather inconsiderate of him. If all her lodgers insisted on being that clean, she might as well shut up shop, for the cost of the water bills alone. She went out onto the balcony to strip the dead leaves off her geraniums, to caress her favourite ivy in its pot, and to contemplate the flashing sign which she had bought three months previously, and which confirmed her as the owner of this small business for which she had struggled a whole lifetime. 'Set me up with a boarding house, Pablito. Set me up with a boarding house, because you won't always find my breasts so attractive, and when you don't I'll need something to provide for me in my old age.' This idea of planning for her old age had made Pablito laugh, but he turned it over in his mind, until the day when the asthma got the better of him and he left her the money just as he was more or less at death's door. She crossed herself and murmured a bit of the Lord's Prayer in homage to the most considerate lover she had ever had. 'I miss you, Pablito! I miss you!' But she didn't really miss Pablito. Not if she was honest with herself. She didn't miss him at all, and it was quite enough to have had to put up with his elephantine weight for the best part of twenty years, although at the same time the thought of him being dead and all on his own in his coffin, was capable of invoking in her a wave of pity and a flood of tears. From the balcony she contemplated her surroundings, darkened by the oncoming dusk, and the irreversible shadows of the area's decrepit buildings. Three bars, complete with prostitutes, an ancient dairy, two boarding houses, half a dozen staircases peopled with the old, and Arabs and Senegalese Africans and all sorts. Houses which had been defeated by old age and then abandoned and forgotten. She would have preferred to set up her boarding house in Ensanche, but Pablito also had to provide for his family, and felt he'd done quite enough in leaving her the money to set herself up with these two floors on calle de San Rafael. The lawyer who had dealt with the will was a randy old goat. He stared cheerfully down her cleavage as he opined that she should be grateful to señor Pau Safon and that he'd been a gent of the old school.

'I've not heard of anyone leaving their lover this kind of money since before the Eucharistic Congress.'

Groups of men up from the country and Barcelona men in their fifties emerged from the shades of dusk and took substantive form as they dawdled undecidedly in front of the prostitute bars. The men. You take them by their cocks, and you can do what you like with them. But these days there's no control on anything. You get these dirty little junkies out on the street, and they end up giving you some lethal disease. Like that dirty little slut who spends her time up and down calle de San Rafael, offering the men a 'literary screw'.

'What do you say to them, child?'

'What's it to you?'

'I was just wondering.'

'I ask them if they want a literary screw.'

'And what's that supposed to mean?'

'Something out of the ordinary. I know what it means.'

'But how are they supposed to know, child. They're all up from the country, or off building sites. From Matadepera, or Santa Coloma. The way you say it makes it sound as if you learnt your trade in a library.'

There she was, again. Marta, her name. She had tried tidying up her unwashed hair and putting lipstick on her lips and eye-shadow around a pair of eyes that suddenly turned black and ferocious. Doña Concha felt sorry for her, partly because she had the drug habit to deal with, and partly because she always had that slimy little shit of a pimp watching her from round some corner. Every now and then the girl would raise her head in the direction of the balcony of the Pensión Conchi, pretending to be irritated by the flashing of the neon sign, but actually in order to catch Doña Concha's eye as she leaned over the veranda. Then she would come up for the sardine or mortadella sandwich and the coffee which Doña Concha was happy to supply any time she asked.

'Come up for a coffee and a bite to eat, any time you want. In my house there's always a coffee and a bite to eat for decent people . . .'

It hurt her to see this girl having to sell her wares in faulty English to wandering sailors. One time she had been badly beaten by a drunkard, because he'd thought she'd been making fun of him when she asked: 'Excuse me, sir, could I interest you in the prospect of fondling a pair of small breasts with two big nipples like teenage heroines used to have in novels of the 1950s?'

And the man had hit her. Twice, and then twice again, and then again. And her pimp came running out of a doorway, screaming hysterically, with a penknife in one hand, the sort that people used to use for sharpening pencils. Doña Concha came down into the street, and cursed the drunkard to kingdom come. She called him everything that a woman can call a drunk to bring him to heel: bastard, filthy sod, son of a bitch, and fascist. It was the 'fascist' which had most disconcerted and intimidated him. Like a defeated army he promptly retreated. Even though he was drunk, he hadn't lost his sense of the times he lived in, and these were democratic times. That was the night that had seen the start of the sardine sandwiches and the milky coffees.

'If you don't eat something, you won't even have the strength to take your drugs.'

This was a convincing argument. As the girl downed her coffee, Doña Concha summoned up the confidence to ask: 'Tell me something. Do you feel anything when a man's on top of you?'

'It depends how stoned I am. If I'm stoned, it's all the same to me. And if I'm not, it's like having an enema.'

'What do you know about enemas, child? In my day

they used to give you an enema, and how, if you weren't careful.'

'They gave me one when I was on a drug-rehab course, because I got constipated.'

'What a way to earn a living . . . ! I started out on the streets, until I got to know Pablito — and a couple of others too, because Pablito on his own wouldn't have given me enough to live on. And then, well, you open your legs and let them get on with it, but you have to show a bit of interest, because when a man senses that a woman's bored he stops feeling like a man, and bang goes your customer. I bet you've never had the same man come back to you twice.'

'I don't remember, and I don't really care.'

So there she was, poor cow, forever waiting. Worried about Marçal, the scrawny pimp whose weight she carried like an exercise in penance, half asleep in some doorway, still high on his last dose. One day they would find him dead in a toilet somewhere, with a syringe hanging out of his arm. Doña Concha crossed herself, and just as she kissed her two crossed fingers she saw her lodger appear down the street. He was a good-looking sort, that he was. A bit bow-legged, and a tendency to lean forward, as if he was trying to sniff something, or see better, or simply as his way of warning that he was about to arrive. But there was no menace in his strong body. Rather, a sense of self-restraint, of an ability to keep his capacity for movement under control, to know his own weight and volume, like a man who knows his own character and destiny. He walked past the girl in the street, and smiled when she threw her proposition in front of him like somebody throwing a bucket of water at the feet of a passerby. Doña Concha backed off, stroked her ivy, locked the veranda door, made sure she hadn't left his room untidy, and emerged into the corridor to sit in her rocking chair in front of the colour TV. Professor Perich appeared on the screen just at the moment that her lodger appeared in the doorway. The man greeted her with a slight bow of his head and a smile, which she returned with a generous welcoming gesture. He retired to his room, and she went back to her day's principal pleasure, the homespun philosophy of Professor Perich.

'The worst thing that can happen to a diver is when he gets a cold.'

The thought of this had her choking with laughter, but her mind was still on her lodger, and she spent a moment puzzling out suitable excuses to confront him for an explanation of the strange medicinal smells. In the end she hit on a strategy, left her rocking chair rocking, and reconfigured her face into the smiling solicitude of the perfect landlady. She stood before his closed bedroom door and knocked.

'Don Alberto? Am I disturbing you, Don Alberto?'

The door opened, and the man seemed to be both supported by and supportive of the door frame, with well-formed muscles showing under a white shirt which turned alternately red and white with the flashing of the neon sign outside.

'Am I disturbing you, Don Alberto?'

'No, no, not at all.'

He had a nice smile, and Doña Concha's eyelids fluttered in a reflex action which, according to old-timers in the area, she had inherited from her Aunt Amparo, who had been a chorus girl with Tina Jarque before the Civil War.

'I was a bit hesitant about bothering you. The thing is, I thought I smelt gas. Silly of me, really. How could I have smelt gas, since the shower heater is electric? But I did smell something, so I thought I'd better knock, just in case something had happened to you.'

As she was speaking she noted that the smell wasn't just in the room. It was actually emanating from the man's body, with an invisible but tangible substantiality.

'It smells like . . . medicine . . . or something . . .'

The man raised his arms to take a sniff, and then laughed lightly.

'Yes, señora, I suppose it does. It's the smell of liniment.'

Doña Concha's eyes opened in surprise.

'Liniment? I've known the smell of Sloan's Liniment all my life, and it's nothing like that.'

'This isn't Sloan's Liniment. It's one that I got into the habit of using in Mexico. It doesn't bother me, but I can see that it might bother others. Sorry about that . . .'

'Anyway, why do you use so much liniment? Do you have a hernia, or something?'

'No. No. I go out running. I go training . . .'

Doña Concha's lips maintained a broad smile, but her brain was harbouring suspicions. What kind of training could possibly need so much liniment?

'I'm a footballer.'

'A footballer?'

Her reaction was half incredulity and half confirmation of what she had heard. Then, later, while the girl was finishing her sardine sandwich and coffee, the lodger hurried out into the night again, as if not wanting to be seen. It suited Doña Concha not to publicize the fact that she was harbouring prostitutes in her kitchen, so she let him go, pursuing him only with a look that was full of secret doubts.

'Tell me something. Do you think a man can be a footballer once he's past the age of thirty?'

'I don't see why not.'

'With all the money they earn, why would a footballer want to come and live in an area like this?'

'How should I know?'

Her literary protégée was having a bad night. She seemed to have no appetite as she nibbled at her sandwich and slouched in the plastic chair, with her legs apart and wearing a pair of tights that were too loose for her. There's nothing so pitiful as the sight of a women in loose-fitting tights, Doña Concha thought, and she averted her gaze from the wretched sight.

'Because you have usurped the function of the gods who, in another age, guided the conduct of men, without bringing supernatural consolation, but simply the therapy of the most irrational of cries: the centre forward will be killed at dusk.

'Because you use your centre forward to make yourselves feel like gods who can manage victories and defeats, from the comfortable throne of minor Caesars: the centre forward will be killed at dusk.

'Because dusk is the hour at which the bio-rhythms of enthusiasm drop, and death and the death rattle resound like a music which is awesome and mournful: the centre forward will be killed at dusk.'

Carvalho finished reading the letter, and raised his eyes to look at the slow-moving, serious young man who had been sitting in his office for the last half hour, with his legs crossed effortlessly, as if they were made to caress each other every once in a while as he periodically changed position. The movements of his arms were equally light and elegant — that's the word, Carvalho thought, as he tried to find an aesthetic quality to complement the simple sensual impression of lightness. Elegant. And modern. Judging by his hair-style and the casual alpaca clothing, the young PR man for the most powerful football club in Barcelona (and in Catalonia, and the world) was there to create an impression — namely that the club's new board of directors represented a new spirit, a far cry from the air of make-do, improvisation and pre-modernity which had characterized the previous management.

'Which centre forward is it referring to?'

The young man arched one eyebrow and composed a smile of benign perplexity.

'Don't you read the papers?'

'No. Ever since I stopped needing to wrap sandwiches, I no longer buy newspapers.'

'Don't you watch television either?'

'It sends me to sleep. I do my best, but I always seem to end up nodding off. Maybe I'm getting old.'

'I'll make it easy for you. The whole world is talking about our club's latest signing. The outgoing board left us with a team that wasn't really up to it. You could say it was burnt out. So we have been working to rebuild it, and what we needed was a star, a major international figure, who would restore the public's confidence in us. We signed Jack Mortimer. The Golden Boot.'

'Is that a metaphor?'

'No. It's a prize. For the best footballer in Europe.'

'They give him a gold boot? Solid gold?'

The visitor wasn't a man who lost patience easily, but he had no great pedagogic vocation either, so he pursued his explanation no further and waited for Carvalho to take the conversational initiative.

'Why would they want to kill a centre forward who cost such a lot of money? Competition?'

'I don't imagine that anyone's actually planning to kill our centre forward. He's probably got something else in mind which he hasn't yet communicated to us. Maybe we're just dealing with the kind of person who's got a thing about famous people. Like the man who killed John Lennon.'

'But I presume that you get hundreds of letters like

this, and just ignore them. So why have you decided to take this one seriously?'

'The first thing we did was to notify the police. We asked them to be very discreet, because of the possible knock-on effect that something like this could have on a club with more than a hundred thousand members and a social expectation involving millions. The police moved behind the scenes, and they told us that it was worth taking this letter seriously. They'd had word from their informants that something was afoot. The police are continuing their inquiries, but they're having to move very carefully. The club has decided that you should also be brought onto the case, in parallel with the police. You'll be able to move less conspicuously than the police.'

'Your club's very much in the news. You've got a hundred journalists at the gates every day waiting for scraps of news. How are you going to hide the fact that I'm involved?'

'I'm glad you asked that.'

'I'm glad too, and I'm glad that you're glad.'

Something approaching a melancholic smile blurred the seriousness on the face of this fastidious messenger.

'We'll have to collaborate very closely. We could end up being friends.'

If he'd had anything in his mouth, Carvalho would have choked on it. But he had nothing, so he choked on nothing. He fell silent and looked bemused.

'I'll be acting as your go-between. It wouldn't do for the journalists to see you having a direct relationship with the club's board. We'll need to find some kind of pretext for you to be moving around the club.'

'Are you a footballing PR man by vocation?'

'If you're going to use the word "vocation" in its proper meaning, you should only apply it to jobs where God is involved. Priests, for example. Or monks. The gods send out a call, and the person in question feels that he has a vocation. Are you a private detective by vocation?'

'I'll need some kind of card or document, something to authorize me to move around on the club's premises.'

'Are you interested in psychology?'

'I find all branches of human knowledge interesting. Take grammar, for example . . .'

'Do you think you can pass for a psychologist?'

'Absolutely the best profession for passing yourself off as something.'

He tossed an envelope onto the desk and waited while Carvalho opened it, took out a sheet of the club's headed notepaper and read what was on it.

'So I'm now authorized to conduct a study on "The Application of Group Psychology in Sporting Organizations".'

'That piece of paper will enable you to talk to anyone connected with our club without raising suspicion.'

This elegant man seemed to take pleasure from leaving things on Carvalho's desk, and this time it was a visiting card which he produced from a very expensive leather wallet like a priest taking the host from the chalice. 'Alfons Camps O'Shea, Public Relations'. Carvalho read the card, and then took another look at its bearer. There was a pleasing correlation between the name and the physical appearance of this young man who was in the process of rearranging his legs and regaining the vertical. He was evidently about to leave.

'Have a think about it. We know your rates, and we have no problems from that point of view.'

'Who says you know my rates? I don't have fixed rates. How about you pay me what you pay your centre forward?'

'Are you a centre forward?'

'As good as. I'm the "Golden Boot" of my profession.'

Camps O'Shea took in the entire contents of the office with one glance, which he then transferred to Carvalho as if to say that he had completed his inventory.

'It doesn't look that way.'

'Don't you worry about that. The rest of the world doesn't need to know. We'll keep it between you and me. I'll draw up a pro forma and a plan of action.'

The man buttoned his alpaca jacket and adjusted it around his anatomy with the same suaveness that characterized his discourse and probably his entire life. He had an air of luxury about him. As he reached the door he was checked momentarily by Carvalho inquiring: 'I imagine you must be pretty keen on football?'

The PR man turned round and calculated the effect that his answer might provoke.

'As a sport, I find it rather stupid and ordinary. But as a sociological phenomenon I find it fascinating.'

So saying, he left, without giving himself time to hear Carvalho muttering to himself: 'A sociologist. That's all we need.'

Carvalho brooded over the questions that he should have asked and hadn't, but his musings were interrupted by the arrival of Biscuter, laden down with every kind of shopping imaginable. He was panting and puffing and each puff ruffled the few long red hairs remaining on his balding head.

'That staircase is going to be the death of me, boss.'

'You look like you've bought up half the market.'

'The fridge was empty, boss, and I prefer to do it all in one trip ... Those stairs'll be the death of me ... I've bought some *cap-i-pota*, and I'm going to make you some *farcellets* of *cap-i-pota* with truffles and prawns. Don't worry, though, I'll make it nice and light. Not too greasy. Mind you, I reckon the human body needs a bit of grease every once in a while. Otherwise it starts squeaking like

a rusty hinge. Then I'll do you some figs *à la Syrienne*.
Stuffed with nuts and cooked in orange juice. Low calorie.
Instead of sugar I'll use honey.'

'You're reading too much, Biscuter.'

'You should take a look at the *Enciclopaedia Gastron-
omica*. I've been buying it in instalments. It's incredible,
the things that people dream up. Who do you reckon it
was who first thought of stuffing figs with nuts and cooking them in orange juice?'

'A Syrian, I suppose.'

As the video came to an end the lights came on. There
was a buzz of comment and small-talk, and the darkness
gave way to a fervour of words and gestures. Behind the
presidential table sat the club's directors, headed by
the chairman, Basté de Linyola, and in the centre,
illuminated like a particularly pampered pet, sat Jack
Mortimer, the golden-haired golden boy, with a face that
was all smiles and freckles. The proceedings were opened
by the club's PR chief, Camps O'Shea, who reminded the
journalists of the reasons for the press conference. He
blinked slightly under the harsh lights of the various TV
channels which were there to record the moment of the
public presentation of a newly signed footballer. Camps
O'Shea then informed them that he would be translating
for Mortimer.

'He's been doing a crash course in Spanish, but he's a
bit shy about his conversational abilities, particularly
when he's in the lion's den with the likes of you,
gentlemen.'

His attempt to break the ice was rewarded with a ripple
of appreciative laughter, and from within the ripple the
first questions began to emerge.

'Will he be learning Catalan as well?'

'Of course! També! També!'

Mortimer contrived to answer partly in Catalan when the question was translated to him, and thereby won himself another ripple of laughter and a round of applause.

'How do you feel about signing for such a powerful club?'

'What do you make of the fact that English footballers have never been a great success in Europe?'

'Are you aware of the social and symbolic importance of the club that you have signed for?'

'Do you expect to maintain your English average of thirty goals a year?'

'Do you prefer to wait for the ball to come to you, or do you prefer to go out and get it?'

'Mortimer, you were married a short while ago, and now you're expecting a baby. Will you call it Jordi if it's a boy? Or Núria if it's a girl?'

This time Camps did not translate the question, but offered the reply himself.

'Señor Mortimer may well decide to choose a Catalan name, but that doesn't mean that it has to be Núria or Jordi. There are other names.'

'Such as . . . ?'

'Montserrat and Dídac, for example.'

'All right, then. Will you call the child Dídac or Montserrat?'

'I said that they *could* be called Montserrat or Dídac, but they could equally well be called Núria and Jordi, or Pepet and Maria Salud, or Xifré, or Mercè . . .'

Some of the journalists were beginning to show impatience with this process of onomastic accretion, and Mortimer sat by, puzzled but none the less smiling, as they proceeded to choose names for children that he didn't even have yet.

'Señor Mortimer, have you tried *pan con tomate*?'

Camps O'Shea patiently described to Mortimer the composition of *pan con tomate alla catalana*: bread, oil, tomato and salt.

'Is that all?'

'Yes, that's all.'

Mortimer gave the matter some thought, and announced without great enthusiasm that he would make sure to incorporate *pan con tomate* into his diet at the earliest opportunity. Then he added, with the ponderous determination of a novice linguist: 'Me gusta mucho la paella.'

'Do you prefer Catalan paella, or Valencian paella?'

Camps O'Shea asked the journalist to explain the difference between Catalan paella and Valencian paella, and the journalist said that it had been a joke. Camps gave him a poker-faced look and continued: 'Are there any more questions?'

'Mortimer, are you one of those centre forwards who go out looking for the ball, or do you prefer to stay in your area?'

When this had been translated, Mortimer pondered for a moment and replied: 'A good centre forward should almost never come out of his area.'

Camps O'Shea got up, to indicate that the press conference was at an end. The press photographers flashed away as if their lives depended on it. Camps ushered Mortimer into another room, followed by the club's directors, with the club chairman, Basté de Linyola, at their head. Once the photographers and the journalists were gone, Mortimer lost his aura as the god of the stadium. Now he looked like a young lad who had ended up in the wrong room by mistake. Especially when you put him next to Basté de Linyola, a businessman and ex-politician who had transformed the club's presidency into a position of ultimate social significance. He had been on the point of becoming, variously, a minister in the Spanish government, a councillor in the autonomous government of Catalonia, and mayor of Barcelona. At sixty years of age he had suddenly discovered tiredness, and a fear that this tiredness would cause him to disappear from the public stage that he had occupied continuously ever since he had become the great white hope of the progressive business community under Franco. The chairmanship of this football club was his last position before retiring, but he had converted it into a hot seat, and he was a man who loved power as the only antidote to his own self-destruction. By the age of sixty, either you have power or you commit suicide — this was what he told himself every morning as he stood in front of the mirror which reflected back unpityingly the tired face of that other being who was growing inside him, and who would eventually turn into his worst enemy. The idea of taking up this presidency after a long period in which the club had been run by uncouth and uncultivated businessmen had struck him as a worthwhile task, to which he brought his qualifications as an engineer and a master in fine arts at the University of Boston, a cultural schizophrenia which had provided him with a few entries for his CV.

'Now that we're here, this club is coming home,' he had said in his first address as club chairman. And the sentiment was well received, as was his observation that the club was not just a club but was the symbolic army of Catalonia.

Now he permitted himself a closer look at Mortimer. He felt both curiosity and a certain populist tenderness towards him. The lad could have been one of his factory workers in Valles, one of those young workers who excited his poetic sense of himself as an enlightened businessman, and who stirred in him the envy that every cultured rich man feels in the face of young men with promise.

His English was better than Mortimer's, a provocation
that would have enraged the learned professor of Shaw's
Pygmalion, and as the golden boy of European football
became aware of this fact, he suddenly became reticent,
as if he was speaking with some superior being who stood
for the bosses and all they represented. Basté de Linyola
passed him a box and told him to open it. In the box were
the keys of three-hundred square metres of apartment
located in a residential area of the city close to the club's
ground, where Mortimer would be able to house and raise
his family during the four years of his contract with the
club. Thereupon the club's vice-chairman, the young
banker Riutort who had connections with Arab investors
and Japanese microchip manufacturers, handed him
another box, in which there shone with almost indecent
brightness the keys of the Porsche that Mortimer had
requested as one of the terms of his contract. The entire
board broke into applause, and Basté de Linyola decided
that it was the responsibility of his PR man to utter the
banalities which the act required. Camps O'Shea spoke
up accordingly: 'Mortimer, may we welcome you as one
more citizen of our city of Barcelona.'

The young footballer was happy, and caressed the car
keys as if somehow expecting the vehicle to appear mir-
aculously in the room. Somebody opened a bottle of *cava*,
and a waiter dutifully poured it. This gave Basté de
Linyola his cue for a toast. He had a complete mental
collection of toasts which he had tried for size that morning before leaving home. He was particularly proud of
the one which he had pronounced on the occasion of the
homage which Barcelona's up-and-coming entrepreneurs
had offered to Juan Carlos when he was still a princeling
in the shadow of General Franco.

'Your Highness, in these bubbles you see the impatience
of a people waiting to make the leap to modernity.'

The toast that he'd made to the president of the reconstituted Generalitat wasn't bad either, on the occasion of his elevation to the post of president of the Chamber of Industry and Commerce.

'Sir, *cava* is our symbol. It has been necessary to give it a new name, but for us it is still what it always was.'

Basté de Linyola's toasts were much appreciated among the so-called political classes, and there were some who suggested that they might reflect the presence of a certain well-known writer as a regular guest on his yacht. Basté de Linyola was aware of this calumny, and cultivated it, in the same way that he secretly wrote pieces for the theatre and composed small items of classical music which he would play in the loneliness of his study, with the voluptuousness of a person buried alive, who knows the hour and the day of his resurrection. But this time he sensed that a simpler toast was required — not least when he looked at Mortimer's smiling, freckled face, poised and eager to absorb the strange sounds that were about to fall from the lips of his club's chairman.

'Mortimer, we hope you're going to score many goals. Behind every goal you score stands a whole city's desire for victory.'

Camps O'Shea took advantage of the ensuing applause to lean in Mortimer's direction and translate what the chairman had said. The footballer nodded with a determined affirmation that some might have found excessive, and his enthusiasm was slightly at odds with the rest of the hall, because by now people were inventing excuses for having to leave. Basté de Linyola himself was the first to move, having first instructed his PR man to be sure not to abandon their new purchase.

'The first few days are important, Camps. Until his wife arrives, you're even going to have to make his bed for him.'

The chairman glanced momentarily at a silent man with a drink in one hand, leaning against a wall poster depicting some important moment in the club's history, and then redirected his gaze to Camps O'Shea.

'Is that him?'

'Yes.'

'Don't you think it's a bit risky having him here?'

'Nobody seems bothered by him. He's our psychologist.'

'Well, let's hope we never need a psychiatrist!'

Camps watched as the chairman left, accompanied by the two remaining directors; then he took Mortimer by the arm.

'I know a place where they do an excellent paella. I've reserved a table.'

'Can we go in the Porsche?'

'Of course. And a friend of mine will be coming too.'

Carvalho abandoned his stance of drooping weariness and fell in behind the footballer and the PR man. He mentally cursed himself for having accepted the job. The prospect of having to share a paella with a spoilt kid and a naive freckled Englishman filled him with foreboding.

No. She hadn't left a forwarding address.

A fleeting narrowing of the eyes betrayed the man's irritation, and disarmed the porter's reluctance to continue a conversation which he had accepted unwillingly in the first place. At first he had decided that he was a sales rep, but when he registered that he wasn't carrying anything with him he had listened more or less inattentively to his questions regarding Inma Sánchez, the tenant on the second floor, and her son. The man had to drag the negatives out of him one by one. She wasn't living there any more. No, she hadn't left on her own. She could hardly have gone off on her own, seeing that she didn't live alone. The boy had gone with them too.

'No. She didn't leave a forwarding address.'

The conversation was at an end, but since he sensed a great sadness weighing on the shoulders of the man before him, he lowered his guard and momentarily abandoned his role as porter in a semi-de-luxe house in a semi-high-class part of town, halfway between Ensanche and the slopes of Tibidabo, with a service lift for flats that had no servants, and parking places for tenants who couldn't necessarily afford cars.

'Was the kid OK?'

'He seemed to be, seeing the way he was going down the stairs four at a time.'

'Four at a time?'

Something told the porter that he needed to give a better impression of the boy.

'He's a good lad. Well brought-up, too.'

'Well brought-up . . .'

The moistness which seemed to appear in the man's eyes was countered immediately by a straightening of his back in an attempt to recover a vertebral condition which sentiment had eroded. He adopted a pose that was almost athletic. He took his wallet out of his back trouser pocket, and from it produced a photograph which he showed to the porter.

'Has he changed much?'

The porter took his glasses out of the top pocket of his uniform jacket and examined the photograph carefully. It showed the good-looking woman from the second floor, her son, and the man with whom he was now talking. As he looked at the photograph, a flash of a half-remembered image passed before his eyes.

'I've seen you somewhere before. On TV, maybe . . . ?'

'Not these days.'

'But you used to be. I'm sure I've seen you on television.'

'I used to be, years ago, once in a while. Has the lad changed much?'

'A lot. He's a teenager now. In this photo he must be seven or eight years old, but he must be thirteen or fourteen by now. Is he your son?'

'Yes.'

'And why would I have seen you on TV?'

'I used to play football.'

'Ballarín!' the porter shouted, as if he'd suddenly hit the jackpot. 'You're Ballarín!'

'Palacín.'

'That's it. Palacín. Well, I was close. Amazing — who'd have thought that I'd run into Palacín today! Now, I tell you what . . . I remember your surname, but not your first name.'

'Alberto. Alberto Palacín.'

'Jesus! Palacín! They don't make centre forwards like you nowadays! Centre forwards these days are rubbish. You don't get players like you, going right up to the goal area and driving it in, straight past the goalkeeper . . . What are you doing nowadays? I suppose you're retired and living off rent. Or is it business?'

'Business, really. Not rent.'

'Well, that's good. You deserved a break after what happened . . . What was it, now . . . ? You were injured, that's it. That animal, what was his name . . . ?'

'What does it matter?'

'What do you mean, what does it matter? The bastard had it in for you. I remember it like it was yesterday. They showed it on TV. In those days I only had a black-and-white set, but when I remember it I see it in technicolour. By the time he'd finished with you, your knee looked like raw meat. What was it the doctors said . . . ?'

Reaching into the recesses of his memory he produced the answer to his own question: 'Fracture of the meniscus, and a tearing of the internal ligament and the front right ligament.'

'A bastard, that. Like having to buy yourself another leg.'

'That's right. Like having to buy yourself another leg.'

The porter cast a critical eye over his leg.

'You don't seem to have a limp, though.'

'I don't limp.'

'That was bad luck, that was. You'd be making a packet by now. You were making good money, but not like they make nowadays. They're all millionaires, but half of them are nothing to write home about. They only play when they feel like it, and if they don't feel like it they run off and hide behind the ref or behind the goalposts. Have you seen that Butragueño play? He looks like an orphan ... And what about Lineker ... A joke ...! And this one they've signed now — it's like taking lambs to the slaughter. The kind of thugs you get in Spanish football these days will teach him a thing or two. In no time at all he'll be wanting to hang up his boots.'

'They're good players. They're all very good.'

'But there's no one like you.'

'No, that's not true.'

'No one, Ballarín, no one!'

The porter took him by one arm to emphasize the point. He took another look at the photograph, and was clearly full of sympathy and willing to help.

'A hell of a girl, you had there. She didn't leave a forwarding address, but you could try asking at the beauty parlour on the corner. The lady spent a lot of time there. It's very well equipped — they've got everything, a gymnasium, a sauna, a hairdresser's ... I'm sure they'll be able to help you.'

As Palacín left, the porter called him back.

'You wouldn't happen to have a photo you could sign for me . . . ?'

Palacín smiled, and then shrugged to indicate that he couldn't oblige.

'I haven't carried photos of myself for years. I used to, in Mexico, but here . . .'

'That's a shame. My grandson would love one. He's got a signed photo of Carrasco.'

Now that Palacín was alone again, he walked down a pavement that was almost deserted, in the shade of trees that had too much September about them. The trees were young, in the same way that the area was young, and the plants hanging off people's balconies, too. Fifty yards down the road was a sign for the 'Beautiful People' beauty parlour, but the watch on his wrist was signalling an urgency of which only he was aware. At any rate, he knew what he'd be doing with his free time the following day, in this city where he now felt such a stranger.

The worst of it had been the taste of reused frying oil which had provided the base for a paella apparently cooked by a gastronomical natural scientist with a mania for combining every botanical and zoological possibility imaginable together into one single dish. Apart from *foie gras*, the paella contained just about everything you could think of, and each species left in his mouth the aftertaste of its death-throes before sinking down to let itself be drowned in his gastric juices. Mortimer was still absorbed in anthropological research, and he ate the paella as if he was consuming the soul of his new country of adoption. Camps barely touched his, maintaining an air of distant reserve, like an English major in the Falklands. Carvalho took advantage of Mortimer's ecstasy to ask him a few questions appropriate to his new-found status as a sports psychologist.

'Do people see you as a superstar in England?'

'Yes, more or less.'

'Were there protests from the public when you decided to sign for a foreign club?'

'No. No. We have a lot of centre forwards in England, and my club did a good deal. The club is a limited company, and the proceeds from my signing will keep them out of the red for a while.'

'Has anyone ever tried blackmailing you?'

'No.'

'Have you ever had threatening letters? Or phone calls?'

'Only one time, when we reached the cup final, against Manchester. Sometimes you get threats from lunatics. But then nothing happens. The fans tend to fight it out on the terraces, and they leave the players in peace.'

'Have you encountered any particular hostility from members of other teams?'

'Off the pitch, not at all. One season I had a bit of a feud with a Liverpool midfield player . . . But these days, every time we have a run-in, it's a kind of a nod and a wink situation. We're professionals. Football's our bread and butter. The dangerous players are the younger ones, because they're in a hurry to make their mark, and the older ones, because they want to show that they're still up to it. There's nothing more dangerous than an ageing midfield player. I got an elbow in the face once, and ended up with a broken cheekbone.' At this point Mortimer got up, in the middle of what was a rather expensive Barceloneta restaurant, and invited Carvalho to participate in an action replay. 'You jump. Jump as if you're about to head a ball.'

Camps half closed his eyes as if urging him to play along, but Carvalho limited himself to getting up and resting his hands on the tablecloth. Mortimer closed in on him, leapt up as if to head off an imaginary football, and lashed out with his left elbow in the direction of Carvalho's head.

'You see? You could end up knocked unconscious and the ref wouldn't even notice. Elbows are the worst, because a kick usually leaves a mark, but refs don't tend to notice elbows. Or when somebody nuts you. There was a Spurs centre back who had a head like iron, and if he nutted you you'd end up out for the count.'

He was obviously intending to do a demonstration head-butt on either Carvalho or Camps, but they both sank back into their seats to deny him the opportunity.

'I'll eat paella every day,' Mortimer promised himself, and he inquired of Camps O'Shea whether it was possible to buy frozen paellas, because Dorothy wasn't too hot on cooking.

'She likes cakes — people in England like cakes — but she doesn't like cooking.'

'Have you been married for long?'

'A year.'

'Isn't your wife going to get very bored in a city that she doesn't know?'

'Dorothy never gets bored. She's been working as a buyer for Marks and Spencer's, but she's into birdwatching in her spare time. She wants to make a list of all the birds in Barcelona. I told her that there are a lot of birds in Barcelona. I saw a lot of birds on the Ramblas.'

'It's a market. They're in cages. They're not native birds.'

Camps moved to temper this discouraging piece of information: 'Don't worry. We have uncaged birds too. If that's what Dorothy likes, she'll find no shortage of birds.'

'I hope so. She does my accounts, too. She's got a good head for figures. Not like me. My business is football. I know where a ball's going to land simply by the shape that the kick takes. It's instinctive. The English papers used to say that I could always tell where a ball's going to end up.'

'Remarkable,' said Carvalho and Camps simultaneously, but each with a difference of nuance which Mortimer was not in a position to identify.

The PR man took advantage of the footballer's need to go to the toilet, to ask Carvalho's impression.

'Not a lot to him. A bit simple, I would say.'

'He has the ingenuousness of all young animals. He hasn't taken too many knocks, yet.'

'As regards our particular field of interest, it seems he

hasn't brought any enemies with him. These anonymous letters are obviously locally produced, designed to produce a local effect.'

'I'm not saying that we should pay them too much attention, but we should still be careful. It could be some lunatic who will give up after a week or two. On the other hand, if he's looking for publicity he might carry on until he gets found out.'

'There are crazy people around who kill their idols.'

'In the United States, maybe. When Europeans get mythomania, they're usually more civilized about it. But you should take a good sniff around, just in case.'

'I'm not going to get much more out of this young man. And one paella's more than enough for me.'

'Didn't you enjoy the paella?'

'No. Rice is a very delicate creature, señor Camps. It looks as if you can do anything you like with it, but it has a very sensitive soul. It's not like the potato, or Italian pasta, although these too are simple vehicles with a volume and texture that carry all kinds of flavours. Rice either has to have an underlying flavour of its own, or its flavour has to be unobtrusive so that it can take in other flavours. For this reason it can only be cooked together with things that have a common paternity. When you combine it with meat and fish, you have to use white rice, and boil it on its own. Then you strain it, and then you can put it with other things that have been cooked on their own. It was the Valencians, the real Valencians, who invented the idea of cooking rice together with other things, but they never invented the gruesome concoction that people serve nowadays — chicken and seafood paella. The Chinese, and Asians in general, are masters of the art of rice on its own, which they combine with whatever takes their fancy, anything from five to five thousand different things. What I find intolerable is that people can serve up a paella like the one we've just had, where the rice has been fried in half a litre of oil that was previously used for frying fish. That wasn't a paella. It was a by-product of a serious burns hospital.'

By now Camps was open-mouthed. At the start he had listened to Carvalho's monologue with his customary air of condescension for the inconsequentiality of other people's opinions, but Carvalho's irritation, and his obvious knowledge of the subject, had triggered his interest.

'Amazing. So you know about cooking.'

'That's *all* I know about. And even then, I don't know much.'

'Is knowing about cooking an occupational requirement for a private detective?'

'No. But it is for being a social psychologist.'

'Fascinating. Could you explain that?'

'I'm not a great talker.'

'That's not the impression I had just now.'

'After-dinner chit-chat has never been my forte.'

'I want to know the connection between cooking and social psychology.'

'Man is a cannibal.'

'That's a good start.'

'He kills in order to feed himself, and then he calls in culture to provide himself with ethical and aesthetic alibis. Primitive man ate his meat raw, and his plants too. He killed and he ate. He was sincere. Then they invented *roux* and bechamel. At that point culture came onto the scene. Covering up what are basically dead corpses in order to be able to eat them with your ethics and your aesthetics intact.'

'Do you eat your meat raw?'

'No. I have a great contempt for the way in which culture in general tries to mask reality, but I lay it aside when it comes to food. The only masking effect that I accept with good grace is cooking.'

'And sex?'

'Adulterated sex is bad for your health.'

When Carvalho fell silent in order to light a Rey del Mundo Special which he had ordered from the waiter, Camps waited for him to finish his lighting-up ritual in the hope that he would continue his explanation. But Carvalho limited himself to the quiet contentment of simply smoking.

'Carry on. I'm very interested in what you're saying. You're a philosopher.'

'That's all I know. I've already told you everything I know, and it surprises me that I've said so much. I'm getting old. I like to know the reasons for the things that I do.' And all of a sudden, as if he'd received some sort of internal message, he rose to his feet.

'I'm going to have to leave you to look after your Englishman. I have to get a move on. I have people I need to catch after lunch.'

Coffee-time is the best time to catch shoeshines around town, Carvalho thought as he left the Barceloneta restaurant, a little wobbly from the effects of two bottles of Brut Barocco which he'd had to drink virtually on his own because Camps was more or less teetotal, and Mortimer barely touched the stuff, not even the *cava* which Camps had promoted as part of the framework of what was quintessentially Catalonian. *Pan con tomate, cava*, the *seques amb butifarra*, the *escudella i carn d'olla* ... Camps had run through the list as if he was declaiming a patriotic poem. On the crowded beaches of Barceloneta, scores of tanned bodies, bronzed with the assistance of atmospheric pollution, were taking the afternoon sun. Two images came to his mind's eye, faded images of days that he had spent on that beach during his childhood, and he was just on the point of turning sentimental when a sudden whiff of oil that had been reused after frying frozen scampi erected an insuperable obstacle to nostalgia. So instead he went looking for a taxi in paseo Maritimo, a street seemingly frozen in time and place as it waited for the extension which would link it to the Olympic Village. In the distance, the houses that had been demolished for the construction of the Olympic sports facilities looked more like a set for a film about the bombing of Dresden. The new city would no longer feel like the city he knew, the city which had lived within the confines of Tibidabo to the north and Barceloneta and the sea to the south. The taxi dropped him in the Ramblas, at the foot of the Pitarra monument in plaza del Arco del Teatro. The young prostitutes, made up to look like even younger prostitutes, were still there, lined up along the pavement outside the Amaya and the Palacio Marc, which was now the seat of the Cultural Council of the Generalitat of Catalonia. The frontage of the church of Santa Monica was showing signs of the plastic surgery which was about to turn it into a Museum of Contemporary Catalan Art, and at his shoulder the bulldozers were poised over the Raval barrio, intent on opening an exit route for those who were trying to escape from the unpleasant realities of drugs and Aids and black and Arab immigrants. As long as there are young prostitutes, there will also be contemporary art, he thought, and this thought proved to him that he had reached the desired level of alcoholic surrealism. Bromide was not cleaning shoes outside the Cosmos, so Carvalho set off down calle de Escudillers, expecting to find his old and balding friend kneeling at the feet of some somnolent citizen. Why, he wondered, don't women use shoeshines? Outside yet another restaurant advertising the delights of paellas and *calamares alla Romana* he found Bromide labouring

over the shoes of a self-satisfied man who was either
Swiss or a rich Catalan from Vic.

'You'll have to wait a moment, Pepiño. I've another
customer after this gentleman.'

'Glad to see you've got plenty of work, Bromide.'

'Touch wood.'

Carvalho leaned up against the counter and treated
himself to a malt whisky with no ice or water. He was
feeling the need to disconnect his capacity for self-control,
but he wasn't sure why. Bromide finished with his clients
and then applied himself to Carvalho's shoes, apologizing
all the while for having kept him waiting.

'People are beginning to want their shoes polished
again, Pepe. Shoeshines are doing good business. The
young ones, mainly, because I just do my usual customers,
and three or four others a day. Why are people wanting
their shoes shined, again, Pepiño? Have you asked yourself that? You should think about it, because you've got
a good brain, and it's worth some thought. If you ask me,
things are changing. Everything. And I'm not talking
about a change like in the 1940s or the 1950s, or the years
when everyone was flush, the sixties and the seventies,
up until Franco died. It's another sort of change. I see it
from people's attitude to their shoes. For ten years people
have been too ashamed to stick their feet under the nose
of a shoeshine and say, "There you go, clean them." They
didn't mind going to the dentist to get their teeth cleaned.
But when it came to cleaning their shoes, they preferred
to do it in the privacy of their own homes, with those
shoeshine machines that put the likes of me out of a job.
For years they all wanted to be so egalitarian, and it
wasn't the done thing to have someone else shine your
shoes for you. So what's it all about? What's happened is
that they're not embarrassed any more, Pepe. So shoeshines are making money again. But I wouldn't say other

things were so great. In fact things seem to be going from bad to worse. What do you think?'

'Do you know anything about someone putting the screws on a centre forward?'

'Schuster?'

'No. First because he's not a centre forward, and second because he's no longer with Barcelona.'

'A centre forward, you said?'

'Yes.'

'No, nothing.'

'Well see what you can find out.'

'Keep your voice down, Pepe, because round here even the Coca-Colas have ears.'

'What are you so scared of, Bromide?'

'Everything.'

'Scared that they're putting bromides in the water so's you can't get a hard-on any more?'

'That's the least of it. People are terrified these days. Everyone's scared, wherever you go. And me too. Things aren't what they used to be, Pepiño. I'll come to your office in a couple of hours, and we can talk more freely.'

'I'll have a glass of wine, please.' Bromide's request had the urgency of a shipwrecked man just rescued from the waves and wracked with thirst. Biscuter disappeared into the kitchen and returned with a bottle and three glasses. He filled Bromide's glass half full, and handed it to him. The shoeshine sniffed it, held it at a slight distance to judge its colour against the light, and crinkled his nose.

'It's not that I don't trust you, but is this stuff decent?'

'Look at the label on the bottle. Val Duero. The boss is in the process of trying all the wines from Ribera del Duero. One after another. Last month he tried all the wines from Leon. With all due respect, boss, I'd say you've been getting a bit obsessional recently. The boss says, and he can correct me if I'm wrong, that he wants to try all the good wines in the world before he dies.'

'So why didn't you fill my glass right up?'

'The boss says that a glass of wine shouldn't be filled to the top.'

'Is that what you say, Pepiño?'

'Biscuter, for Bromide you should fill it right up. Bromide's ways are different to ours.'

Biscuter was upset at being taken to task, so he retorted that Bromide could pour it himself, and thereupon disappeared into the little kitchen next to the toilet, slamming the door behind him, as an indication of a state of internal torment that the rest of them were going to have to work out for themselves.

'The dwarf's in a bad mood, and when I say dwarf, I mean it in a friendly way, Pepiño, because I like Biscuter. But what you said just then really hurt, Pepe.'

'What was that, Bromide?'

'When you said that my ways were different to yours.'

'I wasn't meaning to put you down.'

'I know, Pepe. You're not talking with some little old lady, you know. You're talking with a gentleman legionnaire and a veteran of the Russian campaign. And that's the whole problem. I can still talk to *you* about the Russian campaign, even though you are a commie — or *used* to be a commie — because at least you remember how things were. But I don't know what's happening to the world, Pepiño. People have lost the ability to remember, and it's as if they don't want to be reminded of things. As if there's no point in remembering. No point? If you take away my memories, what's left of me? As far as I'm concerned, this is all a conspiracy of those bloody stupid socialists. They want everyone to think that everything started with them. But they're just like all the rest. I don't recognize anything any more. I've said it before,

and I'll say it again, and I feel very strongly about this . . .
Pepiño, we're surrounded.'

'If you say so . . .'

'I don't know . . . I guess I've been talking to myself. I
didn't dare talk openly when you saw me earlier, because
walls have ears. I don't even feel at home in the places
where I used to feel at home. In the old days, Pepe, I used
to know every criminal in this city, every one of them.
They were like my family. They were in and out of prison,
and they stole whatever they could lay their hands on,
and Bromide was like their memory. Up in my head I've
got all the shit that's ever happened in this city. But it
hurts, Pepe, it hurts, what's going on now. They've colonized us.'

'I presume you're referring to American imperialism.'

'The hell I am. I'm referring to the new class of criminals. There's not a single Spaniard among them. It's all
split between the blacks, the Arabs and the Asians, and
our own Spanish criminals have to go and work for them,
and God help anyone who tries to set up for himself. Do
you remember "Golden Hammer", the pimp I introduced
you to one time? Well, two months ago they found him
dead as a doornail on a demolition site. He thought he
was going to be in the game for life, but he wasn't
watching what was going on around him. And don't go
thinking that the blacks and Arabs you find round Barcelona are the kind who've come off the farms. Not a bit of
it. They're ready-made mafiosos, with good connections
with the police. The other day I was talking to an old
soldier who comes from the same village as me. Valverde
is his name, José Valverde Cifuentes. Well, he told me:
"What can we do, Bromide? The bloody blacks and the
Arabs all look the same. Supposing one of them mugs
you, what are you going to do at the ID parade? You could
identify someone who came from Calahorra, or Marbella,

or Stockholm, but they stick ten blacks in front of you, or ten Arabs, and you can't tell one from the other. And if you do happen to point one out, it'll be curtains for you. The police prefer to turn a blind eye, because what happens if they arrest them? The case finally comes to court, and they know that it's going to cost them more to put them on an aeroplane out of the country, or keep them in prison, than it will to leave them on the streets, so they pretend they don't know what's going on. Or they do a deal with the gang bosses: don't stir it up for us, and we won't stir it up for you. You scratch my back and I'll scratch yours. You know what I mean, Pepe? If a Spanish bank robber does a job — say El Macareno, or El Nen, or La Mapi — then the cops just go round and pick them up, because they know exactly where to find them. But nobody's going to touch one of the immigrants. And that's where my problem starts. Where do I figure in all this? Nowhere. Absolutely bloody nowhere. I've had these Arabs coming up to me, looking like something out of a fashion show, with more gold hanging off them than Lola Flores, and they threaten me: "You just clean your shoes and mind your own business." If anyone had said that to me four or five years ago, he'd have got my box on his head, brushes and all, and I'd have taken my shirt off and shown him my chest with the tattoos from the Legion and the Blue Division: "There, cocksucker, read that, and remember who you're dealing with — a gentleman and a legionnaire." But if you do that with this lot, they just laugh in your face. Even the police laugh at me. Before they used to treat me with respect, because even if you'd only been in the infantry, if you were one of Franco's soldiers, it meant something. But nowadays the gangsters and the police don't know or care what happened in the old days. They have no memory, Pepe — they've stuck their memories up their arses. And that's why we're fucked. So that was what put the wind up me, when you asked me what I know, Pepiño. You know I'd love to help, and I know you'd be generous in return. But I can't, because I don't *know* anything.'

'But surely you know someone who *might* know something.'

'Yes.'

'Well, lead me to them.'

'I don't dare, Pepe. They leave me alone because I pretend to be crazy, but if I go up to one of the Arabs and say: "Listen, I've got a friend who wants to talk to you," they'll just tell me to mind my own business. And I might get a kicking too. I tell you, we've been colonized, Pepe. It's terrible that we've just got to swallow it in silence. Instead of jetting off round the world all the time, Felipe Gonzales should at least see to it that when people rob us or knife us, it's Spaniards who do it. I've always been a good patriot, and it infuriates me when I see how they're selling Spain out. The other day there was an expert on the TV — one of those eggheads who talk out of their arses — and he was going blah-blah-blah, all about how Spain was up for sale, and how anyone with any sense would come and invest here, because they'd make a mint. Of course they would. Even the criminals' hang-outs are up for grabs. There are people who have a seat in Plaza Real, and they wouldn't give it up for two million pesetas, because all they have to do is sit there all day, and they make a fortune. Cocaine, I'm talking about, cocaine . . . So what can I say? If a prostitute's even halfway good-looking, she goes with an Asian. We're getting to the point where there won't be any Spanish pimps left. Sure, your average-looking prostitutes end up with Spanish pimps. But the minute you start talking above-average looks, ten thousand a screw and upwards, they all end up with the foreigners. We need another Franco, that's what we need. I'd like to see Franco back on the scene, waving his sword around. You wouldn't see these foreigners for dust. If people feel they need to go thieving, fair enough, go ahead. But they can stay at home and do it in their own countries, because Spaniards take lessons from nobody when it comes to crime. But it's the same old story. Who invented the helicopter? And the submarine? Spaniards. But who made the profits? The Yanks. Well now the same thing's happening with crime. You've always had Spaniards stealing and killing, but we did it in our own Spanish way. And now we've got these foreigners coming in and running off with the loot, and even the blacks are taking liberties now. Even the blacks, Pepe! I don't understand anything any more. I've said it before, and I say it again — there are two kinds of people in this world: the mafiosos who control everything, and the junkies who go their own way and don't control anything. And poor old Bromide's stuck in the middle, and they treat him like a dog. And I'm hurting all over, Pepe, I can hardly tell you. One day it's my kidneys, the next it's my liver. I can hardly piss, Pepe, I can hardly even piss. When I shake my ding-a-ling, it's like a lump of wood, and I don't know why I bother, because even if I shake it, all that comes out is drops. I could shake it for two days on end, but all I'd get would be drops.'

Carvalho had let him talk on, but even though he pretended to himself that he wasn't really listening, he slowly found himself getting involved. What the old man was saying now was no different to what he'd been saying as he'd got more and more pessimistic over the years, but this time it sounded less rhetorical and more a sincere declaration of impotence. A powerlessness at the core of his being. And his gestures as he pointed to the various aches were the gestures of a man who could hardly bare to touch where it hurt because it was hurting so badly.

'There are doctors, Bromide.'

'The trouble is, they find all sorts of things wrong with you, Pepe. I used to go to one before, a National Health doctor, and he was very good. He'd ask me: "Do you want me to find something wrong with you? No? That's fine. Goodbye, then." And off I went, and for sixty years now I've been fit as a fiddle. But then my doctor retired, and I've not been back from that day to this. Or rather, I did go back one day, and I saw his replacement. He was an idiot. No sooner did he set eyes on me than he started dreaming up all kinds of things wrong with me. Some of them were right, as it turned out, but he was making up the rest. I waited till he went to answer the phone, and I cleared off. If he'd been right about everything he said was wrong with me, by rights I should be dead by now. And the other thing is, I feel a bit awkward about going to doctors.'

Carvalho caught himself saying: 'I'll come with you.'

Bromide stood and looked at him, letting the words sink in. Then he swallowed heavily.

'I'd be embarrassed to go to the doctor with you, Pepe. It'd be different if I was married . . . I've always dreamed of having a wife to go to the doctor's with me, but then you know what a hard time I've had, trying to find a decent woman. I'd like to be married. It's good to go to the doctor's with your wife.'

This time Carvalho heard himself say: 'Charo could go with you.'

All the dirty wrinkles on the shoeshine's face creaked into action and his eyes suddenly shone with happiness.

'Would Charo do that for me?'

'Charo needs a dad to take to the doctor's.'

'You're making fun of me, Pepe.'

'I'm serious.'

Bromide finished off his wine and savoured it with a

tongue that ranged around a mouth that was more or less devoid of teeth.

'I'll see what I can do to find you a contact. But be careful with what you find out.'

Carvalho stuck a thousand-peseta note in Bromide's jacket pocket, and the shoeshine closed his eyes as the money made contact with his body.

Juan Sánchez Zapico was a self-made man, and he had surrounded himself with people who were incapable of seeing that what he'd made of himself didn't actually amount to much. The four apartment blocks that he had constructed in the barrio; the six scrap-metal yards which extended his domain to the outskirts where Pueblo Nuevo meets with San Adrián; a small sugared-almond factory which had all the latest technology, as he never tired of telling anyone who was willing to listen — all this had made him moderately rich, and likely to remain so. This meant that he could dedicate part of his leisure time to being chairman of Centellas, a historic club in a historic barrio. In the early days of football in Catalonia, Centellas had been capable of competing with Barça, Europa, Espagñol and San Andrés. But then, after the Civil War, it was lucky to survive at all. Its continued existence was due in part to the solid support of its fans in the barrio, and in part to the fact that its pitch was located in a key zone for Barcelona's future. The club's directors had resisted the temptation to sell the ground in the period of urban expansion in the 1950s and 1960s, and then later when people began sniffing around for promising real estate in the area around the proposed Olympic Village. The Centellas ground sat on the third or fourth parallel from the sea, almost on the edge of San Adrián, and as such it was fated to be swallowed up by the new Barcelona which was planned to grow outwards from the central nucleus of the Olympic Village, which in turn would become apartment blocks for the new post-Olympic petty bourgeoisie — a marked contrast with the previous population of the neighbourhood: the last remains of the Catalan proletariat, and the archaeological sedimentations of various immigrations.

'All in due course,' Sánchez Zapico would say when the club's more impatient directors started pressing the merits of some of the more lucrative offers-to-sell.

On other occasions he would wax more lyrical: 'For as long as I live, Centellas will live, and without this ground Centellas would die.

'Centellas depends on its ground,' he declaimed, at the end of the speech with which he introduced Palacín to the other players and to around two hundred fans spread out on the club's time-worn terraces, not forgetting three trainee journalists, recently emerged from the Faculty of Information Sciences who were there to cover third-hand news events with fourth-hand tape recorders bought in the flea market in Plaza de las Glorias.

'Our intention in signing Palacín is to improve club attendances. Palacín isn't just a name. He's a centre forward to his core. He's got balls.'

The journalists noted down the phrase 'he's got balls', but then, when their offerings finally appeared in their respective newspapers, they went no further than to say that, in the opinion of Sánchez Zapico, Palacín was 'well furnished'. The new signing merited only one photograph, which, in the event, was not published, although a small headline at the bottom of the last page of sports news seemed keen to stir public interest in the reappearance of Alberto Palacín. 'Centellas is obviously taking next season seriously, as we see from the fact that they have signed Alberto Palacín, the centre forward who was hailed as the new Marcelino in the 1970s, but who then ran into bad times because of injury. He continued his career in American football, and ended up playing for Oaxaca in Mexico. He was a popular player and established himself as one of the highest goal scorers in the Mexican League. At the age of thirty-six, Palacín has committed himself to helping Centellas to promotion to the Third Division. Then, he says, he will retire. On the pitch he looks to be in fine form, although the passing years have clearly left their mark.' This was written by a twenty-two-year-old journalist, in other words, a journalist of no age at all: this was the thought that ran through Palacín's mind as he read the article and had a vague recollection of the youngster who for a few minutes had accorded him the role of a star.

'Don't take any notice of what they say in the papers. I never take any notice of the press,' the club's chairman urged him, thinking that the bit about his age had hurt him. 'A journalist is like a man with a gun. He thinks that just because he's got a pen in his hand, he's got more balls than you. I want you to show balls when you're out there. This club needs players with balls.'

The Centellas manager, Justo Precioso, operated by similar standards. He was an accountant in one of Sánchez Zapico's factories, and had become the club's manager-in-residence after an obscure period as a Second Division player, first as a right-wing defender and by the end as a sweeper. He was a thin, miserable little man, bald, with a three-day growth round his chin and an Adam's apple which looked like a third testicle as it strove to rival the club's chairman in his metaphorical reference to the players' sexual impedimenta.

'Toté, I want more balls!' he shouted to the club's midfield defender. 'Pérez, let's have more balls up front' — this to the man who until that season had been the club's centre forward but since the arrival of Palacín had been playing inside forward.

Every now and then he went over to an old blackboard, to try and plan out moves, but he couldn't always find the chalk, and, when he did, it screeched and set the more sensitive players' teeth on edge. His real forte was training with the players, out on the pitch. 'Out there, that's where it matters. I want to see intelligence and balls,' he would say, as he stood next to the south-end goal, onto which the club's parsimonious lighting had been focused in a sort of half light which left the rest of the pitch in the dark, a ghostly landscape for the antics of these nocturnal footballers.

'I don't want to overdo it with my knee,' Palacín warned him.

'Do you mean just today, or for always?' the manager asked, his Adam's apple suddenly paralysed with alarm.

'Gives me trouble every now and then. When I've had a bit of a warm-up, I'm fine.'

'So I should hope. You just play the way you want to play. But I want balls, Palacín. Midfield players in the regional League are a lot more lethal than what you find in the Second or Third Division. Compared to most of them, Pontón was an angel.' And he winked knowingly, because he had just named the player who had been responsible for crippling Palacín's knee.

During this first training session, the players were watching as much as playing. Palacín was the object of their evaluation, and in skirmishes for possession of the ball they were respectful but also at pains to demonstrate that they were not dazzled by the residual splendour of his past. Especially Toté, the central defender, who marked him so closely that it felt like having a limpet on his back. Each time that Palacín slowed down, protected the ball with his body, and was about to swing on one leg so as to wrong-foot his marker, an elbow would knock him off balance, or a knee in his thigh would stop him in his tracks. During one of these encounters, when Toté's knee made contact with his old injury, Palacín suddenly went wild. He left the ball and went for his team-mate, grabbing him by his vest, and pulling him face to face as if he was about to chew his head off.

'You just fucking take it easy, bastard . . .'

'You too. We don't play like young ladies here.'

'What the fuck do you think you're playing at?' The manager ran up, arms flailing, to separate them.

It wasn't necessary. The two players backed off, knocking the earth from their boots. The manager put one arm round Toté's shoulder and took him to the corner of the pitch, where he gave him a quiet talking to. Then he came over to where Palacín was cautiously checking his knee for damage.

'I'm sorry about that. The man's a bit of an animal . . .'

'Exactly what I was just telling him.'

'No need to get all worked up. Don't let him upset you.'

'Easier said than done.'

'Come on! Let's see you running! Hup, hup, hup!'

The players broke from their statue-like immobility, and started running in Indian file, hopping alternately on one leg and then the other, and moving their arms and necks in a way that made them look dislocated. The trainer ran alongside, moving up and down the line to check how willingly or unwillingly his troupe was performing. He had banned the wearing of watches during training, but some players had them up their sleeves and checked them surreptitiously as they waited for the whistle that would signal the end of the session.

'Look at your arse, man! You look as if you're running sitting down! All of you, I want you to feel your balls, feel them bouncing, OK? Hup! Hup!'

He finally ran out of breath and ideas for things to shout, and gave the long-awaited blast on his whistle. The line of players broke up, and some of them ran ahead to get to the changing room before the others. Sometimes there wasn't enough hot water for everyone to shower, even though Sánchez Zapico had presented the club with a powerful gas water heater, the inauguration of which had been attended by the whole team, the club directors, and their respective wives and children. The water heater was about the only thing on the premises with any future. The changing room was full of leaks and the walls were decorated with damp patches and flaking paint, and whether the players' lockers were lockable or not depended on some arcane logic which no carpenter in the past ten years had ever succeeded in fathoming. Palacín took his boots off and put them on the floor. The two showers were already occupied, so he kept his shirt on in order not to get cold.

'Sorry about that,' Toté said, as he walked past, completely naked, and reached out to shake hands with Palacín.

'He's a decent sort of person when you get to know him,' said a blond-haired player as he sat next to Palacín and began taking off his boots. 'He's not got anything against you. It's just that his contract ends in June, so he's got to put on a bit of a show.'

'I see.'

'My dad tells me that you were brilliant in your day.'

The lad's eyes consumed him as if he was an elixir, an alchemical residue of his former glory.

'I'm a bit over the hill, these days.'

'I was there when you scored in the match with Madrid Athletic, when the whole stadium was on its feet.'

'Other times they were all booing me.'

'You win some, you lose some. That's what my dad says.

He says you had a neck like a pile-driver. Boom, when you headed a ball it would go off like a rocket. He says you had as much power heading a ball as kicking it.'

'That's impossible, son.'

'I know. But that's what he says. I play midfield.'

'Yes, I saw you.'

'What do you think of the way I play?'

'Very good. You play with your head up, and that's very important for a midfield player. But you have to listen out more. Keep eyes in the back of your head.'

'Why?'

'A midfield player has to be able to feel the waves of air coming off the player who's following him, and when he's got the ball and he's looking for who to pass it to, he needs eyes in the back of his head, because that way he knows who's coming up behind him. That's the sort of thing you learn over the years.'

'The trainer says I'm very intelligent.'

The lad gave him a look that was obviously seeking confirmation, and Palacín laughed.

'For sure. It shows.'

Biscuter had tucked himself away in his kitchen; Charo was suffering an attack of indignation, and needing attention; Bromide was sick and scared — Carvalho's family was falling apart, and he decided he needed to spend a bit of time putting it back together. He called to Biscuter to make his presence known, and when his assistant emerged from his lair, with his lank red hair bristling up in tufts and his large mournful eyes wide with surprise, Carvalho had a sudden revelation — that, in Biscuter's case, time actually stood still. Of all the members of Carvalho's bizarre family, he alone had remained unchanged since the day Carvalho had first met him, thirty years previously, in Aridel prison. The little hair

he had was red, and he still looked like a foetus that had
been abandoned by its mother in horror at the ugliness
of the creature she had brought into the world. For all
that he disliked admitting the passing of time, Carvalho
reckoned that Biscuter had to be over fifty by now. Time
passes with its own inexorable logic, and only the artist's
technique can cheat it by freezing it in films and novels.
Time was there, for all to see, in himself, in Biscuter, in
Charo and in Bromide, and in each case it betrayed its
victims in a different way. Charo, by a tendency to put
on weight, Bromide by the fact that he was slowly rotting
away inside, and Carvalho by the fact that he was ever-
increasingly a passive spectator of his own time and of
other people's. For the time being, though, time had
spared Biscuter — perhaps because it had already
marked him from the moment of his birth. Biscuter was
born ugly, and it was as if time had settled its account
with him from the moment that he emerged from his
mother's womb.

'Jesus, boss. So you've finally noticed that I exist!'

Carvalho leapt to his feet abruptly and thumped the
table.

'Not you too, Biscuter! I seem to be surrounded by
manic depressives. Why do I have to spend my life providing a shoulder for other people to cry on?'

'It's not that, boss. The problem is, these days you don't
seem to care if I'm alive or dead. I told you the other day
I'd bought the *Gastronomic Encyclopaedia*. It cost me a
small fortune, and you didn't even ask to see it. And you
never tell me if my cooking's any good or not, or if I'm
doing it right. I've always stood by you, boss, and every
shopkeeper in the area knows it. I'm not asking for a
reward or anything, but people are always telling me how
lucky you are to have an assistant like me.'

'Go and see Charo, and tell her that Bromide's ill and

she should take him to the doctor's. If she starts throwing things at you and saying that I can come and tell her myself, tell her I'm tied up for the moment. I'll ring her later.'

'And I've got no security, either, boss. Do you ever stop to think about that? God forbid, but supposing something happens to you one day? What's going to happen to poor old Biscuter? Out on the scrap heap?'

With a vehemence that alarmed him, Carvalho assured him that this would not be the case. Biscuter was sufficiently alarmed to leave the office at a prudent speed, albeit with the satisfaction of a man who has just spoken his mind: 'That told him,' Biscuter repeated to himself as he went down the stairs, and he had the impression that his words had not passed unheard. Carvalho was perplexed, a state of mind which he found particularly repellent — a philosophical luxury unbefitting in a person of even average intelligence. He needed to clear his brain. He opened the desk drawer and took out a bottle of vintage Knockando, a good whisky for states of fundamental perplexity. He served himself three fingers in a large glass, and drank them in three long sips. This triple charging and discharging of alcohol and inhaled air did him good, and he was just preparing to go out and reconquer the streets and his state of mind when the phone rang. Even before the first words took shape at the other end, a kind of malignant vibration told him that it was Charo ringing to acknowledge receipt of Biscuter's message.

'Would señor José Carvalho happen to be in? Could his majesty come to the phone and oblige his humble servant by telling her exactly what was on his mind?'

Carvalho decided to stick to the bare bones of conversation and ignore the provocative tone. Yes, she would be happy to go with Bromide, because Bromide was a nice person, not like some people she could name. In fact, a very nice person. Not like some people etc. Why in God's name did he have to send a messenger? Had he forgotten her phone number? Surely at least he could have remembered her phone number, even if he seemed to have forgotten her. And sending Biscuter round just showed what a bad-mannered pig he was.

'And a bastard . . . Do I make myself clear?'

She made herself clear.

'I'll be round later this afternoon.'

'You don't have to treat me like a dog that has to be taken for walks. If I need a piss, I'm quite capable of going on my own.'

'All right, so I won't be round later this afternoon . . .'

Since she now had him on the hook, there followed another monologue which eventually resolved into a plaintive 'Just who do you think you are?' And then silence, as she waited for Carvalho to give an answer that she knew he was incapable of giving. And then, finally, acceptance of his 'I'll be round later this afternoon,' delivered in the tones of a man admitting defeat.

Carvalho waited for Biscuter to return — a Biscuter still smarting from his dressing-down — and he explained the Mortimer case to him as if it was vital for Biscuter to be kept informed of its progress. It didn't take long for him to take up his allotted role as a faithful Watson and to apply his analytical shrewdness to the situation in hand.

'It must be the Arabs, boss.'

'What Arabs?'

'The Arab sheikhs, boss. They're buying up all our best players and carting them off to their cities in the desert. They've got the money to build themselves teams that are unbeatable. First they put the wind up Mortimer, and then they sign him. I happened to hear what you were

talking about with Bromide, and I've drawn my own conclusions. He wasn't saying anything we don't know
already. I've been thinking more or less the same
myself — you only have to walk round town to see what's
going on. You've been travelling too much lately, and
either because of your travelling, or maybe because you're
stuck up in Vallvidrera, you haven't noticed how things
are changing round here. It's the Wild West all over again,
but this time it's knives instead of guns. Are you in for
supper? I've got the necessaries to make a *brandada de
urade.*'

'And what might that be, Biscuter?'

'It's a recipe I got out of the encyclopaedia I was telling
you about. It just so happens I've still got a piece of fish
left over from the other day. It won't take long to prepare — all it needs is taking out the bones and adding
oil and garlic, whisk the cream and add salt, pepper and
a drop of tabasco. Put it through the blender and it's
done. Five minutes.'

'Why not!'

Biscuter was happier now, and as he disappeared into
the kitchen he gave Carvalho an update on Charo's state
of mind.

'She's angry, boss, but it'll pass. She told me she's just
about on the breadline these days, what with the Aids
scare and all that, and the only clients she can still count
on are her regulars, and they're all getting old. One of
them's just died, in fact. A chemist from Tarasa. That's
why she was a bit depressed. You know what a softie she
is.'

Carvalho shared the *brandada de urade* with Biscuter,
and they washed it down with a bottle of Milmanda de
Torres, a fact which Biscuter found amazing until he
realized that the bottle's presence was his boss's attempt
at a peace offering. Carvalho ate hurriedly, because he

felt an urgent need to get out into the streets and see or
talk with people who weren't going to burden him with
hard-luck stories or premonitions of hard-luck stories to
come. He used the pretext of his appointment with Charo
and left. He decided to go on foot, so as to observe at first-
hand the changes that Biscuter had talked about.

'Mind how you go, boss. Honestly, the way things are
going . . . The other day I read in the papers that they're
planning to pull down half the Barrio Chino, from
Perecamps on upwards, because knocking it down will let
some fresh air in, they say. The place is beginning to feel
like a graveyard.'

Carvalho was propelled out onto the street by a sense
of irritation. Admittedly he had been travelling a lot, and
admittedly Vallvidrera was a fair way from the city
centre, but it was unreasonable to suggest that he would
no longer recognize the places where he'd spent his childhood. How could they just spirit away all the old places?
Presumably the fashion of imagining that everything had
changed had now reached the lower classes, and Biscuter
was singing, out of time, a hackneyed requiem for what
had once been and what was no more, or for what might
have been but never was. He recognized his old haunts,
as he walked the streets reviewing a geography that had
been his whole life, or almost his whole life, and everything seemed to be where it ought to be. He visited a
couple of second-hand bookshops, and the feel of their
dusty, mummified culture reminded him of his breathless
hunger for books in the days when he'd been a cultural
junkie. He skimmed through a large, expensive book
about Barcelona sporting a label on which the scandalous
original price had been reduced by the bookseller's sense
of common decency: 'Is the dream of free men living in a
free city really realizable? At the moment, Barcelona is
humanizing itself in each strip that it recovers or

OFF SIDE 51

constructs for leisurely walking — that relation of space and time which gives us the freedom to do nothing, to fear nothing and to expect nothing. In other words, what we could call a beatific *desideratum*. Here we have a people that enjoys free things, and to whom one of their own philosophers promised that one day they would have everything paid for, wherever they went, for the simple fact of their being Catalan. These are people who get enthusiastic just collecting snails, or picking mushrooms, or drinking from public fountains and strolling round the city without a penny to pay. The average citizen relates to this city like a son to a mother: he knows that Barcelona is a woman, and he feels himself to be a child of the virgin Mother and the prostitute, of the Bronze Venus and of Pepita with the umbrella, of señora Josefina, of Reus, and many others. Over the years the city's philosophers have tried to persuade us that Barcelona was a marble city, or a city state, or a city-region ... But they failed. People recognize this city as a motherland which each of them is able to possess through the hegemony of his own memory. Some were born here. Others came from elsewhere. But this possessive memory began on the day when, like the ancient Chaldeans, they understood that the basic elements of their world ended with the hills that constituted their encircling horizon.' He either agreed or disagreed with this sentiment, but he couldn't be bothered to decide which. He deflated the bookseller's expectation of an impending sale and exited decisively en route to see Charo. When he arrived at her door, he called up on the entryphone. Two minutes later Charo came stampeding out and flung herself at him in a huge exhalation of rose water and warm flesh. It was a railway station embrace, a wife's embrace for her returning husband, and Carvalho let himself be hugged and kissed, all the while giving her little pats on the back, because he was at a loss what to do with his hands and his guilty conscience. Charo made it easy for him, because she was in a happy, chatty mood, and Carvalho suggested that they celebrate in style. First a film, and then up to Vallvidrera, always assuming she didn't have clients waiting for her.

'Clients? What are you talking about? I'm in a worse crisis than those poor devils in the steel industry. I tell you, Pepe, this Aids business has really messed things up. I've got regular clients that I've had for years, but that's not what you'd call a decent living. I don't want you to think I'm complaining, but I've got some important decisions to make, and I wanted to talk to you.'

Carvalho knew that she'd get her say eventually, for all that he tried to delay the moment. He was willing to talk, but not until they first went to the cinema to see a film in which various people were getting drugged on gazpacho, and a girl was losing her virginity in her dreams, and a bunch of Shiite conspirators were somewhere in the background, making life complicated for a fashion model who had eyes like a doe and skin the colour of cream. Then, as they were on their way up to Vallvidrera, she repeated that she had things she wanted to talk about, decisions that she had to make. But first they made dinner, and then they made love, to the fullest of Charo's expertise and the fullest of Carvalho's capacity to evoke another body whose face he couldn't exactly place, until at last he realized that it was Charo's own — Charo as a younger woman. And as they relaxed afterwards, she with a cigarette, and he with a Churchill Cerdan, flat on their backs and with a blanket to protect them from the October chill of Vallvidrera, Charo finally explained what was on her mind. An old client was suggesting setting her up in business. Something simple. A boarding house, in fact.

'What would you think of that, Pepe? A boarding house would be a good idea, wouldn't it . . . I don't have a penny to my name. Just a bit of money in the bank, but that's going very fast because I'm using it to live on.'

Whenever Charo was depressed, some client always seemed to pop up and suggest setting her up in business, and Carvalho had to be told all the details and was expected to offer advice. Carvalho shut his eyes in order not to catch Charo's eye as he said: 'That's not a bad idea.'

Calle Perecamps was to be extended, and would cut through the meat of the Old City towards Ensanche, forging a way through the defeated fibre of the city and the calcified skeletons of its direst architectural horrors. A gigantic mechanical digger with a head like some nightmare insect would convert the archaeology of poverty into archaeology pure and simple, but even if they demolished the houses, and got rid of the old people, the drug addicts, the pushers, the penniless prostitutes, the blacks, and the Arabs, all of them would have to find somewhere to escape to as the bulldozers drove them out. They would have to find a new home for their poverty, probably somewhere in the outskirts, where the city loses its name and thereby sheds responsibility for its disaster victims. A city with no name is a city which effectively doesn't exist. It appears on no postcards, and only earns the sympathy of the front pages when its auto-destruction complex transcends the limits of tolerability in a permissive society, and it begins to kill, rape, and commit suicide with the lack of self-control which normally characterizes only the desperate and the insane. Streets of old people with almost empty shopping bags, eternally en route from one pitiful purchase to another, from one half-memory to another; what they've done with their lives, and what day it is today. A new generation of whores with varicose veins, who will be entered into the census statistics by a fifth-generation computer, and who will feed, as their mothers fed, on tuna sandwiches and squid tapas floating in a hybrid sauce and (as a concession to modernity) frankfurters doused in ketchup. Alongside the monumental prostitute, weathered by the passing years and the chill of the night, stands the skinny, wraith-like junkie prostitute, her shifty eyes flicking about like those of drunken sailors on a sea with no way out. Two classes of pimps, too: the old familiar type, a pachydermic stud with prominent buttocks and a barrel chest, and the postmodern pimp, wiped out by drug addiction, and with his eyes and fingers slipping like blades over the surface of a mad and hostile world. Dimly lit shopkeepers who are irretrievably up against the wall. Clean-living young men, unemployed through no fault of their own, who hurry through prohibited streets. Mothers, internal exiles in barrios where they have been growing geraniums on their balconies from five or six generations back. The contrast of honest poverty. Families of Moroccan moles and black gazelles from darkest Africa, inhabiting flats that have been abandoned by people fleeing a leprous city. Toilets with no running water. Dead bodies lying in flats barricaded from the inside. Old people, abandoned by memory and left by their own desires and those of others. Lost children kicking footballs around in the squares, up against the doors of Gothic churches that are so old that they're half sunk into the ground, each with a recent history as street-corner tobacconists or the abodes of artisanal cutlery makers. Dog shit, and shit dogs, as faded and fearful as their owners — the women and mature children who look as if they are obliged to take the dog for a walk in order to take themselves for a walk, down the narrowness of narrow streets and worn paving stones. And something approaching the beauty of poverty has etched itself onto the façades of houses that were built shortly before or after the publication of the *Communist Manifesto*, a fact to which they remain oblivious, because this city was already old and has built itself, or rebuilt itself, on both sides of the medieval walls that were demolished in the middle of the nineteenth century. What excited Carvalho's visual memory as he left Charo at the hairdresser's and drove towards the southern parking lot on the Ramblas was not his own erudition, but a radio discussion on the problem of 'Violence in the City', where the contributors were an ex-terribly-modern-novelist, and a communist Jesuit, the former using as his spiritual inspiration a collage of various and opposing spiritual sources, principally a certain Georges Simmel, and the latter invoking Jesus Christ and Karl Marx. According to Simmel, since cities provide no ways of discharging aggression which do not involve great danger to the well-being of society, it becomes absolutely necessary to find ways of channelling that violence. One of the most familiar ways is what experts in ethics have come to recognize as aggression against a substitutive object.

'Let us imagine,' said the novelist, 'that a terrified rabbit decides to kill the fox which has been making its life a misery. Obviously, the fox is stronger than it is. So instead it relieves its aggression by taking it out on a mouse. There's a long tradition of these kinds of urban scapegoats: the persecution of Jews, blacks, Arabs, gypsies, Asians and foreigners in general gives the frustrated and aggressive citizenry a chance to lash out against minorities who are weaker than them and have no way of hitting back. Sport is another effective variant of substitutive objects. The ritualized interplay of aggressive actions and self-control enables the public to participate in a simulacrum of struggle, in an aggressiveness between players. The problem is that today's generation of fans is no longer satisfied simply with simulated violence, but feels the need to materialize it on the terraces, or outside the ground, out of frustration at the feeling that their escape valve has become commercialized.'

'Do you believe, señor Félix de Azúa, that if we made admission to football grounds free, soccer violence would disappear?'

'I think it very likely.'

'Do you have other forms of substitutive aggression on your list?'

'Yes. Nationalism. Excessive patriotism, in the negative sense that it necessitates the existence of an external enemy. Also deaths in road-traffic accidents, and motorway deaths in particular. Industrial societies are willing to take on themselves the costs of deaths resulting from the use of motor cars, but not the cost of deaths arising from religion, politics or sex. Some deaths are permitted, others are not. Urban culture generates a scenario in which laws are able to distinguish between violence which is acceptable and violence which is not.'

'Do you share this point of view, señor García Nieto?'

The communist Jesuit agreed with the theory and the general scenario, and agreed that double standards were applied, but said that the causes of the violence and the disorder lay in the mystified values of wealth and the inability of the majority of people to achieve that wealth, a sense of powerlessness which was becoming increasingly widespread in society.

'Thirty per cent of Spanish society lives below the poverty line. How can it avoid being violent?'

'And fewer and fewer people are going to football matches,' the interviewer concluded, philosophically.

Carvalho switched off the radio. Faced with the choice of either going to the office or examining once more on foot what his mind's eye had reconstructed with the aid of the radio debate, he opted for the latter, parked the car, and headed off towards Arco del Teatro to examine the future path of the bulldozers, zigzagging down alleys that had an air of expectant mourning, and saying good-bye to buildings that had suddenly become ennobled by the death sentence hanging over them, because even the Boston Strangler inspired compassion and acquired dignity in the hours preceding his execution. Going up San Oligario, he emerged onto calle de San Rafael. On the left, Casa Leopoldo, an honest restaurant in the process of preparing its daily offerings; in front, pasaje de Martorell; to the right, calle de Robadors, with its now defunct bars for cheap prostitutes, and a couple of boarding houses, including one which announced itself as belonging to a certain 'Conchi', but whose neon sign evidently reserved its electric energies solely for the night. All the bars were more or less shut, except for one which reproduced a tropical environment reminiscent of some Third World country definitively ruined by foreign debt. Three ageing, early rising prostitutes were staring contemplatively into their coffees, and his presence as the only man in the place failed to arouse their interest. Carvalho went up to the bar and ordered a coffee, and instantly sensed a human warmth hovering by his right shoulder. He turned round to see a girl in such reduced circumstances that she looked more like a memory of her former self. The skin of her face was grey, and the way it was distributed over bones that were well proportioned but meagre reminded you of a skull. She sported a black eye, and a bruise on her forehead.

'Excuse me, sir. Would you be interested in enjoying a literary screw this morning?'

'Any particular type of literature?'

'Type or genre?'

'It's all the same to me.'

'We could screw like a Baudelaire poem.'

'Poetry doesn't turn me on.'

'What the poetry doesn't do, I'm sure I can.'

'What faculty did you graduate from?'

'The Faculty of Fellatio. Do you know what fellatio is?'

'It's a long time since I was at university . . .'

'A blow-job.'

'A blow-job,' Carvalho mused as he grappled with the hidden etymology of this mysterious word.

'At this time of day, you'll get it cheap. The price goes up later.'

'That's a terrible way to do business. At this time of day you should be charging more. There's less competition about.'

The would-be intellectual retorted sharply: 'Do you want it or not?'

Her eyes flicked intermittently to a corner of the bar where Carvalho just about made out a young man with a pigtail, who was watching them in a vacant sort of way.

'Is that your pimp?'

'No. My father. What are you after, here?'

'A coffee.'

'Do you want coke?'

'Do you have coke?'

'No. But I know where you could get some.'

'And that way you get some too. Are things really that bad?'

'Things are as good or bad as my cunt happens to feel like.'

'A professional prostitute would never have said anything so vulgar.'

'What do you know about prostitutes?'

'My girlfriend's a prostitute.'

'I bet your girlfriend's a slag.'

And she turned on her heel, but her legs were too

skinny for the stylish exit she'd intended. She disappeared into the half light at the back of the bar and sat next to her boyfriend. From that moment on, two pairs of venomous eyes drilled into the back of Carvalho's head until the moment when he finally finished his coffee and turned to glare sufficiently menacingly for the two of them to pretend to be scanning other horizons.

Dorothy arrived with six suitcases in tow and an aunt who had reared her like a mother. The aunt was drinking Irish whiskey from a silver hip flask and assuring everyone within earshot that she would only be staying in Barcelona long enough to make sure that her niece was well installed and that the city had good specialists in liver complaints. Since the onset of puberty Dorothy had been afflicted by a delicate liver. This, however, had not prevented her from becoming a good sportswoman and a star dancer at Soho parties until the moment she met Jack, whereupon she had been forced to cool her arse, so to speak.

'Thus spake Zarathustra,' Camps O'Shea announced, as he concluded his unasked-for report on Dorothy's impending arrival. 'Have you heard of Sarah Ferguson? A daughter-in-law of the Queen of England.'

'I can't say I've had the pleasure.'

'You must have read about her in the papers. Oh no — I forgot — you don't read newspapers.'

'I know the name.'

'Well, Dorothy is like Sarah Ferguson, but a bit less chunky. For my taste the Ferguson woman has always seemed a bit on the fat side.'

The word 'fat' was a serious insult when it came from the lips of the fastidious Camps.

'And as for the aunt, let's hope that she leaves as soon as possible, because she insists on sticking her nose in everywhere. She even wanted to see the dressing rooms where Jack will be changing. I told her that Aids is running rampant in Spain, and particularly in club changing rooms. Speaking of changing rooms, we've hired a company to put security guards at all the entrances to the ground, on the pretext that there's been a lot of thieving at the club recently, and we're concerned for the security of our players. Have you made any progress?'

'Yes and no. To tell you the truth, I'm at a bit of a loss. I used to know where I was with Spanish criminals, but with this new breed of imported criminal I don't know if I'm coming or going. The message I get from them isn't capable of being translated. It's very weird.'

'What do you mean?'

'The contacts that I've made have so far led me to a non-Spanish Mafia, and from talking with them it's obvious that they know nothing about what we're hoping they know about, but they certainly know something that they don't want *us* to know about.'

'Isn't the one the same as the other?'

'No.'

Camps had arranged to meet him at the gates of the Montjuich stadium, and they were strolling like a pair of sightseers past the building site where the rebuilding was taking place: the perimeter of the place was to be maintained intact, with the original façade, but the inside of the stadium was to be rebuilt entirely. A homage to memory, as Camps commented unenthusiastically.

'It's not that I think that all museums should be burned and the Parthenon knocked down once and for all. But I do think you can go too far in conserving heritage. If humanity had spent all its energies on conserving its heritage, we'd still be living in caves. Do you find anything particularly striking about this stadium?'

'I couldn't imagine walking through Montjuich without expecting to see it there.'

'Imagine the scene here seventy years ago — what a surprise this building would have been for travellers who happened to come across it. I'm more interested in what our new buildings are going to look like, though. Barcelona is going to be a showcase for world architecture. The new is generally less banal at the start, although sometimes the new is already dead at birth. When I was in France this year, I visited a nuclear power station which is apparently never going to be operational. It was a frightening experience. Rather like walking round some abandoned ancient city. Palenque. Pompeii. Machu Picchu. Spoleto. Have you ever been to Spoleto? The city began life around a temple to Diocletian, and its subsequent growth has maintained that original logic. It's as if the town is growing out of the temple itself. Extraordinary, it is. Here, take this.'

He casually handed Carvalho a piece of paper containing the latest anonymous letter, which was equally menacing and parallelistic as the one before: 'Centre forwards have heads of stone, and bodies of pink coral, and that is why they shatter when they hurl themselves against cliffs.

'And you grow in their shadow, you invalids who will never pose for an epic portrait, and in the destruction of the centre forward you will be reborn, because on his corpse will grow your status as biological remains.

'All these are the reasons why you deserve that the centre forward should be killed, and at dusk. And if you ask me why the centre forward must be killed at dusk, I will tell you that it must be before night comes, and before I am left, alone, in the house of the dead whom only I remember.'

'I'm not so keen on this one.'

'It's got a quote in it, from a poem by Espriu. Basté de

Linyola spotted it. Look at the last sentence, and compare it with this bit.'

Camps handed him another piece of paper, with two handwritten verses which he had presumably copied himself.

> Maybe tomorrow
> more slow hours will arrive,
> of clarity for the eyes
> of this greedy gaze
>
> But now it is night
> and I am left alone
> in the house of the dead
> whom only I remember.

'How's your Catalan?'

'Fairly good.'

'Our killer obviously has taste. Would you like to meet Dorothy?'

'No. But I would like to have a quiet talk with you. I'd like to invite you to my house for supper. I live in Vallvidrera. I'll be inviting a friend of mine too, a commercial agent. He collects autographs of PR men from famous football teams. I'll be doing the cooking, so you'll have the chance of being surprised at my practical abilities, since you were obviously impressed with my theoretical abilities the other day.'

'I feel honoured by the invitation.'

He meant it.

'You can bring a friend, if you like.'

'I don't usually take friends to this kind of revelationary encounter. Sometimes it's better to go without. And why is your agent friend coming?'

'He's a good talker, good at breaking the ice, and he

doesn't have my inquisitorial tendencies. I seem to spend my whole life questioning people.'

'So I noticed. By the way, I have to report another appointment, which we might not find so agreeable. Inspector Contreras wants to have words with us. Both of us.'

'Contreras, eh?'

'Do you know him?'

'From years back. He's one of my favourite enemies. Better the devil you know than the devil you don't. He's become more sophisticated over the years. He started life like a cop out of some low-budget Spanish film from the 1950s. Then he turned into a policeman from the American film noir. Recently he's had more substance to him. I don't know what his role model is this time, because I haven't been to the pictures for years, but he's not the same Contreras that I once knew. When's he expecting us?'

'Whenever suits us.'

'We could go right away.'

They each arrived separately, in their own cars. Carvalho in a Renault on which he was still paying the HP instalments, and Camps in an Alfetta. But they contrived to enter the via Layetana police headquarters together. Contreras raised an amicable eyebrow for Camps, and a disapproving one for Carvalho.

'Parasites like our friend here will continue to exist for as long as they find gentlemen like yourself willing to foot the bill. This is the first time I see you when you're not in trouble with the law, Carvalho. Lucky for you, nobody's been killed yet. A private detective is allowed to investigate a threat. But just you remember, the moment there's a drop of blood, if I see you snooping about, I'll have you. Why don't you retire?'

'I'm a terrible spendthrift. I haven't saved enough money to retire.'

'Aren't you with a pension fund?'

'No.'

'You're making a big mistake. An old detective isn't a detective any more — he's just old. Take it from me. I've got the state standing behind me, but as far as I can see, you don't have a penny to your name.'

'I haven't come here to talk about pensions.'

'What do you think of this second letter? Damn stupid, if you ask me. That's all we need, anonymous poets turning to crime! In the old days maybe we were less educated, but people were more honest. I've never seen such a load of drivel. I miss the old days, when anonymous letters were full of spelling mistakes, and used to start like the letters that people wrote before the war: "I hope that this letter finds you well. I am well too, thank the Lord".'

Camps let out an entirely inappropriate guffaw, and then repeated it. So inappropriate that to Carvalho it indicated a lack of respect and a streak of hysteria. Camps sensed what Carvalho was thinking, and this made him laugh even more, until by the end there were tears streaming down his face.

'I'm glad you find me so amusing.'

In Contreras's eyes you could almost see the handcuffs that he was mentally preparing for the impertinent Camps O'Shea. The latter was having some difficulty regaining his composure.

'Inspector, you're brilliant.'

Carvalho found this sentiment equally repellent. Police inspectors are never to be considered brilliant, and even less should they ever be told so. Camps's apparent neutrality in relation to the police was ill-befitting in a sane-minded citizen. A person is entitled to love the police when he's riddled with authoritarianism, and a vigilant citizen is entitled to be an enemy of the police, but to see the police as somehow part of a spectacle is only possible in times that are essentially ambiguous, times in which people have lost their sense of values. Contreras decided to re-establish the logic of the situation, and came to the point.

'I'll tell you what's behind all this.'

This offering aroused expectant surprise in his audience.

'What we're dealing with here is a polysemic delinquent.'

'Even though it might surprise some people — Carvalho knows who I'm referring to — the police nowadays work with new methods. We have here a clear starting point. What stands out when you take a close look at the first letter, but more particularly the second? Is it the fact that a murder is being announced? No. Or is it that the object of the exercise, if you'll pardon the expression, is a centre forward, an unusual target for a murder, as I'm sure you'll agree? Well, maybe, but maybe not, because we've had boxers being murdered, and those that live by the sword . . . I say this without any disrespect to the worthy profession of footballer, and particularly to the centre forwards of this world, who are undoubtedly a very proper class of person . . . Now, put your imaginations to work, gentlemen. What stands out? The form, gentlemen, the form! The important thing here is the form in which the letters are written. You laughed when I compared the form of these letters with the kind of anonymous letters that we used to get in the old days. Please don't think I was annoyed, because I realize that the comparison was rather comical, amusing, what have you. But the point is still worth making. The author of our anonymous letters is trying to be literary. He is creating an atmosphere, just like they do in films or at the theatre, where you slowly build up the audience, and then, bang, the *coup d'effect*. One problem is that they're written in a transfer lettering, probably Letraset, which means that we might have to go and interview every graphic artist in Barcelona, which could take us half a lifetime, since there's a lot of publishers in this city. But it's useful to remember that we're on the trail of somebody who knows how to write, and who wants to show that he knows how to write. And, as Inspector Lifante suggests, probably somebody with money, and somebody who has moved in Madrid circles. This person is using literary techniques to build our expectations, literary expectations, around a criminal act which has not yet taken place, but which, if it did take place, would provoke a major scandal. Let's be in no doubt about that. If anybody ever killed you, Carvalho, not even God would notice. If they killed me, somebody might notice. But if they kill our centre forward, the whole world will know. Sort through the elements that I've put before you: the centre forward, the popular idol, a literary expectation, and major scandal . . . You'll say we're dealing with a disturbed person. Good. I accept the hypothesis. But let's take a look at the statistics. How many times has a crazy writer ever killed anyone and announced his intentions in advance? In real life, I mean. None, to my knowledge. If you ask me, this is a publicity stunt. It feels like a trailer for a film. I can almost imagine the title: *The Centre Forward will Die at Dusk*. So, this little stunt is up and running. But now we have to analyse the actual content of the letters. Perhaps I'd best hand you over to Inspector Lifante, who is our expert in content analysis.'

He pressed the button on his intercom and roared down it as if either the intercom was broken or Lifante was terminally deaf.

'Come in, Lifante.'

Lifante came in. He bore a remarkable resemblance to an Adolfo Domínguez model, with a jacket that could easily have held two Lifantes, and with a quantity of brilliantine sufficient to have supplied half the western world.

'Lifante, would you mind running through your content analysis for these gentlemen?'

'Are you familiar with the work that Moles has done on content analysis? Or the edited version which Kientz recently published?'

'This isn't a cop,' Carvalho groused to himself. He rained mental curses on a system of culture that was capable of having intellectuals specialized in the art of repression. He had probably graduated from some Faculty of Repressive Sciences. But Lifante's manner finally succeeded in winning him over. In Inspector Lifante, the medium was the message, and for him any crime was essentially a puzzle. He explained that he saw any given crime as a communication which had been interrupted by a noise. He waited for the others to ask him what noise he was talking about, but since they maintained a state of silent puzzlement, he continued: 'With any message there has to be both a transmitter and a receptor, and the message has to be passed via a channel. But sometimes the transmission of the message can be interrupted by a noise. Well, crime acts as that kind of noise. It is a temporary noise which tends to deflect the message. Here a death is being announced. Somebody is engaged in trying to communicate this fact — and I stress the word "communicate". If we succeed in tracing the path back, we will finally arrive at the transmitter, the communicator, that is to say, the criminal in question.'

Contreras gave them a wink as if to say 'This boy's good.'

'One should not confuse content analysis with ideological analysis, although obviously we might find it useful to establish an ideological portrait of the transmitter. Myself, I prefer to relate content analysis to psycholinguistics. I have constructed a method for myself, which uses psychology in order to define the psychological type of the person who is transmitting. Once we succeed in establishing this psychological type, that immediately takes us into the area of sociology, and via a combination of sociology and psychology we will finally be in a position to draw an Identikit of the person's state of mind. And that state of mind will have a face to go with it.'

'And an ID card,' Carvalho added.

The inspector laughed, briefly.

'I probably shouldn't say this, because I am a policeman after all, but actually the person's identity card is what interests me least.'

'I don't like to hear this, Lifante.'

'I'm just hypothesizing, chief, just hypothesizing. I know that the person's going to have to be arrested, either by catching him red-handed, or by tracking him down via his record. But what interests me, scientifically speaking, is this whole process of defining a psycho-social type.'

'Get to the point, Lifante, get to the point. Explain how you do this analysis.'

'Well, first you take the texts and you differentiate the various basic semantic elements. You look at where these are repeated, and this tells you something about the person's obsessions. Now, the problem here is that we have a message which is evidently polysemic.'

'Polynesian?' Carvalho inquired innocently.

'No. Polysemic. Moles has done a lot of research into this, and he tells us . . .'

'Tells who?'

'Don't interrupt Lifante, Carvalho.'

'I used the word "us" in the sense of the plural receptor, in other words, Moles's readers. Anyway, Moles tells us that messages can generally be divided into two sorts: those with a principally semantic content, and those with a principally aesthetic content. In other words, those which tend to prioritize signification and communicability, and those which introduce polysemic elements demanding a certain freedom of reading. For example, "Mummy, my tummy hurts" is a principally semantic message, whereas "I come, in my solitude, and in my solitude I go" is an aesthetic message. This is where the complication comes. The messages that we're getting from our anonymous transmitter are both semantic and aesthetic; in other words they're complex and polysemic. He's telling us: "I am going to kill a centre forward." But the way he says it makes it difficult for us to disentangle, because he's put an aesthetic slant on it. This makes it difficult to isolate the various elements, and to establish their inter-relationship.'

'Get on with it, Lifante.'

They waited expectantly for Lifante to spell out his elements. The young inspector placed the two anonymous letters on the desk.

'Here you have the two messages. I have attempted to isolate and correlate the various elements and what has been the result?'

Their expectant gazes awaited the revelation that was about to come.

'The result is that, unfortunately, it has proved impossible to establish a result.'

'I see.'

Contreras stirred restlessly in his seat.

'But the fact that I haven't come up with specific results still leaves us with a basic conclusion. Namely that here we are dealing with a polysemic personality. A polysemic message implies a personality who is also polysemic, someone torn between a desire to communicate and the need to embroider his communication. If I were a literary critic, which, by the way, I am not, although I hope to be, one day . . .'

'He writes articles in *Police Review*,' Contreras confirmed, with a wink.

'If I were a literary critic, I would say that our man has fallen into a trap which is very common among writers who can't tell the difference between journalism and literature. Our author has sufficient style to say: "I am going to kill a centre forward, and that's all I have to say." But when he tries to be literary, he starts dressing up a basically valueless message with a literary camouflage. Exactly that. A literary camouflage.'

'I'm afraid I don't share your diagnosis,' Camps O'Shea cut in, shaking his head dubiously.

Lifante shrugged and gave another little laugh which gave him the chance to swallow the saliva that had accumulated in his mouth.

'That's your prerogative. However, I'm sticking to my guns. Either you write journalistically, or you write literature. You can't do both at once. If you do, the result ends up a hybrid, which is precisely what we have in this message.'

There was a note of challenge in Camps's reply: 'I'd be interested to hear how you would have conveyed this message without combining the communicative with the literary?'

'This is obviously a key question. We already know what the purely journalistic message would look like: "I am going to kill the centre forward."

'Full stop,' Carvalho interjected, but he failed in his attempt to cut Lifante short.

'And that would be sufficient. The message would be

simple, functional and to the point. Commendable. If I were a true poet, I might have written it as follows: "Centre forward, paled before the fall of night, and usurped gods extract frustrated vengeance." '

Camps appeared to be considering this. Finally he said: 'Not bad, but you'd have to work on the rhythm a bit.'

'OK. What do you suggest?'

Camps and Carvalho exchanged the looks of bored guests at a dinner party.

'It would sound better like this:

> The dusk fallen, the gods usurped,
> In the centre of the world is he who must die.'

'I would say you've improved on the polysemic element, but not on the rhythm.'

'I'm more interested in plurality of meanings than rhythm.'

'Rhythm is an important element of linguistics; it's indicative of particular ways of breathing.'

'I agree that there's a lot to be said about the relation between rhythm, or syntax as a whole, and the human respiratory system . . .'

'Right . . . that'll do.'

Contreras was on his feet, looking as if he was about to thump the desk. Instead his hand hovered in the air, and he did his best to muster a smile from among the folds of his indignation.

'Very interesting, gentlemen, but neither you nor I, Lifante, are paid in order to write poetry.'

Lifante laughed again, and once again swallowed surplus saliva.

'If you have any concrete conclusions to offer us, we'd be delighted to hear them; if not, you'd best go with Bolaños to check out the Guinardó.'

'In a certain sense, yes, I do have a conclusion. First of all, we already know that our writer has a tendency to polysemic hidden meanings. I suggest that this means he's a frustrated writer; as he continues sending these anonymous letters, we're going to find that he'll tend to repeat significative elements in his discourse. All we have to do is wait, and when they arrive we run them through our analytic system.'

'Off you go, Lifante. Time to check out the Guinardó.'

Once the young inspector was gone, silence fell. The silence expressed a variety of perplexities. Contreras, on the one hand, was dizzy with words. Camps had a headful of alternative rhythms; and Carvalho was trying to make some relationship between the bizarre circumstances of this case and something approaching a proper professional situation. Unfortunately the effort defeated him, and he found this disconcerting. In normal circumstances the situations that he found himself in professionally generally had some single common denominator, but this one was proving annoyingly polysemic.

'Contreras, I fear for the security of this city, in the hands of people like your young polysemic inspector.'

'Out of respect for señor Camps, I won't say what I was about to say. I will limit myself to saying that you are an ignoramus and a pest into the bargain. If we'd put this case in the hands of some routine blockhead, you'd be complaining that we're prehistoric and primitive. But the minute we try to bring in new procedures, you treat us with the contempt of the ignorant. Who was it said that people can only be dismissive when they're ignorant?'

'Harpo Marx, I think.'

Camps O'Shea was shrinking progressively further into himself. Carvalho had to repeat his name several times to bring him back to reality — namely that the time had come to leave.

*

The woman had peroxide hair, large, sad, brown, liverish eyes, and a mouth designed for moist but chaste kisses. A hint of carnality in a body that had been formed by gymnastics, ballet, massage, and an orderly life as an independent, upper middle-class lady, thanks to a business concern entitled 'Beautiful People' which her husband had financed for her so that she could have something to keep her amused, and which she had developed into an expanding empire that had already spread halfway down the block. Women were coming and going, in between doing their shopping, or in between the two traffic jams that they had to endure in order to take their children to and from schools which were located in the greener part of Barcelona just before you get to Tibidabo. Since Alberto Palacín cut a fairly fine figure in the place, the woman ushered him in from the main entrance and took him into an office with a desk which was occupied by photographs of her husband and children, and walls which were occupied by certificates proclaiming her expertise in various branches of the bodily sciences.

'What a pity, what a pity. Inma and I were great friends. She wasn't just a client, you know. One time she even stood in for one of my ballet teachers. She had a magnificent body. In fact people used to ask her to do fashion shows for them, and conferences, all that sort of thing . . . No. No, she didn't leave a forwarding address. One day she was here and the next she was gone. I don't want to be indiscreet, but are you a relative of hers?'

'Her first husband.'

'What a pity. Three weeks earlier and you would have caught her.'

'I didn't tell her I was coming back to Barcelona. The fact is, I didn't decide to come until August. You know how it is between separated couples. I used to send her a cheque for the boy, every month, via a bank account. And I still do.'

'Maybe the bank could tell you where she's moved.'

'Banks are usually very tight about that sort of thing.'

'But she must have a forwarding address to be receiving the money.'

'That's true.'

'I'm sorry I can't be more helpful.'

'Do you know how they were getting on?'

'Who?'

'Her and the boy.'

'Well. Very well. I think they were having a bit of money troubles, because her husband, I mean her new husband, was having a bit of a hard time. His business went bust, and he was turning his hand to all kinds of things — sales rep, that sort of thing. I think he wasn't doing too well. I would say that's why they decided to leave, in the end.'

'The boy was just about to change schools, though . . .'

'I presume that's precisely why they chose that time to leave. She didn't say where she was going, though. Do you know her present husband?'

'Yes. Yes. Thanks for your help.'

'It's a real shame that Inma went. She was such an example for our other clients. She had an excellent sense of physical discipline, and it was a pleasure just watching her when she was working out in the gym. We have just about everything here: squash, underwater massage, a swimming pool, a gym, a dance studio, and a small health food restaurant.'

Her enumeration of the establishment's various facilities pursued Palacín to the door, whereupon the woman had to divide her charm between Palacín and some clients who were sufficiently important for her to comment effusively on the marvellous tracksuits that they were wearing.

'We bought them in London in July, in the sales.'

'You lucky things!'

As he reached the street, Palacín looked at his watch. He had time either to go to his training session or to go to the bank to inquire after his son, but not both. Faced with the choice, he plumped for the training, a decision he instantly regretted as he found himself briefing the cab driver on the quickest way to the Centellas ground. Maybe he could ask the manager's permission to leave at one, which would give him time to get to the bank before it shut. But the trouble was that the morning training session was arranged specially for the club's three professionals, whereas the players with outside jobs had to start training at seven in the evening when they finished work. It was the start of the season; he wasn't too confident about how his knee was going to shape up; it was the last contract he would ever get and señor Sánchez had promised him a job in one of his companies when the time came to hang up his boots. He was still dogged by regret at not having gone to the bank, as if he had a particularly ferocious marker on his heels, and his half-heartedness did not escape the eyes of Precioso, the manager.

'You're day-dreaming, Palacín. Keep your mind on the game.'

He was about to make his request, but it hung on the tip of his tongue like a stammer. This sent him into a deep depression from which he was only finally rescued by the chill of the shower as it doused the fire in his brain. He suddenly had a recollection of taking a shower with Inma, and the boy coming in between them, and his little naked body snuggling up against his parents, and the lad laughing mischievously. He had lifted him up, and the three of them had kissed, in the water, under the shower. If he closed his eyes hard, the image shattered, as it had shattered in real life, for ever, at some moment which, when he thought about it, he located at about the time of the contract that had marked the start of his downhill run. Faced with the evidence that he had no great future in Barcelona, he had decided to sign for Valladolid. Inma had followed him like a woman going into exile, and had then lived with him like a woman imprisoned. All through it she'd had to put up with the moodiness of a hero whose head had grown too big for his crown. The end of every game meant the beginning of a via Dolorosa as he scanned the comments on the sports pages. At first they were expectant and benevolent, as befitted a young idol who was in a tight spot; then they turned into a critical but constructive hope that he would soon return to form; and finally came the dismissive phrase that was a prelude to silence. Sometimes he would retreat into the toilet to read, for the hundredth time, some of the more favourable match-reports, as if reading them could restore his sense of confidence in himself and bring back the good old days. On other occasions he would lock himself in the toilet and try to make the tears come, as a way of shifting the weight of anxiety from his chest — an anxiety which felt like the intractable lumps of dough which he used to knead as a young boy in his grandfather's bakery in Santa Fe. As he looked back over his footballing career, he remembered the scenes of triumph: the four goals which he scored against Lorca, in a Third Division match which was being watched by talent scouts from Barcelona and Madrid; the pride of the lieutenant who had taken him under his wing during his military service in Granada, and who, instead of posting him on route marches and sentry duty,

used to pace him on a motorbike around the parade
ground as he did his training runs.

'If you want to be a good sprinter, you have to practise
long-distance.'

And when he finished his military service, there was
the semi-clandestine game which he played, disguised
as one of the Figueres players, so that the Barcelona
management could see him in action. Then came the
signing. And his transfer to Zaragoza. And then his
return. Those two goals he scored in Madrid, with De
Felipe furious at the ball having passed right over his
head before he'd driven it straight into the goal-mouth.

'The Magic Ball'. The headline had run over a whole
page in *Sporting World*, and it was like a crown placed
on the head of this young hero as he leapt about the
pitch, lifting his happiness to the skies. It was as if, in
that toilet, in that luxury flat looking out over Pisuerga,
he had a photo album in his head. Images that popped
up, one after another, produced by some invisible hand
that was picking out each cruel moment.

'What's wrong with Palacín? He can't control the ball,
he can't head the ball, and he can't run.'

His arms trembled as he turned to the sports pages of
the Madrid newspaper with the article commenting on
his 'catastrophic performance' in the game against Bilbao
Athletic. 'A game which is best forgotten, out of respect
for the Palacín we once knew, whom we all saw as the
natural heir to Zarra and Marcelino.' Sometimes, when
he returned home drunk in the early hours of the morning, in order to avoid a confrontation in bed with his
insomniac wife, he would take refuge in the kitchen. Its
territory of crude light, tiles, and shiny surfaces accentu-
ated the contours of his body as he collapsed, and offered
only a chilly silence in response to his murmurings of
self-pity. Then came the fights, the apologies, the remorse,

and again the wait for the following week's headlines, in
the hopes of regaining a confidence which by then had
abandoned him. One day Valladolid beat Madrid on their
home ground, and the papers reported that Palacín had
not only 'played decisive football', but also that 'he succeeded in opening spaces, and running rings round the
opposition defenders, with the kind of style that he used
to show with Barcelona'. The article took him from
depression to euphoria, and from euphoria to alcohol. By
the time he reached home he was walking ten feet tall
and not in a mood for Inma's reproaches. That night he
felt like a winner. He had hit her, and her expression had
changed from one of anger to one of helpless impotence,
a look which was to pursue him through the long years
of their separation like a dark, evil shadow. First came
her decision to go to Barcelona, to cool off and think
things over. The days turned into weeks, and then
months, and when he got an offer to sign for a club in
the US, Inma responded more enthusiastically than
might have been expected. He'd travelled to Barcelona to
see her, and her response had been to hand him a letter
from her lawyer, in a flat which smelt of another man —
of Simago, in fact, the transfer agent who had advised
him in his negotiations with Barcelona, with Valladolid,
and now with Los Angeles, without ever letting on about
his secret affair with Inma. She was putting on weight a
bit, but she still looked good, and the kid seemed oblivious
to what was going on. He gave him a picture of a monster
that he'd drawn. 'That's you,' he said. The picture was of
a giant with two heads — one head was his own, and the
other was a football, growing out of his shoulders like a
cyst.

A phone call woke Sánchez Zapico at seven in the morning to tell him that a hoist in one of his scrap metal yards

had been wrecked on account of having had its cables cut. Sánchez Zapico gathered his thoughts, while his wife beside him snored and sent sour exhalations in the direction of the Murano glass chandelier which they had brought from Venice as a utilitarian souvenir of a trip taken to celebrate their silver wedding anniversary. From the corner of her mouth a trickle of saliva emerged as she slept, and as Zapico lifted the bed covers he was confronted by the sight of his penis as it thrust impatiently out of the fly of his pyjamas. He would have to do something for it, and not just go for a piss. He headed for the toilet with his head full of plans and plummeting lifts, and his cock waving in front as if pointing the way. He locked the toilet door and set about masturbating over the toilet bowl, but his attempts at erotic recollection failed to provide the necessary stimulus. He mentally summoned up the following: the arse of the freckled little French girl at the Solar Sauna; the pendant breasts of one of his nieces as she had leaned over to serve him food at a family birthday gathering; and the body of his wife in one of their more successful moments of coitus, for which the scene had been a ship's cabin on a cruise to the Canary Islands organized by the Barcelona Confectioners' Association — an idealized image of a woman, with her youth frozen in time and embalmed in a corner of his memories. All to no avail. His premonitions of impending disaster proved too powerful for him, and he and his penis were left looking at each other. The little creature retired in humiliation, and he thought to himself: 'Save it for another day, brother.'

Now it was time to confront another bald-headed figure — himself, this time, viewed in the bathroom mirror as his hands automatically sought the wig perched on top of a polyurethane head near by. He put it on and combed it down at the sides. Then he brushed his teeth, and noticed that he had spat out blood with the water. Was he getting cancer? Cancer was waiting round the corner. As he walked to his office he tried to decide on the best phone call to make — the most prudent, but also the one most guaranteed to produce results. A call which would not necessitate further phone calls, but which would also not irritate the beast in question. He wasn't going to wake it at that time of the morning, however, and he sat at his desk, with his hands in his dressing-gown pocket, watching the phone to make sure it didn't run away. When half past eight sounded on the Swiss cuckoo clock that he had acquired on a trip to buy Gruyère cheese and to visit his Geneva suppliers and the world in general, he dialled a number from memory, decisively, and even as he dialled it he felt the strength draining out of his fingers.

'Is that you, Germán? I'm sorry for calling at this time of the morning, but I had to talk with you. It looks like your friends have lost patience with me. You know what I'm talking about. We need to talk.'

'Very well. Now.'

Now. An abrupt 'now' which sent a shudder through his arms, his shoulders, and his entire frame. If Germán said now, then now it would have to be. He shuffled across the floor to his wardrobe. He chose the blue suit with white stripes, and a silk tie which his daughter had brought back from a trip to Italy after she had finished her course at the Hostess School. He went to the kitchen and prepared himself a ham sandwich, and a cup of milky coffee, because you think better with food inside you. He fetched his car from the parking lot and drove the four blocks that separated him from the flat of Germán Dosrius, the lawyer — as it happened, *his* lawyer. When this business was finally sorted out, he planned to issue him with an ultimatum. Whose side are you really acting on? But when he came face to face with him, on a balcony terrace overlooking Turo Park, ushered in by a half-asleep servant, what came from his lips was not an ultimatum but solicitous comments regarding the welfare of the plants which Dosrius was watering.

'I water them every morning. I know it's not the best time of day for watering, but I never know how the rest of my day is going to turn out, and anyway it gives me time to plan my day. When do you plan your day?'

'In the morning, the same as you. In the toilet, in fact.'

'A good place to do it. Very intimate. Shall we take breakfast together?'

'I'll just have a little coffee; I've already had a sandwich.'

And as he was about to drink his coffee, Dosrius broke off from buttering his toast to ask: 'So what's this all about?'

'That's exactly what I want to know. What's this all about, Dosrius? Don't play around with me like this. We've been friends all our lives, Dosrius. Somebody has sabotaged a lift in one of my warehouses . . . It's obvious that it was deliberate . . .'

'It doesn't take much for a lift to break down.'

'Well what about the warehouse fire in the sweet factory, eh?'

'You're insured, aren't you? I'll sort out the paperwork.'

'Look, Dosrius, you talk with whoever you need to talk to, and just tell them to be patient. This is a complicated business. You can't build a house from the roof down. I know that the pressure's on, but everything's under control. Just let me get the season under way, and when things start to go badly, that'll be the moment to provoke a crisis.'

'What if things go well, though?'

'What are you saying? How can things possibly go well?

I've got a team of cripples and an idiot for a manager; we lost a thousand members last season; and we lost three of our first four games in the League.'

'But you've just signed a star player.'

'A star player?'

'Palacín. He's international status.'

'Madre de deu ... Star player — that's ridiculous! See — you're making me so nervous that I've started speaking Catalan.'

'It would do you good to speak Catalan.'

'Stop it, Dosrius. Palacín has a plastic kneecap. I got him from Raurell, who's one of the shadiest agents there is. I signed him against medical advice — in other words, I did a deal with the doctor. The trouble is, you don't understand. I can't be chairman of Centellas and start the season without signing up someone so as to show that I want the club to survive. That was what we agreed. Tell that to whoever you need to tell it to. You know perfectly well that when we met in that restaurant in Castelldefels, with those people you brought, everything was left very clear. You work at your own speed, Sánchez. That's what they said. That's what *you* said. And that's what I'm doing.'

'The Olympics are getting closer.'

'We've already made our agreement. No problem. The ground will be yours.'

'Ours.'

'All right, ours. But don't go getting so impatient.'

'I want to be frank with you.'

But he delayed being frank until he had finished eating his toast and had taken a long sip at his coffee, a sip which seemed to last an age.

'They've no confidence.'

'In whom?'

'They've no confidence.'

'You mean they don't trust me?'

'There are too many loose ends. Imagine what's going to happen if your club members decide to prolong Centellas's death throes right up to the Olympics. By then land speculation will be spreading like wildfire, and any bit of ground within three miles of the Olympic Village is going to be worth its weight in gold. By then it'll be too late. Our group — I repeat, *our* group, as much yours as mine — won't have the weight to compete with other buyers when it comes to buying the Centellas ground. Don't forget, there will be foreign buyers too. Use your imagination, and you'll tremble even to think of it.'

Zapico trembled accordingly, and mustered a feeble smile.

'But . . .'

'No buts, Juanito . . . Just use your imagination.'

'But . . . you must think I'm stupid. It can only be a question of months. We'll be bottom of the League within a fortnight. Even if my idiot manager doesn't do the trick, I've arranged with one of my players to fix Palacín's knee again.'

'You don't mean you've got someone else involved?'

'Don't worry, I've got him firmly under my thumb, and anyway, I'm not dealing with him directly. As soon as we're bottom of the League, and Palacín's been dealt with, I'll call a board meeting, and an emergency meeting of the club members, and I'll say: "Gentlemen, the time has come to call it a day".'

'Supposing they say no? Supposing they start collecting money in the barrio? "Centellas must be saved!" People love saving things that are at death's door.'

'What do you mean, barrio, Dosrius? What barrio? How many years is it since you were last in our part of town? It's not a barrio any more, it's not anything. People these days don't know whether they're in Pueblo Nuevo, Barcelona or Timbuctoo. People these days are worried about finding jobs, not about saving fossilized football clubs — particularly if it's going to cost them money, because they're not prepared to spend money on nostalgia, Dosrius.'

'What happens if the local reds turn up and start campaigning about "loss of cultural identity"?'

'What cultural identity, Dosrius? Are you telling me I'm the president of a library or something, and I never even realized it?'

'Football is popular culture, Juanito. For the commies, everything is culture.'

'Football, culture?'

'Don't be naive, Juanito. You know how commies love to stir the shit. Commies stir the shit because they love giving the authorities a hard time — until they get into power, that is, and then they start giving everyone else a hard time.'

'What commies? What are you talking about, for God's sake? I wouldn't give you tuppence for communists today. You can buy them with a handful of sweets. Real communists are a thing of the past. The people who used to shout their mouths off have all ended up as city councillors, or directors of this and that. The architects who used to measure the height of houses by the centimetre are now building skyscrapers, Dosrius. You're a man of culture, of course you are, you know how things are going . . .'

Dosrius had finished his breakfast, and was keeping his thoughts to himself. He remained silent while Sánchez Zapico began talking himself round in circles.

'Everything's under control. Really, Dosrius, believe me.'

'I believe you, partly because I know you, partly because I'm involved in all this, and partly because there are a lot of interests at stake in this. You should think the worst about the business with the lift. Do you really think I knew about it, Juanito? Hand on your heart, do you really think that I would do anything to harm you?'

'The thought never even crossed my mind.'

'I should hope not. It must have been some lone operator, just as it was with the fire in the warehouse. But you have earned a lot of money from the bits of subcontracting that we've passed your way, and now these people are wanting results. You're going to earn a lot of money when they start building on the Centellas pitch.'

'My cousin's going to earn a lot, and my brother-in-law.'

'And you, Juanito.'

'Sure, and me. So obviously I've got a personal interest in everything turning out right.'

Dosrius looked sad for a moment and reached across to look Sánchez Zapico in the eye as he grasped him firmly by the arm.

'You're a man after my own heart, Juanito. But don't go playing tricks on them, and don't try to fool yourself either. Today it was the lift. The other day it was the warehouse. What about yourself? And your family? There are some very honest people involved in this operation, professional investors, and so on, but there are also criminal elements, and let's not kid ourselves. I'm sure you know what I mean. I can answer for the honest people, but I can't answer for the criminals.'

Sánchez Zapico looked as pale as the morning and as overcast as the sky overhead.

There was something not quite right about his room. Somebody was in it. Even before he opened his eyes he knew he wasn't going to like what he saw. He was surprised to find Bromide standing by his bed with his eyes fixed on the floor, and behind him a tall, thin man who looked like an expensively dressed Andalusian from the hills, or an equally expensively dressed Moroccan from the city. And on the other side of the bed, another character, of more ambiguous appearance, perhaps a mixture of an Andalusian from the hills and a Moroccan from the city, but also dressed expensively. This was his bed. This was his house. This was Vallvidrera. An October morning in 1988, one thousand years of Catalonia, two thousand years of Barcelona, four hundred and ninety six years since the defeat of the Arabs, the expulsion of the Jews and the discovery of America. And he was he, Pepe Carvalho.

'Make yourselves at home. Are these friends of yours, Bromide?'

Bromide looked as if he'd been turned to stone.

'Do you mind . . . I sleep with no clothes on.'

They made no concessions to this fact, so he was forced to emerge naked from under the sheets and go in search of a half-forgotten dressing gown which he found hanging behind the door. He was preoccupied with how he looked. He wasn't exactly fat but he was certainly putting on weight. He needed to go into training. Something not too strenuous, of course. The two Arabs followed Carvalho's movements. Now that he had the dressing gown as a second skin, Carvalho felt surer of himself and went to put his hands into his pockets, to wait for further instructions. But he barely got his fingertips in before the Arab closest to him suddenly showed great interest in the movement, and leaned over to grab his wrists and force him to take his hands out of his pockets again. The Arab searched the pockets to make sure that they were empty, and then resumed his initial static position.

'You speak English?'

They didn't find this amusing, and Bromide shot him a warning glance. It arrived too late. A heavy sideways swipe struck Carvalho on the cheek and knocked his head to one side. As he tried to tense his body, a kick sent him flying against the wall, where he froze, so as not to provoke his assailant further. There was a gun in the hand of the man standing behind Bromide, and he waved the gun to indicate that Carvalho should leave the room first. They followed him to the front room, and Carvalho went and sat on a chair in the corner, to be able to keep a clear view of the proceedings. His personal guard took up a position behind him, and the other Arab shoved Bromide forward. When everyone was in place, the man with the gun said: 'Good morning.'

'Good morning,' Carvalho replied, with a slight bow of his head.

'You wanted to see us.'

'I don't even know who you are, so how should I know if I wanted to see you?'

'The shoe man said you wanted to see us. We don't like people wanting to see us. Everyone mind their own business. That's best.'

'Insha' Allah . . .'

He expected another slap from behind, but the man

with the gun glanced at his partner, and the expected attack didn't materialize.

'What do you want to know?'

'Somebody is planning to kill someone. He's started sending anonymous letters, to say so.'

'Anonymous letters?'

'Letters without a signature. Letters with no name, where he says: "I'm going to kill Mr So-and-so."'

'So and so?'

'Another way of saying someone particular.'

'Very stupid, all this. Don't you think it's stupid? These letters, nothing to do with us . . . We aren't stupid.'

'Somebody has written letters threatening the life of a football player, a centre forward.'

'Meier? Hassan?'

He seemed alarmed.

'I don't know those two. No. It seems it's an English centre forward, who's just been signed.'

'Mortimer. Very good. Very good, Mortimer.'

The man standing behind him also said that Mortimer was very good. So they obviously knew something about football.

'Why come to us? We know nothing about it. We don't go round killing English people. This stupid old man came bothering us for nothing, and you were stupid to send him.'

Any minute now they'd end up talking like Indians in some cowboy film. But the one with the gun was in a talkative mood, and he continued: 'We keep out of trouble with the law. We don't get involved with stupid things. We don't write letters. We have nothing against Mortimer.'

'But we know that something's brewing, and seeing you've got so many contacts, I'm sure you could find out something.'

'And supposing we find out something, what's in it for us?'

There was no answering a question like that. He could hardly give them a thousand pesetas, like he gave Bromide, or even five thousand, when the information he required was obviously worth a lot more. Carvalho was walking on shifting sands, and he began to feel restless and irritated. The price of information these days was a price he couldn't afford. He would have to ask Charo to find him a job in her boarding house when she set up — making beds, cleaning toilets, maybe. A frugal, peaceful old age; who knows, maybe even happy . . . ?

'We don't get involved in stupid things. Get that straight. Stupid. And this old man is stupid too. One stupid person plus another stupid person makes two stupid people. You have come bothering us. We get on with our work and don't poke our noses in where they don't belong. Why did you send the old man? Look.' He cocked the pistol and pointed it at Bromide's head. 'If I kill this stupid man, nothing will happen to me. And if I kill you too, nothing will happen to me. I kill one stupid person, and then another stupid person. What happens?'

There was a moment's silence as he waited for the answer to this conundrum.

'What happens is you've killed two stupid people.'

He gave the man behind him a charming smile, and in return the speaker gave out a hint of a laugh, but then immediately restrained it.

'This old man is good for nothing. Just brings problems. We don't like problems. What about you?'

'You scratch my back, I'll scratch yours. You give me information today, and maybe tomorrow you'll be needing information from me . . .'

'We don't need information. We know everything we need to know. So why don't you stop bothering us? You made us come here and waste time. This is a warning to you. Remember, you're not even safe in your own house.'

'I'll have to report this conversation to Inspector Contreras.'

'Report it to anyone you want. Contreras doesn't want trouble, and we don't make trouble. You make trouble. And this stupid old man makes trouble. When nobody makes trouble, then everyone's OK. Everyone sticks to their job. Contreras is a clever man. Only stupid people make life complicated.'

He poked his gun against Bromide's head to force it over to one side, and gestured to the man behind Carvalho to come round and take up a position by the door. The one with the gun took a look round the room and noted what he saw. As he was leaving he said: 'You have many books. What do you do with so many books?'

'I burn them.'

'That is why you are stupid. If you read more, you would not be so stupid. You have been warned.'

And off they went. He heard them opening doors but not shutting them, and then the sound of a departing car, down on the street. He went to the window, and saw the city spread out below him. Then he looked to find the car, and saw it disappearing off towards Rabassada. It was a big car. Powerful. German. Bromide had not shifted position, and stood there looking like he had a broken neck. He had a scratch on one cheek, and a bruise over one eye. There were tears in his eyes. Carvalho went off to the kitchen and poured a glass of wine for Bromide and a glass of chilled aqua vitae for himself. By the time he returned to the front room, Bromide had sat down.

'There you go. It's good stuff.'

'Thanks, Pepe.'

And he raised his arms as if to absolve himself of responsibility. 'I warned you.'

'I'm sorry.'

'I'm more sorry than you. Someone suggested I went to the Arabs, so I did what you asked me to. They know what's going on. Nothing happens in this city that they don't know about, and it put them in a bad mood as soon as I opened my mouth. What put them in a bad mood was that I knew that they were the people that I had to talk to. A very bad mood. It's like I told you the other day. They look at us as if we're garbage. We're nothing to them. You saw the way they brought me here at gunpoint. If I'd had my machete from the Legion, Pepiño, they wouldn't have looked so clever. But look at the state of me now. Look at me.'

'Stop it, Bromide. I said, it was my fault.'

Bromide yawned.

'They kept me up all night, in a house somewhere down calle de Valldoncella, and then they hauled me over here. I haven't had a wink of sleep.'

'Come on, get your head down. You can sleep in my bed.'

'In *your* bed?'

He lay down on his side, as if trying to occupy the smallest space possible, and gave out pathetic little yawns, like a man drowning in his dreams and gasping for the air that will wake him. Carvalho went to the kitchen. He was hungry, and made himself a sandwich with the *finocchiona* that he'd bought the previous day from an Italian delicatessen. Since he was feeling irritated by his inability to move decisively in any direction, he sat down at the phone with a view to getting the unmovable moving. His first mission was to locate Camps O'Shea and to confirm that he was inviting him to dinner at his house that night. He had a curious, empty sort of feeling inside him, but he didn't give it too much thought. He decided that the next person to be disturbed was

Basté de Linyola, on the pretext of urgently needing to meet him, to clarify a few things.

'I don't see what clarification I can offer that couldn't have come just as well from señor Camps.'

'I can't carry on crashing around in the dark like this.'

'I've a very busy day ahead of me. If you like we could meet for a drink at eight, at the Club Ideal.'

With the phone call over, Carvalho began planning for supper. He was looking forward to the liberating sensation of handling tangible materials and working towards that magic that occurs in the transformation of meat and its ancillary elements — the magic which turns a cook into a ceramicist, into a wizard, who, by the application of fire, turns matter into sensation. What he needed was the self-confirmation of something that he could make with his hands and then give to others. To others. Not to *an* other. The prospect of a supper *a deux* with Camps O'Shea made him nervous, so he decided to phone his neighbour, Fuster, the commercial agent.

'I was just on my way out. Are you phoning to sort out your tax?'

'Not at all. I'm inviting you to dinner.'

'You really ought to think about your taxes. Your second instalment is due next month. What's on the menu?'

'Peppers stuffed with seafood. Stuffed shoulder of lamb. Fried milk.'

'Too much stuffing, if you ask me, but it sounds good. I'll be there.'

When Bromide finally awoke two hours later, he popped his head into the kitchen to find Carvalho preparing the infrastructure for the evening's meal.

'That smells good, Pepiño.'

'How are you feeling?'

'I'm aching all over.'

'Charo can take you to the doctor. I'll have a word with her.'

Bromide handed Carvalho a crumpled thousand-peseta note.

'What's that for?'

'Take it. I didn't earn it.'

Carvalho pushed his hand away and poured him another glass of wine.

For Carvalho, the cocktail trail through Barcelona meant starting at the Boadas, near the Ramblas, with the lady of the house looking beautiful against a backdrop of drawings by Opisso, a nostalgic landscape of a city which by now was definitively nostalgia. He had already explored a route which took in the Gimlet, the Nick Havana and the Victory Bar in search of the perfect dry Martini; sometimes he would arrive at the Ideal in the middle of the afternoon, when the place was half empty, and anybody who felt like it could get drunk with the full complicity of the barmen or in the company of the bar's owners — father and son — each equally expert in purveying cocktails both ancient and modern, and the nostalgia or modernity that went with them. At lunchtime and during the early evening, the Club Ideal tended to be full of well-heeled Barcelona señores, or heterosexual couples made up of aggressive (and aggressed) executives, and their emancipated three-timing wives, for whom the executive himself represented at best only the third in the line of possibilities. By eight o'clock the bar had a broader range of flora and fauna, and from his particular corner Basté de Linyola could enjoy a degree of anonymity thanks to the noise of conversation, the numbers of people, and the subdued lighting as he sat below a portrait of the bar's owner in the uniform of some old seawolf of the English admiralty. Basté de Linyola was a politician in transit, en route to his own nothingness, and the new glories looked somewhat askance at him. His face did not entirely fit with the most powerful football club in the world, in the same way that it would look odd to have Gorbachev as world president of the Rotary Club. It was only a matter of time before Carvalho caught up with Basté, looking relaxed and master of his corner, and consuming a low-alcohol cocktail which Gotarda senior had purveyed with a literary flourish. Carvalho ordered a Martini, looking forward to the prodigy of absolute taste, the chimera which Martini offers as a Platonic ideal, conscious that the secret of its perfection will never be entirely discovered.

'I have to tell you that this encounter is rather ill-advised.' Nevertheless he was smiling. 'Wasn't Sito a good enough go-between?'

'Who's Sito?'

'Sito Camps O'Shea. His real name is Alfonso, but they've called him Sito ever since he was a kid. His father is a good friend of mine. And I am honoured by that friendship. Camps y Vicens. Do you know the name? Building constructors.'

'I'm afraid not. I had to meet you, though. This business is beginning to look like an optical illusion. It only exists in the fact of the anonymous letters. There's nothing that suggests that Mortimer is actually going to be killed. Don't you have some other centre forward that they might want to kill?'

'We have others, but not really in the assassination league. If they do end up killing Mortimer, it's going to make real problems for us. The club is just coming out of a difficult period and we've had to work hard to win back the confidence of the fans and the public. This is the most powerful club in the world, but only for as long as it has a hundred thousand members. If its membership were to fall to seventy thousand, it would be a giant with feet of clay. It's dependent on the money that those hundred thousand pay at the start of each season. If our annual income took a downturn, it could be disastrous.'

'I thought the police told you there's nothing to worry about.'

'Quite right. And we're not worrying. You're a "just in case". My experience in the world of business and politics has taught me that it's always a good idea to have a few "just in case" people around. We live in a society that is falling apart. Everything appears to be balanced and under control, but chaos is just around the corner. People don't believe in anything. They don't even believe in pretending to believe in something. And societies that have lost their beliefs are the kind of societies where you get crazed killers running around.'

'Are you suggesting that we're going to start seeing irrational, motiveless killings, like in the United States?'

'Why not? We already have psychiatrists and private detectives, so I don't see why we can't have mad murderers too. And here it could be even worse, because at least in the USA they still put up an appearance of believing in God. They go to church on Sundays, and feel themselves part of a chosen people. But you don't have that in Spain. Religion of any kind, whether political or otherwise, has disappeared. The only thing that we have left, by way of communion of the saints, is nationalism.'

'Is that what makes you a nationalist?'

'It's the most gratifying thing that a person can be, and the least concrete, particularly if you are, as I am, a non-independentist nationalist. Politics is a curious thing in Catalonia. We have a situation where power is shared between socialists who don't believe in socialism, and nationalists who don't believe in national independence. The whole thing's ripe for lone operators to take over, and when you look at the likes of young Camps O'Shea, the prospect becomes even more alarming. That man has no conscience, no epic memory, no life-project other than going out and winning, without even knowing what he wants to win at, or whom he wants to beat.'

'And how are we supposed to deal with these lone killers?'

'Arrest them while they've still got their guns in their holsters, or if they've got them out, shoot them before they get the chance to shoot first.'

'And what if they manage to do their killing?'

'Turn up for the funeral.'

'You're a big man in this city. Big men in big cities get there because they have more information at their fingertips than the rest of the population.'

'I gather you're implying that I haven't told you everything I know. Don't be naive. I know that you have to buy people, and I know whom to buy. And that's the extent of it.'

As he sipped his drink he seemed to enjoy having an audience. Carvalho was a new public for him, and he enjoyed surprising people with the variety of the elements comprising his intellectual and moral make-up. His English-style cynicism had acted as a point of reference for Barcelona society in the 1960s and 1970s, when the rich didn't know what to do with themselves, and he shone as a prism with a thousand facets, capable of quoting German philosophers at the same time as getting rich without remorse, of flirting with Franco's government and simultaneously negotiating with the clandestine leaders of the Commisiones Obreras in his various business operations.

'So what's your advice on whom and what to buy these days?'

'The same as ever. You buy land, and you buy the

planning people who are in a position to redesignate that land. That has been Barcelona's stock in trade ever since the walls came down. Do you want to invest a bit of money?'

'I don't have the sort of money to be able to start investing.'

'What are you saving for, then?'

'My old age.'

'And I'd say that's not far off. Don't worry, though . . . By then there'll be a lot of good charities around. Charity is back in fashion. Second-hand clothes shops, and soup kitchens for the poor. But if ever you do have any spare cash, put it into land. On the other side of Tibidabo, for when they build the tunnel. Or in the area beyond the Olympic Village. That's going to be a goldmine.'

'How long does my contract run for?'

'Until we come up with the author of these anonymous letters. Does it bother you not to be earning your keep?'

'That's never been a problem for me. If anything my problem is that I don't earn as much as I think I'm worth.'

Basté shrugged his shoulders and waited for further questions. The audience was beginning to bore him, although he still wasn't sure why exactly Carvalho had been so keen to see him.

'From what we've talked about so far, I don't see why it was so urgent to meet.'

'Camps is just a middle-man. I was interested to hear what you had to say.'

'I shall be giving a lecture tomorrow, on "Urban Growth and our Olympic Future". That'll give you an opportunity to hear me in action.'

'I don't like lectures. The last one I went to was all about the art of the detective novel, and as far as I was concerned they were all talking bullshit. By the way, you're pretty rich, aren't you?'

'Rich enough.'

'So why do you want to be richer?'

'Because that's what gives meaning to my life. When I was younger I always felt I'd been cheated, because I would have loved to have been a first-rate artist. In those days I used to paint, and write, and play the piano. Then I decided that politics was what would give meaning to my life, and I was on the point of taking it to the top, but the problem is that nowadays rich people don't get a very good press, and even right-wing voters prefer their leaders to be of moderate means. People are willing to forgive stupidity, but not wealth. So now I run a football club, which is rather a lower order of power, but equally attractive. My intention is to remain rich, and maybe try to become a senator before I get too old for it. That'll provide another couple of lines for my obituary in *La Vanguardia*. My descendants deserve an impressive obituary. I want at least two columns. Anything under two columns isn't worth the effort.'

'I'm cooking dinner for Camps tonight.'

This appeared to amuse Basté.

'I know hardly anything about you, but I should warn you that Sito has no female friends. Or male friends, either, so far as I know.'

'Peppers stuffed with seafood. Stuffed shoulder of lamb. And fried milk. How does that sound?'

'It doesn't do a lot for me, I'm afraid. I'm an everyday sort of eater.'

'I feared as much. There had to be something wrong with you.'

'When I need to eat well, it's usually in order to seduce someone, and in that case I have three or four reliable restaurants that I go to. My father was the same, and my grandfather too. Restaurants may change, but family traditions don't. I'll tell you something which might interest you. My great-great-grandfather was a muleteer from Bages who came to Barcelona. In the nineteenth century Barcelona was only inhabited by riff-raff, Spanish soldiers, and rich people who were old and devoid of imagination and whose riches were about to run out. My great-grandfather became a moderate regionalist, and he was the first in our family to be what you would call rich. My grandfather used to hire gunmen to kill anarchists. My father went over to Franco during the Civil War, and used armed police when his workers started giving him a hard time. For my part, I studied in Germany and the US, I'm a democratic nationalist, and I hire private detectives.'

'So what am I supposed to make of all that . . . ?'

But by now Basté de Linyola was calling over the barman and pulling out his wallet to pay.

Fuster arrived before Camps, carrying a folder which constituted the entirety of his office premises. 'You're a disaster, Pepe, and one of these days you're going to get a pasting from the tax people. Have you organized your second instalment? What are you waiting for? If you can't afford it, go and take out a loan.'

Carvalho had read in the papers that the owner of a big construction firm in Barcelona was paying not much more than himself by way of taxes, and he interrogated Fuster as to the meaning of this mystery.

'I don't think you have much that you could set off against tax. The only things you could claim for would be the expenses you incur running after people. Not like a big businessman. He can even claim the paper he uses when he goes to the toilet between business appointments. Sign Biscuter onto the social security and set yourself up as a businessman. I've told you so a thousand times.'

'Faced with a choice, I think I'd rather go to prison for non-payment than end up as a businessman.'

'If you're short of cash, why don't you take out a loan?'

'That'll mean I end up with even less money. If you have to borrow money to pay your taxes, can you claim it off tax?'

'You must be joking.'

'What about my gun and ammunition? I'm a private detective, a servant of the law.'

'You're not a lot of use to the law, and you don't use much ammunition either. How many bullets have you actually fired in recent years?'

'Two, in ten years.'

'You won't get much of a discount for that. Dinner's smelling good.'

Fuster propelled his Cistercian presence into the kitchen, rubbing his hands as he went and smoothing down his white hair.

'Who have you invited tonight?'

'A young man from a good family who's presently the PR man for the city's principal football club. Camps O'Shea by name.'

'Building contractors, importers of Swedish trucks, hotel interests in Ampuria Brava . . . Very rich . . .'

'This one must be the son who had no head for business.'

'People like that always have a head for business. One day they discover that there's a market for ballpoints with invisible ink, or egg-timers with lunar sand, and they end up making pots of money like their fathers before them. Making money is inherited in the genes.'

'He's the restless sort. Intellectually restless.'

'Very good, Pepe. It'll do you good to mix with people who can more or less combat your tendency to barbarism.'

When Camps O'Shea arrived, he was evidently disposed to be amazed and enchanted by everything he saw.

'What a marvellous place ... Vallvidrera is enchanting ... It's a marvellous night ... I hope you don't mind — I've taken the liberty of bringing you this piece of ceramics by Noguerola, a wonderful ceramicist from La Bisbal .... What a marvellous house. So spontaneous and natural. Did you do the decor yourself?'

Carvalho had a hard time deciding whether this was sarcasm or flattery, because the house was a picture of orderly disorder. Everything in it bore the hallmark of decay, from the damp-stains on the ceilings to the signs of spilt drink discolouring on the upholstery.

'It's as if every single thing in this house wants to tell a story,' Camps enthused as he fingered a tie which Carvalho had left hanging over a lamp bracket. He peered at it more closely. 'Is this Gucci?'

At this moment Fuster emerged from the kitchen, and Carvalho did the introductions.

'Are you one of the Fusters from Comalada, the ones who summer at Camprodón?'

'No, I'm one of the Fusters from Villores, province of Castellón.'

Camps began to laugh.

'I'm sorry, but some provincial names make me laugh. They all seem to have comic associations. Castellón, La Coruña, Pucela ... Spanish place names always seem to sound comic. Either comic or tragic. It's the same in Italian. French and English place names, on the other hand, have a certain dignity.'

Fuster glared at Carvalho, silently demanding to know why he had been invited into this trap.

'This is an enchanting house, Carvalho. You're a very lucky man.'

They sat down to eat, and each mouthful was

accompanied by one of the only two adjectives that Camps O'Shea seemed able to muster that night. He insisted on having the recipes spelt out in detail so that he could note them down carefully in an expensive pocket book with an expensive fountain pen. Carvalho was a great fan of fountain pens, and particularly this one, which looked like the mother and father of all fountain pens. Camps noted his interest, and passed it over.

'Take a look. It's the most classic of the Mont Blanc classics. I have to confess, I'm a bit of a fetishist when it comes to objects. One does not need to be very rich, but one ought to surround oneself with emblematic objects. For example, earlier on I thought that you had a Gucci tie there. You should buy yourself a Gucci every once in a while, because ties should be Gucci. It's unthinkable that a tie should not be Gucci, or that a fountain pen should not be Mont Blanc. Dupont is too common, and Watermans can't touch Mont Blanc for style. The Mont Blanc has *substance*. I could make you a whole list of emblematic items that one should have about one's person. Jeans should be authentic Levi's; jumpers and sports jackets should be Armani; overcoats — cashmere, naturally — ought to be Zegna ... yes, Zegna, even though they're starting to go in for mass production. Zegna overcoats are particularly well made. They use the wool of twenty animals which are only to be found in the mountainous regions of Inner Mongolia. Admittedly, it'll set you back two hundred thousand pesetas, but it'll last you a lifetime. You should have two — one light brown and the other black, and you'll have coats which are suitable for any occasion and which will last you a lifetime. As for personal accessories, a Vacheron Constantin watch, or maybe an IWC; a Burberry mac like Dustin Hoffman wears; Vuitton suitcases; Alvarez Gomez eau de cologne; Limoges porcelain, of course, because

where else is real porcelain made? English shoes, and
where possible made by Foster and Son; Chanel Number
5 for the lady — there's no arguing with that; handbags
by Loewe; silk scarves by Hermes; Dupont will do for
lighters; a good Le Corbusier office chair, because you
can't beat them, particularly for style. Objects confirm an
individual's identity, and his social status. Look at this
ring for example.' He showed him the ring that he was
wearing.

'A Cartier triple ring. I presume you know the story of
this fascinating ring.'

Unfortunately he didn't.

'It's wonderful. This ring was designed in 1923 for Jean
Cocteau. He wanted to give a present to three friends of
his, and he asked Cartier's advice — Louis Cartier, that
is. They came up with this brilliant idea. How could it be
otherwise, between two geniuses? They decided on a
triple ring, as a symbol of the friendship between the
three of them. Today this ring has become a classic and
they sell more than thirty thousand a year. More than
thirty thousand, in fact. And my shoes are Foster and
Son, as you will have guessed. They're expensive, but I
prefer to spend my money on things that ratify the reality
which I have chosen to live.'

He showed them his shoes.

'English shoes have been the best in the world ever
since John Lobb laid the basis of modern shoe-making in
the nineteenth century. These days a pair of Lobb shoes
will set you back anything between a hundred thousand
and a hundred and fifty thousand pesetas, although, if
I'm to be honest, I think that's rather excessive. Each
shoe takes forty-five hours of work, and the people who
wear them, or have worn them, include President Pompi-
dou, the Shah of Iran, and Prince Charles of England.'

'I thought Prince Charles was a socialist. Isn't he

always saying things like society should take better care of poor people?'

'Ideas is one thing, shoes is another . . .'

Fuster almost choked on the spoonful of fried milk that he was about to swallow, but by now Camps was already absorbed in a careful transcription of the recipe which Carvalho was in the process of dictating.

'For red peppers stuffed with seafood, first of all you need good red peppers. Good and fleshy, but not too large. One or two per person, depending on how big they are and how hungry you are. Grill the peppers carefully, so that when you peel them they don't split. Then you have to prepare the stuffing. That takes prawns, clams and shellfish, cooked and combined with a thick bechamel made of equal parts of milk and the juice from boiling the prawn heads, seasoned with an aromatic pepper and tarragon. Use this stuffing to fill the peppers, then cover them with the bechamel, and put them to bake slowly in a moderate oven. The shoulder of lamb is more complicated. It's from a medieval recipe collected by Eliane Thibaut i Comalade, who specializes in old Catalonian cookery. I don't know if you'll have enough ink in your Mont Blanc to write it all down. You need a boned shoulder of lamb, well flattened. This is stuffed with minced lamb, pine kernels, raisins, garlic, parsley, bread soaked in almond milk, and salt. The other things you need for the stuffing are black pepper, cumin, fennel, chives, grated lemon skin, three eggs, a large onion, a piece of lard, olive oil, and thyme.'

'Very medieval Mediterranean!'

'True. Anyway, you mix the stuffing ingredients together, and put them in the centre of the meat. Then you roll it up, making sure that the stuffing is properly packed inside. Once that's done, you truss the whole thing up with bacon rind so that it looks tidy, and be sure to trim any bits that are hanging out. It has to end up looking like a big *butifarron*. You brown this *butifarron* in a cast-iron casserole, with the oil good and hot. When it's well browned, you add a quarter of a litre of water, pack cloves of garlic around it and leave it in the pot, on a low flame. It's important to remember to turn it over every ten or fifteen minutes, and don't let it overcook, because lamb tends to turn leathery when it's overcooked. Once it's cooked, you take it out, remove the bacon rind, and pack it tightly into the middle of a dish. You take the juice that's left over, and add a bit more water, together with the mashed garlic cloves.'

'And what about the sauce that goes with it?'

'That's the legendary *almedroch*, which you can find way back in the *Sent Sovi*, the bible of medieval Catalan cookery. The simplest version is made with garlic, oil and grated cheese, which you work in the same way as an *all-i-oli*, so that it ends up very thick. If you prefer, you can thin it with a little water and season it with spices to taste. Or if you want it thicker, you add the yoke of a boiled egg.'

'That only leaves the fried milk.'

'Camps, don't tell me you don't know how to make fried milk.'

'It sounds so improbable, almost magical.'

'If you say so. Anyway, you mix a hundred grammes of sugar with fifty grammes of wheat flour. Then you add four small cups of milk, and you beat it all together, adding a knob of butter. You put the mixture onto a low flame, and beat it continuously until it thickens. Then you spread it on a platter and let it cool so that it sets. Then you cut it into squares, dust it in flour, fry it very lightly in very hot butter, and serve it powdered with sugar.'

Fuster's yawns were becoming increasingly prolonged,

due more to boredom than tiredness. Carvalho watched for the moment when he would begin his retreat. This Fuster achieved by wandering off into the kitchen, and Carvalho followed him to make sure there were no bad feelings.

'Next time I expect a warning about the kind of beast I'm up against. He's more than I can take. I presume your man already has an agent, so there's not a lot of point in my staying.'

'He gets on my nerves too, but you can go if you want. I only needed you to break the ice.'

'Next time I'll want danger money.'

However, when he went in to say goodbye to Camps he was all 'marvellous' and 'enchanting' and apologies, saying that he had to get up early the next morning. He solicited Camps's opinion as to the best place to buy cutlery, since he was about to change his cleaning woman, his *menagerie*. This last word was uttered with the characteristically correct pronunciation of a man who was thoroughly Frenchified. Camps smiled receptively, and half closed his eyes as he scanned the pigeon-holes of his mind for the requisite information.

'I would say that these days you'll get the best cutlery from Duran the jewellers. They have provided cutlery for the Spanish royal family, for Franco, and for Gregorito Marañon, at whose table I have had the honour of eating, because he happened to be a business colleague of my uncle's. Duran is also a marvellous craftsman when it comes to silver boats.'

'Marvellous craftsman' . . . 'silver boats' . . . Fuster muttered to himself as he withdrew. But in the alcoholic fog of Carvalho's brain the words conjured up a fantastical, floating image of something extraordinary.

'The dinner was exquisite. What a shame your friend

wasn't able to stay longer. He didn't seem very interested in autographs either.'

Camps O'Shea didn't speak, so much as declaim. But the discipline of his good breeding proved unable to suppress his surprise at the extent of Carvalho's culinary expertise.

'Wonderfully harmonious. Everything related to the senses should follow the rules of harmony, except when it comes to excess.'

He examined the Vielle Fine de Bourgine, elaborated in the manner of Joseph Cartron, and asked for the technical specifications of the Nuit de Saint Georges brandy, which he found excellent. Carvalho was even less fond of literary *excursi* on the subject of the palate than he was of literature in general, and he limited himself to a few generalizations on the evolution of the French distilling industry since the ground-rules were first laid down at the end of the nineteenth century. Camps's eyes betrayed a growing fascination at the extent of his host's erudition, and you could almost hear the sound of his mental sphincters operating as his intellectual bowels loosened. He settled back in his chair and sighed.

'Splendid, Carvalho, that was splendid . . .'

But by now the detective had had enough of him, and he went to search through what remained of his library for a suitable book with which to light the fire, to ward off the evening damp of Vallvidrera. Camps followed his movements with a look of easy-going somnolence, but as the ritual proceeded he began to sit up and show signs of perplexity. Carvalho went up to the bookshelves, chose a book and proceeded to tear it to pieces.

'What on earth are you doing?'

'I'm lighting a fire to enhance your sense of harmoniousness.'

'So why are you tearing up a book?'

'I'm going to burn it. All good fires need paper to start them.'

Each page that he tore from the book was like a stab at the heart of his 'harmonious' guest, who finally plucked up the courage to inquire feebly: 'What's the book you're burning?'

'A book on the Pre-Raphaelites.'

Camps's eyes flickered, as if to say, 'Pre-Raphaelites — what do you know about Pre-Raphaelites?' But once again he erred on the side of polite inquiry: 'Why are you burning it?'

'It happened to be handy, it's got a revolting cover, and it represents a bastardized hybrid of two cultural forms: painting and literature, in the worst of combinations, namely the painting of literature. No need to look surprised — I once had to do an end-of-term project on the Pre-Raphaelites. I've been to college, you know.'

'So I see. And you have strong opinions on aesthetics.'

'Tonight, yes. Tomorrow is another day.'

'Supposing that tomorrow you decided that the book would have been worth saving?'

'This book's fate is already sealed. Only once did I save a book from burning. It was called *A Poet in New York*, and I reprieved it for sentimental reasons. Burning that particular book would have been like shooting García Lorca twice, so I decided to save it, despite the fact that the national and international phenomenon of García Lorcism makes me sick. To tell you the truth, the image of Ophelia drowning in the lake has always fascinated me.'

He returned to the Pre-Raphaelites, probably because the flames were now burning precisely the picture in which a drowning Ophelia emerged above the waves like some monstrous, delicate flower.

'We're two of a kind, Carvalho.' The detective looked at

the PR man suspiciously. 'You too have a schizophrenic cultural past which you try to suppress. It shows in the way you seem to feel the need to run things down.'

'Not at all. I have no cultural background, and I feel no need to run anything down.'

'As regards this job, I suppose I have a choice. I could work at something else, or simply not work at all. I took the job on partly because it was such a contrast with my ambitions, and partly because Basté de Linyola, who is a good friend of my family, told me that he was intending to break with the boring traditionalist outlook that has dominated the club in recent years. In addition, I'll admit that it was a fascinating prospect for me, to penetrate this den of heroes. Don't you sometimes imagine the dressing rooms of a major football club as being like the mythical cave where the gods and heroes waited before joining their astral battle?'

Carvalho took a deep breath. Camps O'Shea was leaning forward with his glass clutched in both hands and his eyes fixed on some distant Olympian horizon that only he could see. 'What film did you get the pose from, friend?' Carvalho thought, but he resigned himself to the unavoidable explanation.

'Do you know what astral battle I'm talking about?'

'No idea.'

'When the gods were sorting out the universe, and the heroes were defending it. I've always found the gods rather less interesting than the heroes. Basté de Linyola, for example, is a god, and Mortimer is a hero. The one is not a patch on the other.'

'From what I've read in the papers, I find neither of them particularly interesting.'

'One of them thinks he's interesting, and the other one actually is.'

'Why does Basté de Linyola think he's interesting?'

'He's a more or less frustrated politician. He once had hopes of reordering Catalonia and its economy, and its political structures. Now he's decided that he's going to recreate the country's epic sentiments, by restoring the club to its role as the symbolic unarmed army of Catalan identity.'

'And that's where the heroes come in?'

'Exactly. You know, if we were to make a family tree of the world's heroes, it would have a few surprises.'

'Go ahead, surprise me.'

'The real hero is the warrior. Societies have always felt the need to mythologize their warriors in order to mythologize the symbolic legitimacy of their aggression. Right from the earliest primitive societies, the hero has been imbued with a ritual, a costume, an aura of a chosen person who, by the victories he achieves, fleetingly comes close to being a god. But the gods carry on controlling the show from behind the scenes, and the lords of the earth, that is to say the gods, have adapted the hero over the course of time. Think of the symbol of Saint George killing the dragon — Saint Jordi, our patron saint. Well, Saint George actually derives from an ancient image found in Germanic legends, in which the hero is half man and half dragon — in other words, he contains within himself his own negation. The Saint George that we know no longer has the dragon within him; it is outside him, and he has to kill it. What was happening was that the logic of shop-keepers was beginning to establish itself in the world. Shopkeepers like things to be clear, and they like things spiritual to be one-dimensional. And Christianity took this vulgarity even further. When Saint Michael the Archangel is shown, he is no longer spearing a serpent, or a symbolic dragon, but Lucifer. In other words, evil.'

He took a mental breath and observed from the corner

of his eye the effect that his erudition was having on Carvalho.

'Am I boring you?'

'No. Carry on. I don't have to worry about burning spoken words. They burn out of their own accord.'

'Heroic myths have always been built around a single powerful man, or on a god-man, who overcomes evil and frees his people from death and destruction. Are you with me? Good. I could quote you a bit of Jung, about man and his symbols, which would help you understand what I mean. The hero is surrounded by sacred texts, and cere-monies, and people sing about him, and dance for him, and sacrifice to him, and all this, and here I cite from memory, ". . . overawes the bystanders with numinous emotions (as if these were magical incantations) and exhorts the individual to the point of identification with the hero." When we give a person the possibility of ident-ifying with the hero, and believing in him, we give him a means of freeing himself from his own personal insignifi-cance and lack of importance, and he comes to believe that he himself shares his hero's superhuman qualities.'

'In other words, football.'

'Or any other ritual of victory and defeat. Now, if you project forward into our present mediocre and so-called civilized world, in which wars are almost unthinkable between civilized countries, you find that the sporting hero has taken the place of the previous local Napoleons, and the club manager takes the place of those gods whose role was once to make order out of chaos. Then you trans-fer that schema to Spain, to Catalonia, and to our club. Our club represents Saint Jordi, and the dragon is the enemy without: in other words, Spain, for those who have high symbolic aspirations, and Real Madrid for those who are more down to earth.'

'And you enjoy all this.'

'It fascinates me. I find it entertaining.'

'But you don't actually enjoy it.'

'I find very few things enjoyable, Carvalho. For me, it is sufficient that something fascinates me and that I find it entertaining.'

'I envy you. It's been years since I last found anything entertaining, let alone fascinating.'

'One has to regain one's sense of superiority. Heroes are strictly for the masses.'

'Because you have usurped the function of the gods . . .'

'I beg your pardon . . .?'

'The first bit of the anonymous letter . . .'

'Oh yes. "Because you have usurped the function of the gods who, in another age, guided the conduct of men, without bringing supernatural consolation, but simply the therapy of the most irrational of cries: the centre forward will be killed at dusk." I know it off by heart.'

'Somebody else disillusioned with the degeneration of mythology.'

'In fact I've given a lot of thought to what our author's trying to say. I don't at all share the police verdict that he's a loony. Have you considered the possibility that this might be a paraphrased fragment of some book?'

'Whatever way you look at it, he's got to be a loony. Only a loony would actually read books like that, let alone start paraphrasing them with an obvious taste for parallelistic rhythms . . .'

'Parallelistic rhythms! That's the last thing I expected to hear from you.'

'You've succeeded in stirring my cultural roots. In the same way that every once in a while a woman is capable of stirring my sexual roots. Over the years I've tended to store all that away at the bottom of the trunk.'

'Might I ask how old you are?'

'You might.'

Carvalho poked the fire for a moment. Then he picked up his glass and offered a toast.

'For Pepe Carvalho, who will be too old in the year 2000!'

'At least we've got our freedom, Marçal.'

'If only it wasn't so cold.'

'The summer's not even over yet — this flat seems to trap the cold. Not one door shuts.'

From where they were lying on the mattress they had a view of the front door of the flat propped shut with a chair, and on the chair a bucket full of water, partly to increase its weight, and partly so that if anyone tried to enter, they would knock it over and warn of their arrival. The door was lockable only from the outside, not from the inside.

'Give me a shot.'

'Can't you wait? I've only got two, and you know you're going to want one later. I'm dying for one myself. I'm jangling all over.'

'Give me a shot, please.'

He asked it as a favour, but she knew that shortly he would turn nervous and aggressive.

'When the rain comes, this flat's going to be leaking like a sieve.'

'We'll have to find another flat which isn't stuck right under the roof.'

'We'll have to try another block. The flats downstairs are all occupied.'

'Old people and cats.'

'We're just two junkies without a cat.'

'Two junkie cats. Give me a hit.'

She noticed that he was no longer asking 'please', and she raised one hand to the cut on her forehead.

'Look what you did the other day, when you started getting twitchy.'

'That was your fault. You had a gramme, and you'd hidden it.'

'I haven't seen a gramme in years.'

'But you had enough for four or five shots, and you didn't want to give me any.'

'Have you seen yourself in the mirror recently?'

'What about you. Have *you* seen yourself?'

They raised themselves on their elbows on the mattress, and each provided a mirror for the other. He saw himself in her eyes, eyes that looked somehow bigger because of her thinness, and she saw herself in his. Looking as if her head had been shrunk.

'Come on, you bitch, give me a shot.'

He dropped the yellowing sheet from round him, and stood naked against the light that was coming in through the closed shutters and the glass-less windows. Outside, the noise of the barrio was growing, and the afternoon advanced, ripened and finally died in the last rays of the sun as it lit the peeling façades.

'If you want your drugs, go out and earn them. I've had it up to here with me being out walking the streets all day, and you lying around here doing nothing.'

'Listen, you're the one who got me involved in all this, and I'm the one who protects you. If it hadn't been for me, by now you'd have ended up in some back alley with a knife in your guts.'

'You — you couldn't even protect yourself.'

'Do you want me to hit you?'

'Hit me, then! Hit me, if you've got the balls.'

'I'm warning you, eh!'

Was this a warning, or was he perhaps asking her permission? Every time he hit her she felt as if it increased her self-awareness, as well as increasing the sense of hatred and impotence that was growing within her. Several weeks previously he had started to vomit and had almost passed out. She was very relaxed about it all. This was her chance to get her own back for all the blows of the preceding months. She had taken off her shoe, and had begun beating his broken body as it lay there uttering groans of bewilderment, until the blood began to flow, and she was able to use it to trace red streaks across his dirty, naked skin. Streaks of blood, rivers, which she traced with an index finger, starting at the source and directing them as the fancy took her.

'Give me the stuff, or I'll hit you.'

'There you are, take it! I hope you fucking die, you useless pig! We're finished! When I go out, I'm going to ring your father to tell him to come and get you. He'll put you on the farm, cleaning out pigsties.'

'I'll kill the pair of you. You and him.'

'If he wants to waste his money on you, that's his problem. If you ask me, you're a basket case. But if he wants to blow his cash . . .'

'And who's going to save you? You started all this, and it's all your fault that I'm where I am now.'

'Don't make me cry! Here, take it . . .'

He too had emerged from under the sheets, and their two naked bodies confronted each other, face to face, with their sexes like two dark brush strokes, and looking each other up and down, while their eyes avoided each other. She leaned over to get something out of her shoe, a small, weightless white packet. She threw it across to him, but it was so light that it travelled no more than a yard before dropping onto the mattress. Marçal dived to grab it, with a surprising degree of agility. As his hand closed around it he stood up and went to look for a cardboard box in the corner of the room. From it he took a hypodermic syringe with the needle already in place, a rubber strap, and a lighter. She turned her back on the scene and went over to the window, standing up on tiptoe to see out into the street. The neon signs outside were beginning to light up, and señora Concha was out on the balcony checking to make sure that hers was working. She fondled the ivy which hung from a pot on the balcony like a tress of hair.

'Do you reckon she keeps her savings in the house?'

He didn't reply. She turned round to find him searching for a vein, with his tongue between his teeth, and breathing slowly, totally absorbed, as if he was threading a needle. When he finally found a suitable vein, he released the strap and gave a sigh of relief as the liquid passed from the syringe into his body. She couldn't resist a smile, like a mother smiling over her child's regained appetite.

'Is it good?'

'Brilliant! Jesus, you've no idea how much I needed that.'

'I was asking whether you think she keeps her savings at home . . .'

'Who?'

'The woman who invites me up for coffee.'

'I suppose so.'

'Before we leave this place, we should give her a going over.'

She returned to her vantage point. Señora Concha was no longer on the balcony, but her lodger, the man she'd said was a footballer, was coming out of the street door.

'Look, it's the footballer. Footballers earn good money, don't they.'

But he didn't hear her. He was lying back on the mattress and smiling contentedly at the paint peeling off the rafters.

'Do you remember what we read in that book? How did it go . . . ? "Drugs are not just stimulants. Drugs are a way of life." '

As he lay there, at peace with himself, she seemed to see again the friend from her student days with whom she had embarked on this adventure of living life to the limit. Driving the wrong way down the Castelldefels motorway. Forging his father's signature on the cheques that had enabled them to set off on trips that otherwise she could only have dreamt about. Their travels took them to the Bosphorus, and they didn't stop there. Nepal . . . Goa . . . Burma . . . She was intelligent but poor, whereas he was mediocre but sufficiently well heeled to enable them to pursue their craziness. Until the point when, fairly soon, they had to admit that they were in trouble and they had to be repatriated from Melbourne, his fare paid by his father, and hers by Caritas. From then on he had followed her, holding her hand, down the path to self-destruction, while he went through the motions of being her protector.

'I've had to go out and prostitute myself for you,' she used to tell him, as her way of poisoning his few moments of lucidity.

But that wasn't the truth of it. The truth was that this happened to be the way they lived. It was a way of living, like any other. 'Excuse me, sir, would you fancy a literary screw with me?' When he became unbearable she would call his father, and the 'king of the scrapyards' would come to fetch the boy and pass him into the care of his young wife, the boy's stepmother, for her to look after. Until the point when the boy was on a drying-out session and stole his father's wallet and cleared out one of his bank accounts. The father gave him a beating that broke one of his eardrums. She at least didn't have the option of running to her family for help. Her mother had returned to her village so as not to run the risk of meeting her in the street, and her sister and brother-in-law had even gone ex-directory so as to prevent her treating them to periodic insulting telephonic soliloquies.

'Hello, Montse, love, it's Marta. Are you still living with that drivelling imbecile? Does he still poke your cunt with his hook to see if you've got crabs?'

Montse would give a terrified yelp and hang up, but sometimes she didn't, and her husband would come on, with all the baritone moral indignation that he could muster.

'Marta? Marta? This is intolerable. I don't know why you carry on behaving in this despicable way, but you're destroying your sister's life.'

'Hey, it's Captain Hook! How goes?'

As soon as the brother-in-law heard the words 'Captain Hook' he would hang up. He had overcome the loss of one of his hands, and had managed to carve himself a niche as one of the most respected lawyers in the Catalan Association for the Disabled, and he didn't appreciate people making fun of his handicap.

'At least we've got our freedom,' Marta declaimed, in the general direction of her naked bed-mate, as he lay there prostrate, drugged and contented.

'The ships sail to the four horizons, Marta, and bread doesn't float. It's a rose.'

A nondescript pile of clothing turned itself into a tight-fitting low-cut dress as Marta slipped it over her head, and as she put on her shoes she remembered to check that her other dose was in one of them. She preferred to take hers in the morning, when she returned from walking the streets, almost always fruitlessly. She took the bucket off the chair, and as she removed the chair from behind the door the door almost came away from its hinges on top of her. She turned as she went out, to see her companion at peace with the world.

'Shut the door behind me, as and when you manage to get up.'

As she went down the stairs she wondered why exactly it was that they always went through this routine of jamming the door shut. What could anyone possibly hope to steal from them? Their microscopic stash? The milk pan and the frying pan which were the sum total of their kitchen equipment? How could anyone be so much worse off than themselves? Or maybe it was just that she needed the ritual of the chair and the bucket of water because it gave her a sense of keeping danger at bay.

'The important thing is to have style. People should always live with style.'

As she emerged onto the street, her mind was working on producing an update of her come-on routine. 'You look like the sort who's got an Olympic torch between your legs. How would you like to come up and give me a light?'

When his instincts told him that he ought to find out more about a particular person, it was usually because his instincts didn't trust the person in question. And his instincts that afternoon told him: 'Go to Basté de Linyola's lecture, because you might learn something about the Barcelona you live in, and you might find out what makes the man tick.' And, as generally happened when mutually conflicting obsessions were struggling inside him, his legs made the final decision and took him off to the College of Lawyers, where Basté de Linyola, in his capacity as an ex-member of the College's board, was about to hold forth on 'Urban Growth and Olympic Hopes', after an introduction by Germán Dosrius, the board's cultural attaché. The word 'growth' reminded Carvalho inescapably of his childhood. He was forever being told to take things to help him grow, in an era when nothing could help you to grow, and 'Olympic Hopes' sounded to him as exotic as the techniques that are used by head-shrinkers, or the mysterious business of the caviar harvest in the Caspian Sea. He was evidently present at a select gathering, although he caught the occasional glimpse of anthropological remnants of the progressives of the mid-sixties and seventies, who now sported white hairs in their beards and moustaches and who had that look of poor souls who have been betrayed by history — the look that progressives began to cultivate at the start of the 1980s. As for the conference room, it inspired the kind of respect that the Law is supposed to

inspire, and both the speaker and his introducer looked
as if they had just emerged from the premises of one of
Barcelona's most expensive tailor's. They were so well
dressed that even Carvalho noticed it, and were so
respectful of the customary rituals of 'I feel honoured'
and 'If I might be so bold', that it looked as if there was
going to be more preamble than lecture, until, finally,
Basté was introduced to the audience as 'one of the last
gentlemen in Barcelona' and as a man who was part of
the history of democracy in the city, in Catalonia, and in
Spain as a whole. He took over from Dosrius and began
to speak for himself.

'Ladies and gentlemen, I am greatly honoured to have
been given this opportunity by the College of Lawyers, to
speak on the subject of this city, of *my* city. At the present
time I find myself occupying a position which is highly
symbolic of the spirit of our society, not only in Barcelona,
but also in Catalonia as a whole. It has been said that
our team is more than just a club. Some people say that it
represents the symbolic and unarmed army of Catalonia,
a nation without a state, and therefore without an army
of its own. This may indeed be true. However, I am not
here to speak of my present responsibilities, or of our
team, or of hypothetical future armies of Catalonia. I am
here to speak of the great adventure that lies before us —
of building and rebuilding Barcelona. Rebuilding what
was not built so well in the first place and recreating it
in line with the challenge that has been placed before us
by the Olympic games. The challenge is to stage the
games in such a way as to perpetuate the spirit, the tradition, of the Olympics, and at the same time to give
expression to the democratic times in which we live . . .

Carvalho was out of training for public meetings. As
soon as Basté de Linyola paused for breath, he negotiated
with his skeleton a change of position. However, he

neglected to negotiate similarly with the lady sitting behind him, and out of the corner of his eye he observed her look of disgust as he blocked her view of the speaker.

'Democracy obliges us to think about the way things are, and to adopt a set of criteria within a framework of what is actually possible. People in the past have said that the poor quality of our present heritage means that it needs to be destroyed, and that we should then build on that destruction. But cities cannot destroy even their worst parts without doing themselves more harm than good. One has to accept both the good and the bad parts of what the past has passed to us, and practise an urbanism and an architecture which improves the parts which can be improved, and demolishes only that which absolutely has to be demolished. In line with the philosophy expressed by the slogans which you see all over the city nowadays, "Barcelona, More than Ever", and "Barcelona, Look Your Best". "More than ever", because now more than ever we are in a position to take a leap towards the future, with the stimulus of the challenge of the Olympics; and "Barcelona, Look Your Best", because this city is going to be acting as the showcase for Catalonia and for Spain as a whole in 1992, and what is at stake is our image in the great world market of public images. All this has to be done with a sense of democratic seriousness and responsibility. We must not let ourselves be carried away by speculative adventures, but at the same time we must not let ourselves be paralysed by the kind of unimaginative conservatism which on occasion dominates public policy-making in the guise of progressive, left-wing thinking. Obviously, without progressive thinking the world would never have advanced to where it is today. But at the same time, when progressivism becomes tired and self-seeking, living on its own rhetoric, it can do more harm than the worst kind of conservatism. This city is either going to grow, or it is going to be paralysed, and this will depend on whether, on the pretext of defending the city from speculators, we end up letting ourselves be ruled by mistrust, in the sense that every attempt at creating growth becomes suspect and we end up falling between two stools: doing nothing ourselves, and not allowing others to do anything either. There is a time and a place for critical thinking, but when it becomes an end in itself, it becomes pettifogging and nit-picking and ends up denying its own purpose, because it simply ends up blocking innovation. This city must certainly maintain control over its growth, but not to the point of paralysing it. Here I would address myself to our socialist council, even though I know that they are sensitive to the spirit of what I am about to say: you should spend more time watching your friends and your fellow travellers than your enemies. At times one's friends can be one's worst enemies . . .'

A passing fair impression of a philosopher. And something of a town-planner too, because he began to map a vision of the city that expanded outwards towards Maresme and Valles, via the absolutely necessary, 'I repeat, absolutely necessary', tunnels that were going to have to be constructed.

'Is there some law that says that a city, a living organism in a state of continual expansion, should limit itself to existing within the natural frontiers that imprison it? Has that ever been the spirit of the people of Barcelona? Of course not. Ever since the twelfth century, they have pulled down successive city walls and expanded the city until they came up against the boundaries imposed by nature herself.'

Forty-five minutes into this exposition, Carvalho's bones were developing a low opinion of their master's lack of imagination in finding ways of rearranging his vertebrae in relation to the pain in his arse. At the point when its annoyance finally developed to the point of forcing him to get up and leave, Basté de Linyola smiled. He looked at his watch, and then held it up for his audience to see.

'This watch indicates present time, a time in which all things are possible. It's also telling me that I should sit down, so that you can begin the questions. To paraphrase one of our best poets, there is nothing so wretched as a mass where only the priest does the praying. Ladies and gentlemen, thank you for your attention.'

Charming applause for a charming man; whispers and a rustle of papers as people looked at each other, wondering who was going to be the first to break the ice. The chairman gathered up the elements of the banquet which the speaker had laid out for them, and worked at creating an auspicious climate for discussion.

'I think we shall find it hard to be as inspired and informative as our friend Basté de Linyola. But perhaps, as a hors d'oeuvres, I might be so bold as to pose a question.'

'Be so bold!'

'I shall.'

They laughed.

'You said that there is a *filum*, a thread, or rather, you didn't actually use the word, but that was what I understood you to mean, between the search for a democratic set of ethics, and its content. In other words, the non-validity of democracy when, in the name of itself, it paralyses progress. Now of course, we would have to agree a definition of what progress actually means . . . In fact we would have to agree on definitions of several things . . .'

He laughed. They all laughed.

'Unfortunately we won't have time to agree on definitions of all the things we would need to agree on. But this *filum*, which is, in itself, conjunctive and almost linear, in the sense that Pearson gives, for example . . .'

'Indeed . . .'

'. . . Pearson, in as much as he works within a linear framework, uses *filum* in both a conjunctive and a linear sense . . . In fact possibly more conjunctive than linear . . .'

'It depends, actually.'

'Of course. Everything depends on the context and one's frame of reference. The point of reference seen as a privileged viewer — the observer observed, to use Morin's image — and the context as an otherness, which, of course, is never static. Otherness is never static . . .' Here he fell silent, blinked for a moment and tried to recover the thread of his argument. 'So, where do we go from here . . . ?'

He wasn't going anywhere.

'Well . . .'

'Perhaps you'd like to ask a few questions?'

'Absolutely . . . There was something I was wanting to ask you . . .'

'About morality being the negation of itself, perhaps?'

'Something along those lines. I see that our friend Basté is a philosopher, among other things, and that he is familiar with Hegel.'

'Not as well-read as you, though, Germán.'

All public speakers are basically the same, thought Carvalho. Mainly interested in projecting their own egos and screwing everyone in sight, male and female alike.

'In other words, if I might sum up the complexity of the proposition, because our audience deserves the courtesy of clarity: you are perhaps saying that when we confront the problems of Barcelona's growth, we have to be democratic but daring at the same time?'

'Yes, yes, exactly. Very well put. Faced with an

opportunity like this, a democratic approach that was over-cautious would simply not be up to the job in hand. People say that this city originally grew in the interests of its upper classes, but that what it has become is now of benefit to all. In a similar spirit, Barcelona is going to have to put its trust in those who have the ability, the will and the knowledge to engineer the changes that the city needs.'

'Ladies and gentlemen, I hand the speaker over to you. Might I suggest that his last statement provides us with a good vantage point from which to begin.'

'Do you think that we ought to complete the Sagrada Familia?' 'I'm all in favour of Barcelona hosting the Olympics, but what about the traffic problem?' 'Do you agree with the way they've cleaned up Gaudi's Pedrera?' Basté was good-humoured and relaxed as he answered the questions one by one. But he tensed visibly when a progressive who was either before or past his prime stood up and asked aggressively: 'What role do you think should be played by our tenants' committees and neighbourhood associations in overseeing this growth? Who is going to undertake the task of identifying and naming the crooks and speculators who are planning to make a killing out of all this development?'

There were murmurs of disapproval at the word 'crook'. A few years previously it would have been accepted as an amusing sub-cultural diversion, but now it appeared as radically destabilizing — precisely as Basté went on to observe: 'When democracies become stabilized, people's language should moderate too.'

They applauded.

'But don't think that I'm trying to duck the question. The role of our neighbourhood associations must be ethical, in the sense that we have been trying to give the word. They must be capable of taking action, but also of allowing other people to take action, putting their trust in those who are capable and willing to take initiatives.'

'Capable and willing of getting rich quick, you mean.'

'So far as I know, there's nothing in the Spanish constitution that says that people aren't allowed to get rich. On the contrary. And in fact, if there had been, I would have voted against it, and so would a lot of other people. If being rich had been against the law, then probably you and I would not have been able to hold this civilized dialogue today.'

'Well now that you're all going round pretending to be so very educated and civilized, I'll tell you what I think of what you've just said: every age finds the words that it needs in order to conceal its real motives.'

'That is a normal condition of human life. It happens among all peoples, at all times.'

The audience was getting bored with the level of abstraction, and a lady stood up and brought things down to earth again: 'Would you say that we have made enough of an effort to give our Catalan sportswomen a chance to win an Olympic medal?' Basté was courteous in proclaiming that all of Catalonia's women deserved an Olympic medal, and he was also sufficiently well documented to reveal a precise knowledge of the poor state of our, I stress *our* sports environment at all levels. But, he said, a country which, without any particular liking for music, had managed to produce a Pablo Casals, could equally well surprise the world by suddenly producing champions.

This was the moment that Carvalho chose to extricate himself from the audience. He hesitated for a moment, unsure whether to take the left exit or the right — a delay that was sufficiently long for Basté to recognize him, and for his eyes to narrow momentarily. However

Carvalho didn't return the recognition, and as he headed for the exit he crossed paths with the ageing radical.

'I gather he didn't convince you.'

'They might not look it, but they're the same as ever.'

'And so are you.'

'Unfortunately not. And that's the way they like it. We will never again be the people that we used to be. As far as I'm concerned, they can stick the city up their arses, and much good may it do them.'

Basté had not succeeded in convincing him, but neither had he had the opposite effect. Having had the opportunity to assess him in a civic environment where people treated him like a patrician, Carvalho now needed to see how he operated in his other scenario of creator of heroes. He transferred himself to the football ground, to see the effect on Basté of having to switch between so many roles in the course of one day. As a patrician orator he had struck Carvalho as a cynic, and when the detective reached the ground and showed his 'Social Psychologist' pass, he thought to himself that surely Basté could not really take the rituals of the football world seriously, for all that this powerful club was built more like a cathedral than a football ground. The players were sitting on the grass absorbing a theory lesson from the manager, who was expounding the principles of ball control, with his back to the fans with time on their hands who regularly attended the club's afternoon training sessions.

'According to Charles Hughes, to create openings, you have to apply the following principles: you have to scatter the opposition across the pitch in all directions; you have to change direction frequently, either by suddenly changing the trajectory of the ball or by connecting the trajectory with another team member; you have to pass the ball quickly, and not hog it; you have to be able to conceal your own intentions; you should not dribble the

ball longer than is strictly necessary; and when you've
got control of the ball, there are four other principles
that you have to bear in mind . . .' And so he went on,
elucidating his principles, until Carvalho finally got
bored, and was confirmed in his conviction that human
beings are divided into two basic categories: those who
lecture, and those who are lectured.

The cashier referred him to a senior clerk, who, having
listened in an unctuous bank-managerial style, lapsed
into meditation for a moment and decided that this was
a job for the bank's manager. Palacín waited for the manager to finish a meeting with a man who looked a lot
more nervous coming out than when he had gone in. The
manager was patting him on the back as he went: 'Cheer
up, young man.'
     And he shook his hand in order to transmit to him the
vibrations of confidence that were appropriate for what
was the sixth- or seventh-largest bank in the country.
Then he dissolved his smile and assumed an air of gravity
as he came across to usher Palacín into the office.
     'I don't think we need to . . .'
     'There is no conversation which deserves to be had not
sitting down.'
     So they sat down. The manager listened to his brief
explanation of how he was trying to trace his wife through
her bank account. He asked for his identity card, and
then called an assistant to bring him the file for that
particular account. He studied it with all the seriousness
that he would give to the bank's annual report, until
finally he offered Palacín a smile and a ray of hope.
     'I don't foresee any problems in providing the infor-
mation you're looking for.'
     He called over his assistant, and they didn't even need
to finish their conversation for Palacín to feel the anxiety

suddenly swelling in his chest like a ball of wet dough. His son and his ex-wife were no longer in Spain. They had left an address for the money he deposited to be sent on. The address was in Bogotá. The manager communicated this information to Palacín, and handed him a piece of paper on which was written an address so far distant that for Palacín it was as good as extra-terrestrial. He stared at this more or less useless piece of paper, and something like a desire to cry seemed to box off his soul. It was a moment before he heard the manager saying: 'Do you need anything, señor Palacín? Hello, señor Palacín . . . ?'

He stammered his thanks and rose to his feet with the note in his hand.

'I hope you will continue to honour us with your business.'

'Yes, of course.'

'I can assure you that we have a very good team of people in this bank, and they are here to work for your interests and those of your family. Have you heard about our new issue of bonds that can be converted into shares? They can be converted at any moment that you decide the market is right. Would you be interested . . . ?'

'No. Not for the moment, thanks.'

'If you have second thoughts, you know where to find us.'

Palacín found himself standing outside the bank, torn between two directions, neither of which made much sense. He could either go and do the recovery exercises which the manager had prescribed for him, or he could go and hide in his room and allow himself to sink into the depression that was flooding over him. He called a taxi, and took a moment or two deciding on his route. Finally he plumped for the depression, and asked the cabbie to drop him at the corner of calle de la Cadena

and Hospital. He sleepwalked towards the entrance of
the *pension*, and as he arrived he noticed that something
was stopping him from going up. He was hungry, or at
least he ought to have been hungry. At any rate, it was
lunchtime, and he headed off down calle de San Olegario
in search of a place to eat. He went into one that looked
less dirty than the others, probably because it was better
lit, and settled himself at a plastic table which a waiter
promptly draped with a paper tablecloth. The words on
the menu swam before his eyes, but he already knew
what he was going to order — a rare steak and a salad.
He picked up his fork and toyed with the lettuce leaves,
searching out the two slices of cold meat where they sat
in the vinegar dressing, and it was the girl's smell that
he noticed before her voice, a smell of sweat and cheap
cologne, as she inquired: 'Do you have a light?'

'I don't smoke.'

'Good for you.'

There was something familiar about her thin body, and
particularly about its subdued way of being, as if she was
waiting for something, which, whatever it was, would
hold no interest for her when it finally arrived. She interpreted his attempt to decide who she was as an invitation
to sit down at his table.

'Am I bothering you?'

'No.'

'I've seen you around,' she said, as if, by saying it, she
had somehow regained possession of a part of him after
a long absence. 'I'm sure I know you from somewhere.'

'I know you from somewhere, too,'

'There's something very familiar about you, you know.'
She leaned back in her chair in order to get an even
firmer grip on his perplexity.

Palacín had a curious sensation of being in the presence

of a female invertebrate whose skeleton wasn't even up to bearing the weight of her skinny body.

'I know! You're the footballer!'

'You're too young to remember me. It's been years since I was last in the news.'

'You're the footballer from señora Conchi's.'

Now he remembered her. Her profile at the end of the kitchen, a coffee in her hand, and the air of bored resignation as she endured the landlady's chit-chat.

'Are you staying there too?'

'No. Señora Conchi invites me up for a coffee sometimes. As a matter of fact, yours truly is a prostitute.'

He twitched momentarily as he took in this piece of information. His brain took a moment registering what she had said, and when it did he suddenly felt tense, both with himself, and with the vibrations that were coming across from this unnerving presence.

'Would you fancy a literary screw with me?'

'A what?'

'I was forgetting, you're a footballer. Literary screws wouldn't do a lot for you. How would you fancy scoring a goal between my thighs?'

'No.' He said this so abruptly that he felt the need to qualify it in case she felt offended. 'Not today.'

'This is the best time. Just after you've eaten. A little siesta. Footballers need a bit of relaxation. So you just relax, and I'll do the business. My clients don't even have to move. A thousand pesetas, plus the price of the room. Clean and decent . . . I might not be pretty, but I screw with a lot of imagination. You just score the goal, and I'll do the rest.'

'Maybe I can get you something to eat?'

She was expecting this, because she raised one arm and called the waiter over to ask for a coffee and brandy.

'You can have something to eat too, if you want.'

'I know I'm skinny, but I'm not starving. I save eating for when I go to see that crazy old woman. She enjoys mothering me. Tough shit on her.'

The harshness of her words were matched by the electric brightness of the gaze which she fixed on him from the depths of her dark-ringed eyes. All of a sudden she smiled and placed a hand on his arm.

'I don't need anything to eat, but if you fancied getting me a line of coke, you'd be doing me a favour, and you could have a good time too.'

'I'm not into cocaine.'

'I know where to get some.'

'For me too?'

These words had been spoken by some *alter ego* that he had inside him, but none the less he didn't retract them. All trace of irony had disappeared from her face; now it showed only wanting, and a willingness to please.

'As much as you want.'

'I've never taken it before.'

'I'll show you how.'

'Where?'

'Don't you worry about that. You just give me the money and I'll go and score. Give me fifteen thousand pesetas. Are you carrying that much?'

He nodded, but delayed reaching for the wallet in the back pocket of his trousers. They looked at each other as if to see who was going to speak first.

'Don't you trust me?'

'It's not that.'

'Yes it is. It's all right. I understand. You follow me. We'll go to Plaza Real, and you'll see how I get the stuff. You keep at a bit of a distance, so as not to get involved, and I promise you, if you've never tried it before, you'll never forget it.'

He paid the bill and followed her down calle de San

Pablo to the Ramblas. She was running more than walking, and he was trying to hide his excitement as he followed her with his hands in his pockets, his head held high, and his legs trying to look as if they weren't really hurrying at all. When they arrived at the arcades in the square, she went on ahead and slowed down a bit, as if on the look-out for punters. She had already spotted a pair of men drinking beers on one of the terraces. She went over to them, looking for all the world as if she had just run into a pair of old acquaintances. She put up a good performance, but the two men weighed her up with a look of calculated irony in their eyes. However, when she tucked the money under the tray that still bore the remains of a *moules marinières*, the two men's air of remoteness suddenly disappeared, and one of their four hands reached into a pocket and re-emerged to shake the woman's hand as she turned on her heels to leave. As far as Palacín could see, she had just met a couple of old friends, and when she came back over he immediately began to repent of his impulse. In fact he hurried ahead of her to tell her that she could keep the money, because he was no longer interested in the cocaine.

'I've got it. It's in my bag.'

They returned to calle de San Olegario, went down calle San Rafael and turned into an entry that smelt of cats' piss and fossilized filth. They went up the broken brick stairs and arrived at a door covered with layers of paint accumulated over the best part of three centuries. She inserted a heavy iron key into the lock and turned it, but the door barely shifted.

'Shit. The son of a bitch is inside.' She kicked the door a couple of times and shouted: 'Come on! Move the bucket and open the door!'

It was a while before there was any sign of life from inside, but then came the sound of something metal being put on the floor and a chair being dragged aside. The door opened to reveal a corridor full of junk. In the middle of the corridor stood a young man in his underpants, with a bucket of water at his feet and his eyes seemingly unable to focus on what he was seeing.

'OK, scram. I'm here with a client.'

'With a client? I thought I told you not to bring people up . . .'

'Scram, I said.'

The young man studied Palacín and the woman in turn, and all of a sudden it dawned on him: 'You're not here to screw! You've been out to score! I know you, you bitch! You never come here to screw!'

'Scram, or you'll get no more dope for a month.'

'What's it worth for me to go?'

'I'll make it worth your while.'

He walked in front of them to a room which a lone mattress in the middle of the floor had transformed into their bedroom, and from the floor he picked up a pair of crumpled trousers that would have looked good on a scarecrow, together with a pullover which he put on with nothing underneath. He didn't look at them again, even when she followed him out. Once he had left, she put the chair and the bucket back in their rightful place. Then she ran back down to the room and gestured to Palacín to sit on the mattress.

'I'm afraid we haven't any chairs. I'll go and get things ready.'

She disappeared and returned with a mirror and the tube of a ballpoint pen without its inky heart.

'Do you want me to strip?'

'No. It's OK.'

'Any time you want me to strip, just say the word.'

She sat next to Palacín and unclenched her hand to

reveal a small white paper packet. She opened it and showed him the fine white dust inside.

'There it is. Life itself. Better than life, in fact. Better than anything at all. I think they won't have cut it too much. I know the dealer, and he might be a son of a bitch but he treats his regulars properly. He's a decent sort.'

She traced two lines of coke across the mirror and sniffed one of them up one nostril, using the barrel of the ballpoint. She breathed in deeply and let her head fall back as if she was trying to absorb the dust deep inside her. Then she handed the mirror and the tube to Palacín.

'Block one nostril, silly. How are you going to sniff it up if you use both nostrils.'

Palacin saw the line of dust disappear, and noticed a slight tickling sensation in his nostril, which made him twitch as only air began to come up the tube.

'You'll see — it's brilliant.'

Her voice had changed. Her eyes had become beautiful. Beautiful and kind. As if they were kissing him.

When Gerardo Passani had been hired as the club's coach, the appointment had been made bearing in mind the role that Mortimer was going to be playing in the tactical scheme of things. Passani had a worldwide reputation for his theory of the double midfield, which some Italian journalist had chosen to define as 'schizocentrocampism'. Basically the theory involved expanding the midfield to six players who doubled up into an advanced midfield and a rearguard midfield; up front a lone centre forward would open spaces and wait for balls from the three advanced midfield players, all of whom had been selected for their speed and their ability to shoot from outside the area. These six men were the key, and on the manager's blackboard they were represented in the following formula:

$$6 = \frac{3A}{3R} = 6AR$$

The formula never failed, and the final outcome produced a surprising logic, as Passani stressed, because the six who opened the formula were not necessarily the same six as the six who closed it. He stressed the point: six does not invariably equal six; it might equal 6AR. In other words, having been recreated via the process of the double midfield, the six midfield players became something more than just six midfield players, because they assumed a double quality as both attackers and defenders, simultaneously complementary and interchangeable. During the first month of training, Passani was very insistent on his tactical system during the theoretical sessions that he organized for the players, and when Mortimer joined the team — still recovering from an injury incurred during an England game — there was no problem in adapting the tactical schema, because the particular characteristics of Mortimer's style of play made him the ideal final point, the receptive and transformatory destination of the work of his six team-mates, whether you saw them simply as six, or as 6AR. Passani derived a second formula from this complementarity, which he summed up as follows:

$$6 = \frac{3R}{3A} = 6AR + M$$

From this it could be deduced that the opposition defenders might at any given moment find themselves facing an unstoppable mathematical formula in the shape of the following:

$$3R + 3A + M = 6ARM$$

This would be too much for the limited abstractive

capacities of the average Spanish footballer, reasoned Passani, who, although Italo-Argentine by birth, had learned most of his footballing theory in English clubs. What was certain, however, was that the remaining four players had been showing signs of an inferiority complex ever since the first match they had played under this schema. This was because they saw no place for themselves on the digital electronic screen which Passani controlled via a remote control button.

'What about us, coach? How do we fit in?'

Passani was of the opinion that the other four players, although important, did not form part of the decisive punch, and therefore did not need mathematicization — a neologism which sounded very elegant in his half-Buenos Aires, half-Genoese pronunciation: *matematicasion*. However, since the four were obviously getting frustrated at having been left out of his game-plan, he was obliged to conjure up additional letters which he then tried to embody into a wider, more general formula. Each of the other players received one of the four final letters of the alphabet: the goalkeeper was W, and the three defenders became X, Y and Z. They too played a twin role in a doubling up advance-and-rearguard operation which at any moment could be reinforced by the 3R that were moving in front of them. Passani contrived to sum up his overall strategy in the following eloquent formula:

$$W + XYZ(A)(R) + 6RA + M = 11.$$

It was evident to all that only Mortimer was favoured with his own personal initial, and not all the players were happy with this. However the fact remained that Mortimer was the star of the show, and was the man that the fans were coming to see, so the protests evaporated almost as soon as they were formulated. There was no preferential treatment as regards access to equipment,

or lockers in the changing rooms, or use of the showers —
although both Passani and Camps O'Shea tried to persuade the rest of the team to leave the covered pool in
the changing rooms free for a bit so that Mortimer could
do the floating exercises which Passani had prescribed
for his muscles. That afternoon, as the players relaxed
after a training session, Passani explained further: 'The
aim is effectively to create twenty players out of the basic
eleven. You can do the sums yourselves: Mortimer and
the goalkeeper are fixed numbers — in other words, one
plus one. However the three defenders and the six midfield players double up so that they become two times
nine — i.e. eighteen — and if I'm not mistaken eighteen
plus two makes twenty.'

At the start, Mortimer showed misgivings about Passani's formulas, because, he said, he was never any good
at maths. However he was eventually pulled into line by
the manager's ponderous verbosity — not least because
Passani was able to express himself in English (a qualifi-
cation that had been considered essential for any
manager hoping to get the best out of the fans' future
hero). Mortimer jotted down the manager's theories, and
went over them every night with Dorothy and her aunt,
both of whom had a better head for maths than he did.
The English threesome were apparently unaware of the
fact that Carvalho was following them around in the hope
that he might spot some clue as to the origin of the
threatening letters. The club's players had assumed that
Carvalho was carrying out some kind of complicated
research project. He was evidently studying the players,
but he didn't bother them, and after a while they hardly
even noticed that he was there.

Carvalho soon began to be bored by the endless theory
and practice sessions, and Passani's baroque syntax was
starting to get on his nerves. The detective welcomed the

end of these sessions, and the moment when the real
Mortimer emerged, with the air of a young man-about-
town, to be received warmly by Dorothy and her aunt
and to be wrapped in a more or less invisible protective
cocoon which comprised a couple of policemen and two
private security guards, plus Carvalho when he decided
it was worth trailing round after them in the hopes of
identifying likely or possible threats to Mortimer's well-
being. More to the point — and professional reasons
apart — Carvalho enjoyed feasting the eyes of his desire
on Dorothy's body, which was trim and well proportioned
despite her incipient pregnancy. She had the looks of a
healthy red-head, the owner of a carnality which was
contained in loose one-piece outfits, belted at the waist
in order to establish their own brand of double midfield,
like two fragments of one single magnetic, erotic field
onto which Carvalho's eyes settled like a vulture, with
his nostrils twitching like a vampire. Vampire. Carvalho
had recently begun to think of himself as a vampire, ever
since he had noticed a tendency in himself to lust after
the young blood of girls who could easily have been his
daughters, a circumstance in which the principal moral
problem was how to overcome the aesthetic taboo of
incest. On occasion he would pursue his theoretical
reflections to the point of concluding that he found it
necessary to seek rejuvenation through young bodies, but
this mechanism of legitimation was a shade too sophisticated for his taste. He fancied young flesh, it was as
simple as that — but the fancying was in inverse pro-
portion to what he actually dared to do, which was becoming increasingly limited by his sense of the ridiculous and
his sense of an encroaching old age which he didn't really
feel in himself, but which he was beginning to notice in
the way other people looked at him. From a distance,
Mortimer was enjoying his role as a young, playful

husband, exchanging kisses with his wife several times
an hour, while the aunt talked and talked as if she wanted
to leave her entire philosophy for the couple to continue to
savour once she herself had returned to England. In the
aunt's opinion, Spain was rather too much for Jack and
Dorothy, and on occasion, from a neighbouring table in
some high-class restaurant, Carvalho was able to study
the lady's deontology, and particularly her preoccupation
with the lack of seriousness shown by Latin peoples in
the matter of consumer goods.

'Never buy anything that hasn't got the sell-by date
clearly marked, and if there's any doubt, either don't buy,
or only buy English goods.'

One afternoon they had employed his services to go in
search of various famous charcuteries, to find one which
dealt in English products. 'And if you can't buy English,
buy German.' After England and the Scandinavian countries, Germany was the most serious country in the world.
You could never really *like* Germans, but they had their
good points, and seriousness was one of them. One afternoon, a scruffy passer-by came across to Mortimer and
asked for his autograph. As if by magic, the footballer
found himself surrounded by four large men, all falling
over each other, and the poor autograph-hunter was
dashed against a Mortimer who was alarmed more by his
protectors than by his presumed attacker. The aunt began
a distribution of choice English invective to left and right,
and Carvalho was tempted to intervene — except that he
hadn't been hired as an interpreter, and he lacked sufficient authority to bring order to this chaotic vocal octet,
comprising the police guard, the English tourists and the
much-trampled hunter of autographs. Finally the four
vigilantes coordinated their efforts to the point of success-
fully tearing up the man's autograph, and they would
have done the same for his face had it not been for the

intervention of some bystanders who took offence at the unfairness of the odds, and who had caught a whiff of police-state arrogance from the four large men. Mortimer stood back and let it all happen. He had an air of passivity about him, perhaps because he reserved all his intervention capacities for the football pitch — for those few square metres which were his world, where he was the centre forward, the precise point, the *nec plus ultra* of the life and histories of the spectators — the thousands of them present and the millions of them present only in spirit. Only heroes can act like that, thought Carvalho, borrowing a conceptual framework from Camps O'Shea, and he felt the envy that heroes rightly inspire, because the footballer knew the limits of his kingdom, and had the added pleasure of sharing it with Dorothy.

He followed the three English expatriates as they wandered abroad in this indeterminate part of the world's southern quarter, and when they'd been delivered safely home he went to a phone box to ring Charo to inquire after Bromide. She wasn't in, but he managed to find Biscuter at the office, and was duly given an up-date.

'They had to rush him to the hospital, because he couldn't even get up this morning. Charo called a cab and took him to casualty, but there's no need to worry, boss, she rang to say that he's over the worst of the crisis.'

'Over the worst of the crisis,' Carvalho repeated to himself, and he wondered at Biscuter's capacity for synthesis. Then, as he left the phone box, he found himself standing almost face to face with the Arab who had been so concerned for the world's stupidity. He smiled slightly. They were in a street in a rich, upper-class area of Barcelona. Neither the Arab nor Carvalho were on their own patch, but perhaps the Arab felt slightly less at home than Carvalho.

'Call me Mohammed. That's what you Spaniards like to call us, isn't it.'

Carvalho assumed the condition of 'you Spaniards' and invited the Arab for a glass of wine, always assuming that his religion didn't bar him from drinking.

'I'm not a very good Muslim. I don't drink in Morocco, but I do in Spain. When I'm with my fellow countrymen, I don't drink, and they don't either. We don't like to cause a scandal. Only stupid people cause scandals.'

Maybe this was the only pejorative term that he knew, and Carvalho began to feel a bit less stupid than he had on the previous occasion, and lost something of the respect that he'd had for the man, because there's a great gap that divides a man who knows how to control his adjectives from one who does not. He decided to find a bar that was small but not so plush that the Arab would feel uncomfortable, and all of a sudden they came upon a diminutive wine shop which, by some miracle, had contrived to survive in this particular location on Paseo de la Bonanova. The bar announced itself as the Cerveceria Victor, and no sooner had Carvalho entered than he was bombarded with a host of visual data that informed him that something unrepeatable had just happened in his life: he had gone into a time warp. Outside the door lay the new, democratic, Olympic, yuppie Barcelona; inside there was a small homage to nostalgia for Franco's Spain: a wine-coloured den where even the beer barrels sported the colours of the Spanish flag, and where the posters around the walls were uniformly nostalgic: Onésimo Redondo, Ramiro Ledesma Ramos, General Muñoz Grandes with his Iron Cross and Colonel Tejero with his iron moustache, Adolfo Suárez in the uniform of a Falangist commander, pictured above a slogan: 'Do You Swear, Judas?' And El Nacional wine, and El Legionario cognac. And a certificate awarded to the Cerveceria Victor in recognition of its involvement in the *El Alcázar* defence campaign — not, in this case, the Alcázar de Toledo of the Francoite Crusade, but the extreme right-wing daily paper published out of Madrid. The only sign of anything progressive in the place was the Arab, and this for the simple fact that he came from the Third World. There was no aggressiveness in the gestures of the regulars as they leaned up against the bar, drinking glasses of wine taken from the wood, or glasses of beer, and eating olives. They were frugal, severe, somewhat embittered by history and were attended to by mine host, who was as slow and taciturn as the rest of them. The aggressiveness was to be found in the emblems and icons; they kept their historical resignation to themselves. Carvalho sat down, fascinated, and watched as the Arab studiously absorbed the visual detail of the environment.

'Franco. A lot of things about Franco here. Is it a museum?'

'Not exactly. But it will be soon.'

'Franco, a great warrior. One of my father's uncles fought with Franco in the war against the communists.'

And by so saying the Arab established his right to be in the place and there was nothing to fear. The ideology of the bar was so coherent that even the sports posters had a firmly Spanish stamp: either Espagñol, or Real Madrid. Seamless fundamentalism. Pure Francoite fundamentalism — so pure that time had rendered it innocent, as innocent as any cause that has outlived its time and has been converted to an archaeology of sentiment. Two of the locals were discussing the shortcomings of the Spanish national squad and the probability of Real Madrid having a splendid season now that they'd signed Schuster. Signing Schuster for Real Madrid was on a par with the sister of José Antonio Primo de Rivera marrying Adolf Hitler. Europe would have seen something then!

But the most delightful thing about the bar was this sense of nostalgia, a nostalgia which Carvalho found repellent but at the same time more or less harmless. The Arab on the other hand looked strangely as if he was feeling more and more at home as the wine began to take effect.

'Another Franco, that's what you need.' This was the Arab speaking. The mafioso boss of old Barcelona. 'Another Franco would sort out all the idiots and the criminals like a dose of salts. He'd put people back in line. No more stealing. No more killing. In my country things went well for a while because the king is strong. He doesn't let people take liberties. But things are beginning to go downhill, badly, because there's the socialists, and even communists, and Allah says we should not be friends with communists. With socialists, yes, maybe, but not with communists. Franco and Hassan would have done great things together.'

He apparently didn't notice Carvalho's increasing air of boredom, and continued expounding his views on history, philosophy, and life in general, with his vocabulary apparently expanding by the minute, although every now and then his discourse became a shade exotic as he used an Arab word, or quoted proverbs that had to do with dates and camels. The Arab was fast turning into a caricature of himself. And when Carvalho brought him back to the here and now, asking him what exactly he was doing so far off his patch, the alcoholic haze cleared from the Arab's eyes and he once again became suspicious.

'The other day you didn't tell me everything you wanted to know, and it's important that I know as much as you. You should always know just enough to get by. Only stupid people know too little, and only stupid people know too much.'

He was off again with his exasperating mono-

adjectivality, and Carvalho regretted having interrupted
his ideological speculation. After ten glasses of wine and
myriad coffees with brandy, the Moroccan was finding the
world a wonderful place. Apparently forgetting that a
lifetime of beatings had taught him the virtues of caution,
he not only struck up conversation with the locals, but
even proposed that they should all join in with the Hymn
of the Legion, which he assured them he knew word for
word. 'One day I shall live in the high part of the city, of
any city. Allah is great, and the sons of Allah have been
chosen to bring back reason to the world. Up until twenty
years ago nobody would give two cents for an Arab. And
now we make the whole world tremble. Look at Khomeini.
Look at the rich Arabs who are buying up everyone in
sight. They're buying everything you have. They've even
bought this mountain you live on, Tibidabo. I guarantee
the name comes from the Arabic. All the place-names in
Spain come from the Arabic.'

'You've got things divided up well. Khomeini preaches
holy war, the sheikhs buy up everything in sight, and you
spend your time thieving in the Barrio Chino.'

'We just get the leftovers. But other Arabs richer and
cleverer than me will bring the cause of Allah to these
barrios. And they'll sort out all your stupid people.'

By now Carvalho was bored with the Arab. He paid the
bill and turned to leave. But the Arab felt unprotected in
the bar without Carvalho to guarantee his safety, and he
followed him out as if he hadn't finished saying everything he wanted to say. Night was falling, and the street
was almost deserted. Carvalho needed only to take one
of the streets leading up Tibidabo and he'd be home. The
Arab, on the other hand, had to go in exactly the opposite
direction. However, whereas Carvalho's nostalgia
remained confined to the territory of his childhood, where
poverty and the pneumatic drill were now throwing

everything out of joint, the Arab's big hope was to climb out of precisely those ruins in order to scale the heights towards the likes of Basté de Linyola, Camps O'Shea and Golden Boy footballers. The Arab was as drunk as Carvalho, but it was less apparent, probably because he appeared to be speaking in Arabic. Not only appeared, but actually was, and, what's more, right into Carvalho's ear.

'I can do without the readings from the Koran, Mohammed.'

But he continued his Koranic recital, and just at that point Carvalho saw a deserted slope leading down to a garage serving a block of flats. There was nobody else in sight, so Carvalho gave Mohammed a push which knocked him over and sent him rolling down to crash into the garage door. For a moment the body of the fallen man tensed, in the reflex manner of an animal accustomed to defending itself, but he was drunk to the tune of a bottle of Vino Nacional and ten coffees with El Legionario cognac, and no sooner had he tensed himself than he untensed again. He was set upon by a Carvalho who had suddenly flown into a fury for no apparent reason, and who began kicking him and punching him, until a woman standing at the top of the slope let out a scream and Carvalho pulled himself together and the Arab registered the fact that he was on enemy territory.

'I know where you live, stupid.'

'If you so much as set foot in my house again, I'll slice you up like a salami.'

When the Arab disappeared with the fleetingness of a shadow in the night, Carvalho thought of his threat and started to laugh. Like a salami! He suddenly had an image of himself chasing after the Arab wielding a salami like a club, and he found it so funny that he couldn't walk for laughing and had to sit down. The woman was still standing at the top of the slope, along with two youths who were sitting on motorbikes and toying with their throttles so that their bikes let out intermittent roars of impatience.

'I saw it all. One of those dirty Arabs attacked this poor man and then he ran off.'

'Shall we go after him?' asked one of the motorized angels.

Carvalho gestured to dissuade them.

'No. He wasn't attacking me. The Arab is innocent. It was me who attacked him. He wouldn't give me his jellaba, so I beat him up.'

'What's the man saying?'

'Man bites dog, señora. Does happen, sometimes.'

'He's drunk.'

Once the word was out that Carvalho was drunk, all trace of solidarity evaporated. Carvalho cast an impertinent eye over the assembled company, and they felt threatened. The youths revved their bikes and as they drove off they called back that he was a bastard and an arsehole. Carvalho leapt out into the middle of the road, arms akimbo, and started yelling after them to come back if they were any kind of men. He was promptly assailed by cars sounding their horns because as he stood there he had become the final obstacle in the way of their return home. He hurled various shades of abuse at them, and then took to the shadows of the deserted upper-middle-class streets that lead up from paseo de la Bonanova in the direction of Tibidabo. His body was aching all over, not from the blows he had received but from those he had given, and he tried to explain his act of aggression as a gesture of vengeance for poor Bromide, or perhaps as a simple racist impulse. However neither of these explanations satisfied him, and as he walked he searched his brain for some kind of answer.

'What made me hit him?'

He went back over everything that had happened,
everything that had been said, by himself and by the
gesticulating Mohammed, and suddenly something
approaching a ray of light illuminated the inner recesses
of his perplexity.

'He deserved it, for being stupid.'

The woman grew on his sex like a phial of blue glass,
like a giant soapy woman, like the best evening of his
life, between leaves of bright-coloured trees painted in
Caran d'Ache colours. The room was like an April country
scene in Santa Fe, in Holy Week, laurel and palm-leaf on
his sex, moistness of thighs and the marble of a colonnade
reaching towards a warm hand on his sex, a giant's eyes
and a flight up towards a cloud which blinked on his sex
soft rains of fragmented light, and his sex was not his,
but was he himself, as both the viewer and the centre of
the kaleidoscope. His ears were somewhere else, searching for some call which had perhaps existed, but from the
ceiling that had suddenly turned kingfisher blue, he saw
his own eyes, laughing as they travelled in the best sea
that he had ever seen. California Bay. Cape San Lucas.
Pelicans and sea lions. Fans of eyelashes which closed in
on his sex.

'Well, that's about it, I suppose . . .'

Night was falling on his confusion.

'The nights are drawing in.'

It was the first human voice that he had heard for
centuries, and with it arrived coherence, and an aware-
ness of the cardinal points of the room, which had
suddenly become horrible, and there, clinging to his
sweaty body, the incrustation of the bare mattress, as
bare as the body of this real and concrete woman who
repeated: 'The nights are drawing in.'

'What time is it?'

When she told him, he felt an immediate anxiety, and then took a few moments working out why.

'My training session . . .'

'What are you training at, snorting or screwing?'

The cynical tone of the woman was the final blow that shattered the glass of his enchantment, and Palacín leapt to his feet. But it felt as if he'd left part of his head behind, as if his skull was now composed of two irreconcilable hemispheres.

'God — how can I go training in a state like this . . . ?'

'It won't last long. You get the best bit of the high straight away. Take a deep breath.'

Her body had turned ugly again, and her eyes cynical, but there was something approaching concern in her voice.

'Where do you train?'

'At a stadium in Pueblo Nuevo. Centellas.'

'What do you play? Football? At your age? And what's the team you play for? A priests' seminary?'

He dressed without replying.

'And they pay you for that?'

'They do. The ground's a shit-heap. You can't get a decent shower and the changing-room door doesn't even lock. One of these days someone's going to come in and clean the place out.'

'You've got a good body. It's been a long time since I last enjoyed looking at a man's body. Are all footballers as goodlooking and shy as you?'

'Every footballer's different.'

'I find it funny that somebody as serious as you could be a footballer.'

When she saw that he was leaving, she got up and shouted angrily: 'Hey! What are you playing at? What about paying for the goods?'

'I'm sorry. I thought it was included in what I gave you for the coke.'

'Coke is coke, and screwing is screwing. At least you could give me a couple of thousand pesetas. Didn't you like my literary screw? What more do you want? Sex and cocaine!'

She tucked the two thousand pesetas into her handbag while she grumbled something about the vulture who was always rifling through her bag, and by the time she looked up, Palacín was no longer there. She shouted after him down the stairs: 'Don't say anything to Conchi! The old bitch is too nosey for her own good.'

Palacín was on the landing by now and noted the message, while at the same time finding himself forced to negotiate his way past a body lying at the door. The young man who had earlier been expelled from the apartment was asleep on the floor, breathing gently, with his eyes half open. The slight movement of air caused by Palacín's passage was sufficient to wake him, and he lay there looking up with an expectant air.

'Did you leave any for me?'

'Any what?'

'Coke.'

Palacín shrugged his shoulders and carried on down the stairs.

'You never think of anyone else . . . you only think of yourselves . . .'

The young man hauled himself up with the aid of the banister and yelled down the stairwell a string of remonstrations that only he could hear. Then he came back and walked unsteadily towards the bedroom where the girl was struggling to get her tights on straight.

'Is there any left for me?'

'I'm sick to death of you . . . and this flat, and this street, and this bloody city.'

'Don't be such a bitch, Marta. Give me a bit . . .'

'I've had it up to here with you. You're like a parasite growing in my cunt. I can get shot of the rest of them, but not you. And all because according to you and your father I got you involved in this. But you're wrong there. Any time there's shit around, you'll find your way into it. That's because you *are* shit.'

'Just one little line, Marta.'

'What are you going to do with a line? You've got veins of plaster.'

'Just one trip.'

She was dressed now, and from the handbag in which she kept all her worldly possessions she extracted a small white paper packet and threw it onto the mattress. As she passed by him, he tried to show his gratitude by caressing her with the back of his hand but she brushed him off and made her way downstairs. In the street the cool early evening air smelt of exhaust fumes and dustbins, but even this stagnant air wasn't able to spoil the glory of the setting sun. It suddenly reminded her of a sci-fi film which she'd once seen. In the dark corners of a contaminated city, the film's heroes — some of them humans and some of them robots who looked like humans — were chasing each other and killing each other in a battle which suddenly ended when the boy and the girl decided to make a run for it, to escape, towards the sun, to the countryside. All of a sudden they emerged into light, as if the city had been at the bottom of a well. There *was* a way out. She thought back over old escape plans that she had once had, but her mechanisms of mind and memory had fallen into disuse. I can't even remember things any more, she thought. However a fragment of a poem which she had once enjoyed, and had decided to memorize, filled her brain like a flash of light.

>So it was me, then, who taught you,
>Who taught you to take revenge on my dreams
>By cowardice, corrupting them?

Books and a typewriter. Peaches. A conversation with her mother, woman to woman, calmly, one afternoon. How could she ever hope to return to all that?

'Will you be coming up later?'

She raised her eyes, and there stood señora Concha, leaning over the rail of her boarding-house balcony.

'Sure.'

And she walked on towards calle de Robadors, but with such lack of interest that in the end she decided that she couldn't be bothered. She still had the three thousand pesetas from the coke deal and the two thousand which the footballer had given her; her nerves weren't jangling for once, and she wasn't in the mood for lone reminiscences. She retraced her steps and shouted up to Doña Concha: 'I'll be up now.'

Doña Concha was waiting for her at the door, and her milky coffee was waiting in the kitchen.

'Right now I'd prefer a sandwich and a glass of wine.'

'That's what I like to hear. I've got some very good wine. A bit sweet, perhaps, but very good. I like good wine. You have to give yourself a treat every once in a while. You don't take your money with you when you die, do you!'

'You must have some little corner stuffed with greenbacks.'

'I've got an account with the savings bank, with not a lot in it, and I keep the rest at home, just in case. But it's well hidden, because out of the six guests staying here I only trust one, and that's the footballer. Oh — and an old age pensioner who's as good as gold.'

'Does the footballer have money?'

'He paid four months in advance, and he seemed to have a fair amount of money. He's single, with no vices . . .'

'All men have vices.'

'Well, he lives a very simple life. Come and look. I'll show you his room.'

A single bed; a bedside table rescued from some second-hand furniture shop; a wardrobe that had been restored to life with laminated plastic; a table on which there was a pile of carefully folded sports newspapers; and a framed photograph of a woman and a boy. Marta took the picture and studied the slender beauty of the woman with the powerful mouth, and the frank laughing features of the young, fair-skinned boy.

'Who are they?'

'No idea. He doesn't talk about his private life. Take a look in here, in the bathroom.'

A shower and a toilet bowl, and over the wash-basin a shelf on which were scrupulously arranged his razor, his aerosol shaving cream, his aftershave, his toothpaste and toothbrush, his cologne, and his deodorant, all lying next to each other in an order which was evidently immutable. Behind the mirror was a cupboard with three shelves full of spray bottles and aerosols which were incapable of keeping their smells to themselves. A hospital sort of smell.

'They're all liniments and special sprays for muscle pain. Look at it — there's a year's supply there!'

'The thrifty sort! And where does he keep his money?'

'I haven't the faintest idea. Who keeps money about the house, these days?'

'You do.'

'But sometimes so well hidden that even I can't find it.'

'I bet one of these days you'll kick the bucket and the mice'll end up eating your money.'

Doña Concha crossed herself.

'You should never talk about death, dear. Not even in jest.'

The club masseur was complaining because someone had hijacked his bottle of liniment.

'I'll kill the bastard who's stolen my liniment.'

'Keep your hair on. I've got it.'

'I'm the one who does the massages in this club. That's what I'm here for.'

The bottle passed hand to hand from one player to another, all of them in various states of undress, and when it reached the masseur he held it up to the light of the dressing room's sole and tin-shaded light bulb.

'You've wasted three quarters of it. Come Sunday you'll have to do your own bloody massages.'

'Can you do me a bandage for my knee?' Palacín asked.

'That's what I like to hear. If any of you needs liniment, come and ask me. That's what I'm here for. But you're not seriously thinking of going out to play with a bandage on, are you? You should stop molly-coddling your knee.'

Like the manager, the club's masseur was also employed by Sánchez Zapico, and the two of them had something in common — a similar thin, hunted look, a similar feeling that they were creatures to be reckoned with within the four walls of Centellas, but amounting to nothing outside it. The manager was giving his final instructions.

'You, Toté, I want you to play libero, but watch out for their number eleven, Patricio, because he's likely to have the upper hand over Ibañez. I'm not saying this to put you down, Ibañez, but he's got a good half a yard on you with every step he takes. I want to see your balls take you there, even if your legs won't, Ibañez. If you neutral-ize Patricio, you'll neutralize Gramenet, because Patricio is Gramenet. And you, Palacín, I want balls. A lot of balls!

If I have any technical advice to offer, it's precisely that — balls! A centre forward without balls is like a potato tortilla without eggs! Ha, ha!'

'Thus spake Confucius,' said Mariscal, the midfield player who was a second-year student of Information Sciences.

'As for you, Brains, I want you to put everything you've got into this. You're a lot of Confucius and not a lot of balls. I want you to play with your head up and your prick as your gunsight. When you see Palacín opening spaces, pushing the ball forward, watch out for the off-side ... be very careful about the off-side, because linesmen nowadays get their flags up quicker than a prick in a brothel. Now: do you remember the game-plan? A, B, D. Let's see, who's A?'

'Me,' shouted Mariscal.

'And B?'

'Yessir.'

'And who's D?'

Palacín raised his hand.

'That's right. And you, Monforte, I want to see you in there with the opposition, putting it about with your elbows. You know what I mean. And I want a lot of balls, because if we lose today we'll drop out of the bottom of the league. By next season they'll be putting us up against teams from the orphanage. It's Palacín's first match today. I don't want you playing just for him, understand? But I want you to take him into account, because the poor bastards who are coming to see the match will be watching for Palacín. And you, Palacín, forget about your knee, for God's sake.'

'I'll make sure my knee's got balls!'

'That's what I like to hear. Now, come on. Join hands!'

The Centellas manager had introduced a number of psychological techniques into the dressing room, and his

particular favourite was the moment of communion prior
to the match, when the players all joined hands and
shouted: 'Centellas, Centellas, All Together'. Then they
formed into a raggedy line, on boots badly worn by the
abrasive nature of the bare earth pitches that they were
accustomed to playing on, where grass, in so far as it
existed, was nothing more than a memory of its former
self. They went up the wooden stairs to the pitch, remembering to take special care over the non-existent fourth
step which had been broken since the season of 1979–80.
The terraces were half full or half empty, according to
your point of view, and from the fans came the sound of
scattered applause and a few catcalls, because they
hadn't forgotten the three successive defeats that the
team had suffered in their last five league games. But
when Palacín stepped forward to be photographed by a
nephew of the club's chairman, he was applauded as the
club's big hope, and he couldn't resist raising his arms in
a V-shape, whereupon the applause increased and
showered onto him as if his raised arms marked the outer
edges of a basket designed to receive it. He hadn't played
a competitive game for the best part of eight months,
ever since he'd left Oaxaca, where he'd been a substitute,
and the atmosphere of the game that was about to start
filled his lungs with a painful euphoria. It fell to him to
kick off, under the eyes of a fat ref who began to sweat
from the moment he struggled to toss the coin. The way
in which the stadium was built, with a running track
round the pitch, meant that the public were kept at a
distance, and Palacín preferred it this way, because he
needed to disappear from the game every once in a while,
to conceal his tiredness. He looked round and picked out
Pedrosa, his likely marker: a young lorry driver with legs
like tree trunks and a right elbow that was legendary in
the second division. Pedrosa had also spotted him, and

was sizing him up from a distance with the hungry look of a hunter and a growing confidence in the light of Palacín's apparent fragility. He had received explicit instructions from his manager: 'You're off the leash now, Pedrosa, don't forget.'

'OK, I know, I'm off the leash . . .'

'You know there's no one who can match you one for one. Think of Palacín like he's an old fox, and remember that he plays as much without the ball as with it. Remember that he's got a knee like glass, but the rest of him is dynamite. Keep the pressure on all the time. Stick to him like glue, and don't let him move that ball more than half a yard. In a yard he'll leave you standing, Pedrosa. And don't forget, you're off the lead, so go for it . . .'

'OK, OK . . .'

Palacín kicked the ball back when he heard the ref's whistle, and ran forward to meet his marker face to face. He stood in front of him, with his back to the opposition's goal, and obstructed his view of Mariscal who kicked the ball up the centre of the pitch. Behind him he felt the heavy, sweating, panting presence of Pedrosa, and the contact of his body was like a wall of flesh which he leaned against when he saw the ball coming his way. Using him as a support, he turned on his heel and put his foot out to stop the ball a couple of feet in front of him. Then he broke away from his marker to start his run towards the goal. All of a sudden he felt his knee give, and although he continued his run he wavered for a moment and lost control of the ball. It was another ten minutes before he got a ball in similar circumstances, and this time he slowed it slightly, detached himself from his marker, and ran parallel with him, preparing to shoot for goal. He kicked the ball forward into the empty space that had opened in front of the Centellas right-wing, and he headed straight for goal, jostling with Pedrosa as he went. The ball came across, ready for a header, but he was unable to reach it, because just as he began his jump his weak knee was caught by a well-placed blow from one of the tree-trunk legs of his marker.

'If you touch my knee again, you'll leave this ground with a faceful of stud-marks.'

Pedrosa spat at the ground at his feet as he turned away and ran to stand guard over his goalie, who had fallen on the ball and was looking to right and left, challenging anyone to try and take it off him.

'He's a thinking player. But he's been out of the game for too long.'

'And he's getting old.'

The spectators were beginning to exchange opinions on his performance so far.

'A centre forward needs time to develop.'

'Give Palacín any more time and he'll be over the hill. Past it. He must be forty if he's a day.'

The first half drew to a close, and Palacín felt more psychologically than physically tired. The club's manager continued with the gesticulating and unintelligible strings of recommendations that he had embarked on at the ref's first whistle, twitching about like an electrocuted animal on the manager's bench. Now he was leaping around his players distributing criticism and ranting about the failings of their respective genital apparatuses. There was a special chapter devoted to Palacín. The voice was lower, and the syntax more composed: 'Don't stick so close to Pedrosa. Keep free of him, for heaven's sake, Palacín. You know what the game is. Even you can beat him once you get a good run with the ball in front of you.'

The troupe nodded and stared at their boots, and some changed their dirty, sweaty shirts.

'Stop that, Confucius! How many times do I have to

tell you?! Don't take showers in the middle of a game. You'll chill your muscles. How can you be so bloody useless? Why do you have to wash so much? You're worse than my daughter.'

By the time they came out for the second half, the afternoon was wearing on and the failing light made the terraces look even older, dirtier and more derelict, and likewise the little stand from which Sánchez Zapico was presiding, surrounded by the other club directors and their families. The chairman had one eye on what was happening on the pitch, and the other on Dosrius, who was mingling with the spectators on the terraces, a philosophical onlooker apparently unconcerned by the way the match was going. Every now and then their eyes would meet, and Sánchez Zapico would narrow his eyes as if to confirm an implicit agreement.

'God, that was close . . . !'

Palacín had control of the ball. He dummied and left Pedrosa sitting at the edge of the area with his heavy arse almost wedged into the ground. Then he gave a kick that sent the ball across the goal-mouth. With painful slowness it missed the goal and slid past the post. The roar and the applause from the spectators put renewed lightness into Palacín's step as he ran back to his original position, and out of the corner of his eye he caught the vicious look that Pedrosa was sending his way. As play resumed, Pedrosa closed in, but Palacín was expecting him, and dug the studs of one of his boots into his thigh, as he jumped over his tree-trunk leg. The ref gestured as if to pull the yellow card from his pocket, but he went no further than shaking his head bad-temperedly as he struggled for breath. It was in the twenty-second minute that Confucius, the student, emerged from an absence that may or may not have been deliberate and dribbled past three of the Gramenet players, to reach the goal line.

He passed the ball back to Palacín. The centre forward took in the wide open goal, and the goalie standing like an impotent statue of clay which he was now going to beat. The ball thudded into the opposition goal and lifted the net like a breeze lifting a pretty girl's skirt, and the magic word became a collective shout: 'Goal!' From where he lay on the ground, Palacín glanced first at the linesman and then at the ref. The goal was allowed, even though the Gramenet players were clustered round the ref arguing that Confucius had been off side.

'He was not off side! I saw it with my own eyes!'

'You, ref, you couldn't see anything, because you're blind as a bat.'

'The only thing you see is the bribe they gave you.'

The ref pulled out two yellow cards, or rather the same one twice, in the way that someone threatened by a vampire might brandish a cross for protection. The Gramenet players backed off and returned to the middle of the pitch with renewed urgency, while the Centellas team performed a victory war-dance around Palacín, glorying in the applause from the fans on the half-full, half-empty terraces, which as far as they were concerned could have been the most prestigious stadium in the world.

'Don't fall back now! Go for the bastards! Let's have some balls now,' shouted Precioso, partly in order to spur his players on, and partly to liven up the fans on the terraces behind him.

Sánchez Zapico was engaged simultaneously in applauding delightedly and at the same time registering the meaningful looks that were coming from the direction of Dosrius. The pressure of the Gramenet attack meant that Palacín had to shore up the defence, and every time he got a ball out of the area with one of his power-headers, a group of spectators chorused 'Olé!' Palacín had thrown his marker off balance, and now they changed roles, as he moved to deny him any chance of shooting, exploiting the blind, bull-like nature of his movements. The ref used his last puff of breath to give the final whistle, and some of the fans came down off the terraces intent on touching their hero. Two boys handed Palacín an exercise book and a biro for an autograph, and as he was signing he felt a profound tiredness creeping up from his feet. His team-mates were slapping him on the back. He responded to the handshake offered by the man who a short while previously had been trying to kill him.

'Congratulations, maestro.'

'Till the next time, matador!'

By the time they reached the changing rooms, their manager was claiming the credit for their victory, arguing that it had been a result of his tactical planning, although he was willing to recognize that in the second half they had put more balls into the game.

'Confucius, if it wasn't for those passes that you manage to conjure up every once in a while . . .'

'Every team needs at least one intelligent player.'

The other players started jeering at Confucius, and Palacín took advantage of the general air of complacency to get first use of the scant supply of hot water in the showers. Then, as he dressed, he received a pat on the back from Sánchez Zapico, whose face had suddenly become a picture of tiredness. Palacín left the ground and turned down offers of a lift to Barcelona. After a match he preferred to walk, and he walked with a light step. Soon he was viewing the ground from a distance as if it had nothing to do with him. The Centellas club was surrounded by working-class barrios, a cheap geometry for anonymous immigrants who had added a touch of floral display to windows and terraces in an attempt to incorporate a bit of nature into that nightmare of glass, cement and brick. The Centellas ground was like a

presence of something out of place, like a sort of urban
folly. Like the ruins which tourists visited on the outskirts
of Oaxaca, attributed to the Zapotecas or the Mixtecas;
like the pyramids of Monte Albán which surge up out of
the countryside, and which include the Temple of the
Dancers, claimed by some to be a celebration of dance,
but by others to be a pre-Columbian hospital for the sick
and the crippled. Or like that stadium for ball-games
where legend says that the captain of the winning team
had the right to tear out his rival's heart. He walked
until he was tired, and until he entered another set of
ruins, the ruins of the abandoned factories in Pueblo
Nuevo, with their big sheds and their railway sidings
rusting among the weeds, and the leaning bulk of threatening, macabre buildings which still retained something
of their brick-built beauty, and whose long-extinct chim-
neys reached towards the ceiling of the night, all waiting
for the demolition which would shortly be creating the
environment of the Olympic Village. When he reached
the Pueblo Nuevo cemetery, he took a cab and asked the
driver to drop him at calle del Hospital. The cab driver
had his radio on, and he was able to catch the final items
of the sports news. It was Mortimer, Mortimer all the
way. Mortimer had been the hero of the day.

'Jack Mortimer, the golden boy of European football in
the season of 1987–88, has now become the idol of the
Barcelona fans at the start of what promises to be a very
good season. This man is solid gold, and will set the
turnstiles clicking in every club in Spain . . . Now I'll hand
you back to the studio.'

He turned off the straight line of pasaje de Martorell
that marked his homeward route and went in search of
the Boqueriá market, with its bars for black men and its
huddles of beggars in the La Garduña parking lot. As he
passed the Jerusalem Bar, he saw her sitting at the

counter, staring obsessively into a small glass of beer. He carried on walking, but stopped a few yards further on and turned back. He wanted to find a way of striking up conversation with her, but didn't know how.

'Well, look who's here. The footballer!'

'I just happened to be passing.'

'I thought as much. Would you like something to drink? Do you want a beer?'

He ordered a beer, but barely touched it. He had something to say, but didn't dare say it.

'What are you doing round here? Looking for something?'

'Could you arrange the same as the other day?'

'No problem. Very simple. Do you have money?'

Palacín nodded, and the girl got off the bar stool as if it was burning a hole in the seat of her pants.

Basté de Linyola ushered the president of the Generalitat of Catalonia and the Mayor of Barcelona into the lift serving the chairman's box. He was rewarded with contented smiles and a slap on the back.

'That was an unforgettable game.'

'Congratulations.'

'*Ja tenim equip!*' exclaimed the general commanding the Barcelona military region, parading a recently acquired commitment to showing that the army these days regarded the Catalan dialect with favour, on the grounds that it was one of the 'treasures of the pluralism of a united Spain'.

The club's directors had lit their Montecristo Specials at the moment when Mortimer had scored his second goal, and by now some of them were on their second. They were no longer moving their cigars in and out of their mouths as if they were guests for whom it was difficult to find house-room, nor were they biting on the foreskins of these delights as if they were being subjected to oral rape; now the cigars had become welcome guests at the party, and were ushered in and out of their mouths like much-cherished princes as they emitted smoky signals of relaxation and contentment. The personalities from the world of politics and culture who had been specially invited to be present at Mortimer's debut allowed themselves to be sought out by radio reporters, and tried to find a suitable language with which to connect with their respective political and cultural audiences. So, on the one hand, a representative from the Convergencia i Unio, the ruling party in the Catalan Assembly, declared that 'If this club goes forward, then the country goes forward too, and vice versa,' an admirable sentiment which compromised him neither with the club nor with the country; on the other hand, an organic intellectual of the Partit dels Socialistes Catalans, also a member of the European Parliament, expressed the opinion that: 'Up until now the club has been inward-looking, but now the team seems ready to take on a new sense of the other. A sense of the other in which they will be scoring goals.' The radio journalists were in their element, waving their microphones under the noses of the city's notables as if offering a chilly hertzian kiss in exchange for a bit of free public relations. The stadium vomited spectators out from its various orifices into the dusk which was settling early, thanks to the end of summer time. Now that the game was over, they turned on their transistor radios so as not to miss the post-mortems. After an away game the previous Sunday, Basté de Linyola had declared: 'Mortimer's debut will give the team a new identity'; this Sunday he felt up to substantiating his expectation: 'Mortimer's debut has given the team a new identity.' All this stuff had to be listened to. It was a necessary part of being able to survive the working week that was about to start. Then came the results of the other games. And the pools. And the league tables. And who had been sent off. And comments on how the refs had behaved. The players themselves were no longer the protagonists of the scene, because by now an army of young radio reporters, microphones at the ready, were preparing to squeeze out, drop by drop, the last mortal juices of the day's various battles and their heroes.

'Pere Rius? Pere Rius at the computer centre — are you on-line?'

No, it wasn't a call to mission control at Houston prior to a space launch.

'Pere Rius is at the computer centre, and he's going to tell us how many minutes Mortimer had control of the ball.'

'Eight minutes.'

'How many shots on goal?'

'Six.'

'How many goals?'

'Two, as well as laying one on for Mendoza.'

'We couldn't hope for better. Mortimer has shown today that he's the kind of centre forward the club so badly needs. It's only the fifth day of the season, and already Mortimer's presence has given an incisiveness to the forward players which has been missing for the past two seasons. It has taken just one afternoon for the fans to discover Mortimer for what he is: the king of the pitch. It's not often that we see a player so instinctively able to control his area. He shakes off his markers. He opens spaces. He knows how to wait for the ball with his back to the goal, and swing round in an instant ready to shoot.'

The fans emerged slowly from the stadium with smiles of satisfaction on their faces and the name of Mortimer hanging from their lips like a festive garland. As Carvalho reached the stairs that led down to the changing rooms, he paused to watch as an impressive air of solitude descended on the terraces, and then went off in search of Camps O'Shea. He found him leading the club's manager into the press room. The dozen private security guards were posted discreetly about the place, their eyes and muscles alert for any eventuality. The floodlights of the various TV channels bathed the changing room door in a harsh light which caught the players unawares as they came out and made themselves available to answer a string of leading questions.

'What difference would you say it has made to have Mortimer joining the team?'

'Why did you pass so few balls to Mortimer?'

'How do you feel when people say that your team consists of ten people plus Mortimer?'

'Is Mortimer the start of a new era?'

'How does it feel to be playing next to a superstar like Mortimer?'

In the harsh light of the TV lamps it struck Carvalho that the players looked so young that it was easy to forget that they were the solid, determined, uniform figures that he had just seen dominating the pitch, invested with all the significance of heroes of the afternoon, as Camps O'Shea might have said. They looked more like little boys who had been landed with a role which was actually beyond them, and whose main interest was to get their photos taken so that they could file them in their photo albums. And there was Mortimer, as a kind of blond shadow whom they accepted because he gave them a place in the limelight as the privileged colleagues of the hero of the hour. And when Mortimer himself came out and stood framed in the doorway of Gate 1, the mikes and the cameras were only for him.

'Did you give a hundred per cent this afternoon?'

'Do you expect to keep up your English average of two goals per match throughout the season?'

'What difference do you find between the Spanish style of defence and the English?'

'What did you feel when the fans all started chanting your name when you scored?'

Mortimer used an interpreter that the club had placed at his disposal in order to explain that the day's win had come about thanks to a good team effort and the manager's strategy. The interpreter managed to render this in a surprisingly large number of words, which could have been expected, seeing that he was considered one of the best translators of James Joyce into the Catalan. Camps O'Shea had hired him in the manner of a literary patron, so that when he wasn't interpreting for the club, he'd be able to continue with his translation of *Daedalus*, which, hopefully, would have the same select cult success as had been enjoyed by his *Ulysses*. Now he appeared to stumble as he replied to the journalists' questions, as if he was the dummy to Mortimer's ventriloquist. He replied either in Castilian or in Catalan, according to the language of the questioner, and contrived to have the kind of accent attributed to English people when they try to speak foreign languages. Mortimer recognized Carvalho and winked in his direction, with the amiable smile of a like-able adolescent aware of his role as the saviour of a Sunday afternoon's football which would help thousands of people to suffer the harsh reality of Monday morning with the hopes of another Sunday, of another exhibition by Mortimer, and of other goals on which they would eventually construct a new legend. Carvalho followed the crowd of journalists, photographers and TV cameramen, who were insatiable in their demands for Mortimer to continue answering the kinds of questions that were asked every Sunday, but which in this case were magnified by the status of the star. Camps O'Shea arrived from the press room, where a scattering of hardened hacks had now finished their ritual of asking the club's manager all the usual questions, and he cleared the way for their new star to approach his Porsche, which was staked out by security guards at each of its four corners.

'OK, gentlemen. Time to let him go. You've got a whole season ahead to pick his brains. Save a few questions for next Sunday.'

This didn't stop one of them thrusting a microphone right under Mortimer's nose as he sat at the wheel, and as he moved to drive off he all but took the arm off the journalist holding it. The journalist returned the mike to his own lips in order to give the final touches to two hours of communication with his audience: 'Mortimer seems satisfied, but he tells us that he wasn't firing on all cylinders today. The golden boy of European football in the season of 1987–88 obviously still needs to get acclimatized to the Spanish style of football, and only time will tell how he'll handle an experience which has broken plenty of other good foreign players. It's one thing playing on your home ground, backed up by fans who will protest against the slightest foul, but it's another thing playing away at some of those grounds where the opposition's tactics tend to be, shall we say, over-vigorous. Anyway, I'll return you now to the studio with one final observation, in the commendably honest words of the club's manager: "With players like Mortimer, any coach is bound to win." We'll hold you to that, mister. If the club doesn't win, it won't be Mortimer's fault. He's ready to set the heavens ringing. So, now we leave this great stadium, with the impression that a new god has taken his place on the altars of our city: Jack Mortimer, the golden boy of European football in the season of 1987–88, has now become the idol of the Barcelona fans at the start of what promises to be a very good season.'

Carvalho emerged from the stadium in the wake of the departing fans, who were moving slowly like ants in an ant colony, following in the footsteps of the people in front of them, slowly divesting themselves of their condition as a collective subject and recovering the memory of their own realities as each step took them nearer home and back to everyday reality. Night had fallen suddenly, as if to assist in the expulsion of the multitude from the stadium and its surrounds, and everywhere you looked there were streams of people and cars attempting to flee this scene which had now given all that had been expected of it.

Several groups of young fans were giving loud cheers for their club, although what they were actually cheering was themselves, and the sole topic of conversation was an open-ended post-mortem on Mortimer's style of play and the goals he had scored. Next to the big stadium rose the other sporting facilities of the powerful football club, but nobody had so far succeeded in dislodging from the locality the cemetery of what had once been a town in its own right, but which had now been swallowed up into Greater Barcelona. Carvalho had a half-memory that one of the former glories of this selfsame club was buried in that cemetery — one of those players whose exploits were as invented as they were real. The player had asked to be buried there, because that way, even though he would no longer be able to see the goals scored in the stadium, at least he would be able to sense them from the shouting of the fans. Maybe you'll be able to hear the goals, but will you ever know who scored them? Carvalho stood next to the cemetery railings in silent communication with this former glory, a part of the scrapbook of his childhood days when that player used to be billed as the main attraction on the posters announcing the next game. The posters used to hang in the windows of the most frequented shops on the street — like the bakery where the inevitable black bread of the post-War period was baked; or the laundry which boasted the four daughters of señora Remei, four plump girls who courted a chorus of lascivious wolf-whistles every time they crossed the street — the co-owners of a collective carnality inappropriate in a post-War period characterized by austerity and rationing.

'Today's goals were scored by Mortimer,' Carvalho said, out loud, as he stood next to the railings. He waited for a moment, half expecting a reply.

There was none. He shook his head, began to doubt for his own sanity and went to retrieve his car, which had been beached high on the pavement by the departing fans. He pointed it in the general direction of Vallvidrera and switched on the radio, which was devoting itself to an endless chewing-over of the afternoon's footballing highlights, and an equally endless listing of the results, the pools draws, the league tables, as well as the opinions and pontifications of managers and players alike. The droning noise of the sports news became a kind of aural wallpaper as he engaged his brain in demolishing the notion that the Mortimer case had even the slightest degree of plausibility. Who on earth would want to kill the kid? Why? What motive could there possibly be? Every day that passed meant more money in the bank for Carvalho, but he was a man who found pointless work even more repellent than useful work. Either way, work makes you tired, whether you're working usefully or pointlessly. All at once something caught his attention on the radio. The commentator was busy clearing out the rest of the day's junk, and he was in the process of giving the results for the third division games, and other results. All of a sudden a name illuminated a corner, a half-forgotten memory in the storehouse of Carvalho's memory:

'Centellas 1 – Gramenet 0.'

Centellas. Did Centellas really still exist? His recollection was of going down a road with his mother in the 1940s. They used to leave the city, sometimes going to the south, other times to the north, seeking out particular houses in the countryside where the black-market was able to supplement the routine and scanty foodstuffs provided by your ration card. To the north, in between orchards and allotments run by full-time or Sunday market-gardeners, he remembered the perimeter wall of the Centellas Football Club, faced with cement, and topped with broken glass. For Carvalho, the club's name and the memories that it brought flooding back were an inextricable part of his childhood, and to discover that it still existed, and that Centellas could still win one-nil (and beat Gramenet, what's more) was like suddenly finding in his trouser pocket a crust of the black bread that they used to eat after the War.

Dosrius agreed: 'Yes. One-nil.'

'Things aren't going too well.'

'We shouldn't be in too much of a hurry.'

'It's starting to get urgent now. If we're going to make anything out of the rescheduling of the Centellas ground as a residential area, it's vital that we keep a firm grip on the agreement — while of course making sure that nobody knows that any such agreement exists. I think we were all clear on this.'

'You need patience, Basté.'

'I'm a very patient man, as well you know. Patience is almost always a good thing, except when it's stupid, and in this case it's beginning to be stupid. I don't trust Sánchez Zapico.'

'He's the one who's got most to lose. We've set him up as chairman of Centellas, and he knows that he's there for a reason. But he's right when he says we should let him go at his own pace.'

'Dosrius, the team won. And that creates fans. Imagine what might happen if they win their next away match. It's going to mean more people coming to the ground, and every bar in the barrio is going to start hanging up photographs of the team, and the kids will be ... In a situation like that, nobody's going to want to shut the club and sell the ground.'

Dosrius opened his wallet and toyed with some

banknotes, without venturing so far as to give business overtones to his conversation with Basté de Linyola. He knew that Basté liked rituals, as long as they were brief, and he had learned the art of combining ritual with brevity. Basté regained his humour, and returning behind his rosewood desk he indicated that he could begin.

'Sánchez Zapico's problem is that he always tries to be all things to all people. At the end of last season, the Centellas board were putting pressure on him to beef up the team. They escaped relegation and instant death by the skin of their teeth. If you like I'll show you the gate receipts. Right. Sánchez, who is far from stupid, sells them the idea of putting out feelers to Alberto Palacín, a centre forward who, by the way, once played for your team, about ten years ago, and who also played in the national squad once or twice. I don't know if you remember, but Pontón, who had a reputation as a bit of an animal, gave him a particularly nasty foul which left him just about fit for the knacker's yard. And that's more or less where he ended up. He went to play in the American League, then signed for Oaxaca, and he was working out his last contract when he got the call from Sánchez Zapico. Sánchez consulted me about it, and I gave him the go-ahead. Palacín had a pretty good name as a player, and people remember him, but actually he's all washed-up. His personal life is a disaster. He's separated from his wife, and he's got himself hooked on cocaine.'

Dosrius paused for a long moment to watch the effect of this last piece of information on Basté. There was a flicker of interest — brief, but sufficient to show that it had been registered.

'As soon as he arrived in Barcelona, I had him followed. He booked himself into a cheap boarding house in one of the streets of the Barrio Chino, if that's still what it's called. I can't keep up with the changes these days.

Anyway, I had to wait for a few weeks, while he settled in with his team, and while he spent some time trying to locate his wife and son. He only ever left the boarding house to go to the stadium, or to try and trace the whereabouts of his family. His wife has shacked up with Simago — I don't know if the name means anything to you. He specializes in buying and selling footballers, and signed up a number of good players in the early 1970s. That was before things started going badly for him — so badly in fact that he had to make a hasty exit to America, because he was being pursued by creditors on all fronts.

'Anyway, Palacín discovers that his wife has disappeared, and starts getting depressed. One day he runs into a young prostitute from the street where he lives. He uses her as his dealer, and they go off and have fun in her apartment — if you can call it an apartment . . . From what I gather from my informant, the girl lives in a derelict building. And this may interest you . . . She's living with Marçal Lloberola, the youngest son of a man whose name will be familiar to you. Lloberola, the king of the scrapyards, as he is known all over the port. A mint of money behind him, and a hundred-year family history of calling the tune in the Port of Barcelona. The woman is Marta Becera, an ex-student friend of Marçal from his college days. They've been together for about ten years now, and they're both heavily into drugs. They're pretty much made for each other. So, Palacín takes up with the girl, and six days ago they went off on their first cocaine trip.'

'And has there been a second time?'

'Indeed there has. Last night, in fact. When the game was over, Palacín went for a stroll on his own in the area round the stadium. Then he took a taxi, which dropped him at the corner of calle del Hospital and pasaje de Martorell. He went to considerable lengths to find the girl, and they went off to score cocaine in Plaza Real again. Then they went back to the flat for sex. He's well hooked, and one of these days he's going to crack. Without his help, Centellas is as good as dead, and I would say it was a miracle that he managed to score that goal yesterday. But he does have style. I was there for the match, and it's obvious that he might make himself a following. I said as much to Sánchez when we contrived to bump into each other, and he was worried. He thinks it might complicate things.'

'Hooked on cocaine, eh?'

'Yes.'

Basté wrinkled his nose.

'I don't like the sound of this. It could get very mucky, Dosrius, and I can't afford to get involved in that sort of thing.'

'That's what I'm here for, Basté.'

'That's not what I meant to say.'

'You don't need to say it. I said it.'

Basté habitually used Dosrius as his lawyer every time he found himself involved in some particularly delicate set of negotiations — the sort of business deals that his ex-wife had criticized him for, calling him a speculator and a cynic; the kind of deals that sat uneasily with his image as a man who, for the last thirty years, had created for himself a public image as a political progressive, and as an enterprising businessman able to preach the philosophy of the creativeness of neo-liberalism by his own example. Dosrius had understood from the start that his role was to take the facts with which Basté supplied him, and then supply him with solutions without explaining too much about the procedures, while all the time taking sole responsibility for the ways in which these ends were to be achieved. The Centellas land-grab operation was going to involve more than a dozen building firms and

industrialists, all of whom were willing to place their
trust in Basté because he had a good business sense and
enjoyed considerable social standing. To such an extent
that they didn't even demur when, during their few discreet meetings together, Basté placed them all in seats
that were lower and less comfortable than his own, while
he shifted his well-preserved skeleton and his concert-
conductor arms into a Charles Eames rotating chair
which his father had imported in the 1930s, and which
Carlos Basté de Linyola had carried with him from one
office to another as a sort of good-luck mascot. To those
occasional meetings, Sánchez Zapico had contributed his
brutal ordinariness, and the rat-like acuteness of his
business sense, while Dosrius brought technical clarity
and Basté the apostolic blessing. Even though in the past
his name had figured among the princes-elect of the new
democracy, he had won the definitive respect of his colleagues from the moment that he had decided to take
over as managing director of the richest and most powerful football club in Barcelona. This was a position that
they understood.

'You know better than anyone that time is at a pre-
mium. Everything is in place and ready to move. The
offer that we shall be putting before the board will include
housing, a public park, a service area with a day nursery,
a civic centre, and, just for good measure, a community
centre for senior citizens. The council will give us medals,
and there's a very large amount of money waiting to be
made. But these kinds of deals can go off the boil very
fast; if we lose the initiative the vultures will be on us,
and there's absolutely no guarantee that we're going to
end up first in line.'

'Sánchez Zapico is the key to all this.'

'Sánchez Zapico can only be counted on for as long as
he has no other option. He's not much more than a rag

and bone dealer who's become rich, and a manufacturer of no account. What can you expect from a manufacturer of sugared almonds?'

'A free hand.'

'You have a free hand.'

'And you can be sure that your hands will stay clean.'

'You shouldn't have said that.'

He felt uncomfortable. He was not a man capable of accepting the slightest hint of doubt about himself. He was a man who liked to look into the mirror each morning and see an image that corresponded to the image that the city had of him. Everyone has his role, and his role was that of a respectable citizen.

'I was thinking . . .'

'I'm glad to hear it.'

'No, no need to get alarmed. I wasn't intending to explain the solution that has occurred to me, but I should warn you that it's probably not going to be easy. You're going to have to accept this, and Sánchez Zapico is definitely going to get jumpy. We're moving to completion now, and the other day I fired a warning shot over his bows and he didn't like it. He turned up at my house at eight in the morning and started ranting. But he's nobody's fool. You shouldn't underestimate him just because he's in the confectionery business.'

'I don't underestimate him at all. I just try to avoid playing golf with him. He's managed to make himself the laughing-stock of the golf club at Sant Cugat. Even the caddies laugh at him behind his back. And what about that wife of his. She looks like a hairdresser out of some bedroom farce. Very uncouth.'

'According to my scheme of things, Sánchez Zapico will call a meeting of the group, and you're going to have to be ready. He's a man with a short neck, and he charges with his head. I might remind you of the dossier which I prepared on his activities, and particularly on the period when he was smuggling photographic material in the 1960s, and the prostitutes that he was running during the period before he discovered massage parlours.'

'I never even looked at it.'

'Well, keep it safely under lock and key. I don't think it's going to be necessary to bring it out — I'll only do that if it's needed. But he's likely to turn nasty, and he knows a few things about me. About you, he knows nothing. Nobody knows anything about you.'

Dosrius took the opportunity of the silence that followed to ponder the fact that the sum total of what he knew about Basté de Linyola would not be capable of staining even the white cuff of the man's shirt, because in effect Dosrius was the instigator and the man behind the scenes. Ten years as a labour lawyer, paid for by money leached out of the clandestine labour unions. Another ten years as a business lawyer, most of them spent in the fastidious shadow of Basté de Linyola, acting as a pageboy to the immaculate patrician. He had progressed from shoes bought in Can Segarra, which had destroyed his feet, to Italian shoes or made-to-measure shoes, and had developed a habit of travelling abroad without luggage and buying new clothes in each city where he stopped, as if in search of a new skin every time.

'If you'll pardon the biblical quotation, Dosrius: "What you have to do, it were well that you do it quickly".'

'I'll reply in equally biblical mode, Basté. "May the Lord be with you, and with thy spirit."'

'Would you like to go away somewhere, Marçal? Why don't we go? Get out of this place. Green fields and pastures new.'

'What with? Shirt buttons?'

'My trade travels with me.'

'With your trade we're better off staying here.'

'You're right, I suppose.'

They clung to each other like two shipwrecked souls on their mattress island.

'I like the idea, though.'

'Would you like to leave?'

'Leave Spain?'

'Sure. Just get on the road and go.'

'Where to?'

'Who cares.'

He raised half of his naked body on to one elbow and examined her, lost in thought; then he gazed upwards as if searching somewhere up among the rafters for an escape hatch through which they could empty their lives, as if down some liberatory drain.

'Let's make the most of this sweet moment, Marta.'

'This sweet moment . . .! Ha!'

'Don't laugh at me. I'm almost happy.'

'You're right. Let's make the most of this sweet moment. What kind of life are we going to have if we carry on here? The same old shit, day after day.'

'You're right. It would be good to go. I'd like to go somewhere where there's sea. There's sea here, but it's not what you'd call proper sea. Morocco. I'd really like to go to Morocco.'

'We could go to the desert.'

'We could go to the desert,' he repeated, with a certain lack of conviction. Then again: 'What with, though? Where will we get the money? Every time we've tried hitch-hiking, even a blind man wouldn't pick us up. Remember what happened when we went to Port de la Selva in the summer?'

'We need money.'

'If you're thinking we can ask my father, forget it. He's

even gone and hired a private security guard to make
sure I don't get within half a mile of him.'

'Who said anything about your father?'

'What are you planning then?'

'For the moment I'm not planning anything. I'm following my nose. Sniffing the air. Using my imagination. You
should try it. One morning we're going to get up bright
and early, and we'll leave this dump behind us. We'll have
the whole world before us — anything we want. Do you
remember that film about the robots and the Chinaman?
I suppose not. Your brain's shot — you can't even remember any more.'

She looked at him as if he was a kind of freak who by
some quirk of fate had ended up as her bedmate and
companion in life.

'I think your brain's melted, Marçal.'

'Well, you're not so clever yourself . . .'

But he had to admit she was right. Sometimes it really
did feel as if his brain had melted, and he couldn't even
turn his head without feeling the liquid swilling about.

'How old are you?'

'I don't know. Thirty, maybe.'

'Thirty-two. Same as me. How long do you think you're
going to last, the way you're going . . . the way we're
both going?'

'Going to last . . . ?' he mused, with an air of perplexity.

'There's still time,' she said, seizing his arm with one
hand. 'We'll have to break a few eggs, though, if we want
to make the omelette. Are you game?"

'How should I know? You're flying, Marta. You're
always in a good mood when you're flying.'

'There's still time, and we are going to need money.'

'Here we go again. Sure . . .'

He ran through all the possible sources of money that
his imagination could muster, but each time he came up

with either the sullen face of his father saying no, or the pitifully small amounts of cash that Marta sometimes carried in her handbag.

'Imagine that we've hit lucky. Imagine us turning up in one of those cities where everyone wears white suits and Panama hats. Fans on the ceilings and jugs full of fancy coloured drinks, and we'll be Lord and Lady Muck.'

'The kind of place where they have billiard halls.'

'Billiard halls. That's right! A billiard hall.'

'I'll shave my beard off, and just leave a moustache.'

'In winter you'll wear a cravat, and in summer you'll wear silk shirts.'

'I used to have silk shirts. I loved them. My mother used to give me a silk shirt every birthday.'

'Exactly.'

'Amazing! That's the first time I've thought of my silk shirts for years. I wonder what they've done with them. They must still be at home. And they're mine.'

'You'll have *new* silk shirts. Imagine it — there you are, in your silk shirt, and you're leaning over a billiard table. You have to be very good looking to play billiards — in fact you've got something of the billiard player about you. And everyone will be saying: "Who's the goodlooking player?" And maybe I'll be the owner of the joint.'

'You know what — you'd look really good as the owner of a billiard hall. No, I'm serious. You've got that kind of "je ne sais quoi".'

'And everyone will be wondering where these two good-looking creatures come from? And you and I will lay false trails for them. I'd love them to think that we came from Australia. Everyone should be from Australia.'

'We could even go to Australia.'

'Why not? Somewhere where we can make a new start.'

'Seeing we've almost got our degrees, maybe we could give private lessons in something.'

'Like what? Sniffing coke and screwing?! Idiot!'

All of a sudden the spell was broken and everything was the same as before. Including the iciness in Marta's voice, and the ferocity in her eyes which tried to cover up for her confusion.

'What's up with you? Don't spoil it, Marta.'

'What exactly are you going to give classes in, eh? Tell me. That'll be just like going backwards for us, won't it. We've got to jump forwards, not backwards. As if we've just been born.'

'Sounds good.'

'OK — now listen carefully. What would you be prepared to do to make it happen?'

'I'd give ten years of my life — twenty, even.'

'Don't be so generous with something you probably haven't got. Half an hour will do. In half an hour we could change our luck.'

He didn't want to irritate her by being blind to the obvious, so he preferred to pretend that he was thinking deeply while he waited for her to unveil what she had in mind. He turned over the possible options, and all of a sudden he came up with a start.

'You're not thinking of . . . ?'

'Not thinking of what?'

'You're not thinking of doing a hold-up?'

'You're talking movie-language.'

'I mean a robbery . . . or something like that.'

'Something like that.'

'Marta, I'd never have the nerve. If it was just mugging someone, OK. But I haven't got the nerve for a robbery — I'd be too scared of ending up in prison. It would kill me. I'd be dead within three days. They'd separate us.'

'You've mugged someone, haven't you?'

'Yes.'

'Well, it's something like that.'

'Mugging someone isn't going to give us enough money to travel abroad.'

'It's something like mugging, but there's pots of money attached. Come over here.'

She got up from the mattress and hauled him across to the window. The street was cool and busy with the sounds of the late afternoon, and the sun was providing a golden halo for the last flats up calle de Robadors.

'There it is. Thirty yards away. Right on our doorstep. The old lady's absolutely loaded, and she let on to me that she keeps it all in the house because she doesn't trust banks, and probably because she doesn't want to pay tax on it.'

She left him standing at the window and went to get her bag. When she returned she handed him a key.

'I made it the other day. It's a copy of the spare key she keeps in the bread bin in the kitchen. We can go in any time we like and search until we find the money. In the afternoons she goes out for a walk, and none of her guests are in during the daytime, or at least only a useless old invalid who can hardly move out of his bed. I'll give him a coffee and a sandwich to keep him happy.'

'Too easy.'

'We deserve something to be easy for once. The woman enjoys handing out charity when she thinks people are down on their luck, and she's decided I'm a poor cow who can't live without her generosity. She doesn't need the money. She's done everything she ever needed to do in life, and now all she does is sit and watch the flashing sign of her dirty boarding house, and wander round the balcony to keep an eye on what's going on down the street.'

'Too easy.'

'I've thought it all out. All we have to do is grab the money and run. You can go and steal a car from the other side of town and park it in the parking-lot behind the Boqueria. It's an open car park, so there's no one to check who comes and goes. It's not even two hundred yards from here. We'll break into her place, take the money, and we'll just drive till the petrol runs out. Then, with the money we'll have, everything will be easy.'

'Too easy.'

'So easy that even you couldn't fuck it up.'

'Supposing things go wrong, though?'

'What could be worse than this?'

And she invited him to look at her, as bare and wretched as the four walls around them.

'How about Morocco.'

'Wherever you like. The desert. Billiards. Silk shirts. Give me your hand. Reach out of the window.'

And he did. A hand reaching out to the afternoon. Like a claw.

His last conversation with Charo had left him feeling uneasy. Once again his soul was making its presence felt, like a tumour which always seemed to reveal his darker side. The day's business had driven the problem of Bromide clean out of his head, and all of a sudden he had an image of Charo and Bromide united in a moment of solidarity which he didn't recognize, and which in part repelled him. He was disturbed by a sense of something approaching a guilty conscience, and before going to see the shoeshine he tried to mend his bridges with Charo. Her voice was sad but affectionate at the other end of the line. When he suggested that they should go out together for a meal, her sadness gave way to cheerfulness, and they arranged to meet at Casa Isidro in calle de les Flors, a few yards from the Gothic surprise of the church of Sant Pau del Camp. Charo arrived dressed and made up for a night out, but with a touch too much Eau de Rochas about her, which threatened to ruin the delicate aroma of what they were about to eat. It was this that decided him to sit facing her, instead of next to her as Charo would have preferred. To make up for this he let her elaborate on the long voyage of analysis, tests, consultations and medical opinions on which she had embarked with Bromide.

'You can't imagine the terrible state of the health service these days, Pepe. When was the last time you went to the doctor's?'

'When that Siamese took a pot shot at me.'

'Don't remind me, Pepe — it gives me the creeps even thinking about it.'

Charo was a mature, goodlooking woman. She was ageing with dignity, and something in him approaching tenderness was interrupted by the timely arrival of the menu in the hands of Isidro and Montserrat, the couple who ran the restaurant which Carvalho frequented as a gourmet and a connoisseur. When Carvalho asked disingenuously, 'What's new today?' they replied without batting an eyelid that they had foie gras with a green lentil dressing, a hors d'oeuvres of foie gras, sweetbreads with lime, salt codfish au gratin with garlic, farcellets of cabbage stuffed with lobster and saffron, *lubina à la ciboulette*, sole with mulberry, and *riz de veau*. They concluded their exposition of the day's attractions, unaware of the profound disturbance which they had occasioned in Carvalho's spirit and his unease at being faced with so many choices and the necessity of having to decide.

'I'll have a bit of everything,' he said, ironically.

Unfortunately Isidro took him literally and was about to go and place the order. Carvalho had to revert to linear language to disabuse him. Charo stayed on familiar territory: a hors d'oeuvre of foie gras, and sole with mulberry, and Carvalho opted for the foie gras with green lentils, followed by the *riz de veau*.

'When Bromide was younger, he used to complain that God had left men very poorly equipped to deal with all the beautiful women in the world. I tend to feel the same nowadays about cooking. I'll never live long enough to try everything I want to try.'

'Your problem is that you're greedy, Pepe.'

'My problem is insatiable curiosity. I have the curiosity of the voyeur who has a sense that there are some things that he's never going to see.'

'Some people might say you're getting old.'

'People don't know the meaning of the word nowadays. The only people who know what the word means are people who are old already, and I don't feel that I'm old yet. Imagine it! They've even succeeded in disappearing the word out of the language. These days they talk about "senior citizens". It reminds me of the years under Franco, when workers had to be called "producers". To be a "worker" was politically obscene and dangerous. These days, to be "old" is biologically obscene and dangerous.'

'Don't depress me more than I am already, Pepe. Come on, cheer up and have a drink.'

Charo always made him nervous when she had a few drinks inside her.

'This is a lovely wine, Pepe. Voluptuous.'

'What's the matter with Bromide?'

'Don't, Pepe, you're going to start me crying. Leave it till the end of the meal. What's for dessert, Pepe?'

'Why not profiteroles, or orange terrine au Grand Marnier.'

'In that case, no. Let's talk about Bromide now, because I'm looking forward to this meal, and I want to be in a good mood to enjoy the sweet.'

'If we're going to talk about Bromide's problems, maybe we'd best do it with the foie gras!'

'That's not funny, Pepe. Stop it — you'll put me right off my food. You know, it was ever so sad at the hospital . . . Have you ever seen Bromide's underwear?'

'No.'

'Well, it never even occurred to me to tell him . . . The first day, when I took him for his X-ray, or abdominal radiography, or whatever they call it, I'm telling you, Pepe, when the poor thing stood there in his underpants I didn't know which way to turn. He had the kind of pants that my father used to wear. They were full of holes, with urine stains in the front. And his vest looked like a moth-eaten old floor-cloth. So I made sure that the nurse was in earshot, and I said: "For goodness sake — couldn't you have put clean underwear on?" And he got all in a temper, Pepe, and said that all this stuff about clean underwear was nonsense, and that we come into this world naked, and we go out naked, and that during the Russian campaign they used to wear newspaper next to their skin instead of underwear, and that Franco set up the Health Service so that workers could go to the doctor's looking how the hell they wanted. And he said the bit about Franco when the nurse was in the room, and the woman gave him a really dirty look. I thought to myself: "Charo, this woman's going to kill him," and I gave her a smile as if to say that Bromide was a bit crazy. I started telling him off for talking like that, and the nurse looked at me and asked if he was my father, and I felt ashamed to say that Bromide was my father, with his underwear looking so dirty, so I said that he wasn't, but I said it a bit too quickly, and Bromide noticed, and he looked even more miserable, Pepe, and I felt a lump coming in my throat. I felt so annoyed with myself that I added: "But it's as if he was." And when he heard that he started getting all emotional.'

Carvalho became aware that the delivery of foie gras and green lentils that he'd loaded carefully on to his fork had coagulated as it hung in mid-air. He imagined the scene in the fulness of its grisly detail and its terminal sadness, and he cleared his throat in order to make way for the food.

'What about his health, though?'

'Looks bad, Pepe.'

'What sort of bad?'

'You name it, he's got it. Anaemia, cirrhosis, one kidney not working properly, and that's not the end of it.'

'In that case, maybe they'd best not carry on looking. They'll probably end up discovering that he's pregnant.'

Charo gave such a snort of laughter that part of what she had in her mouth ended up back on her plate, and this made her laugh even louder, so that by the end the whole restaurant was staring at her.

'I'm sorry, Pepe. I can't stop!'

Carvalho opted for total absorption in his meal, and Charo conducted a secret dialogue with herself until she finally subsided into a state of mild hiccups, and tears which initially were the aftermath of the laughter but then turned into tears for Bromide.

'It's unfair, the way people are left on their own when they get old.'

'If we had to make a list of everything that's unfair in this world, I'm sure we could find worse. Anyway, you went along to lend a hand; Biscuter has offered to help when we need him; and there's me too.'

'He's going to die, Pepe.'

'No.'

It was a dry, irrational 'no', as if the idea that Bromide might die was an act of violence on his very being. For a

moment he tried to imagine his emotional world without
Bromide in it, but he couldn't. It was inconceivable that
one day he would go looking for Bromide in the bowels
of the city and not find him. Bromide was like a little
insect that lurked in the dirtiest cracks of the city of
Barcelona, an insect that was fragile, soft-hearted and
wise.

'The hell he's going to die.'

'Don't take it like that, Pepe. We all have to die one
day, and Bromide is ever so ill. He says it's because of all
the muck that we're forced to eat and drink. You know
his mania about how the council's putting bromides into
everyone's tap water so that people don't screw so much.
Now he's saying that they're poisoning everything so that
people start popping off, and that will solve their unem-
ployment problem. He says that this was all arranged
when Reagan met Gorbachev. And what we need is
another general like Muñoz Grandes, to stop people step-
ping out of line . . .'

'In other words, the same old story. Listen. Let's finish
with Bromide for the moment, because I'm not going to
enjoy my food otherwise. Leave it for the coffee. Instead
of a glass of Calvados, I'll ask for a glass of mineral water
and we can talk about what we can do for him.'

'I'd put him in a home.'

'Bromide? In a home?'

'Somewhere where they can look after him. He can't be
expected to end his days sitting on his shoeshine box, or
dragged up an alley somewhere.'

'He's not a baby, and he's not mad either. Let him
decide. But I'm telling you, once they decide to put him in
a home it'll be the death of him. It's only breathing the
shit in the barrios that keeps him alive.'

'And the poor man was so confused. He doesn't seem to
know what's what any more. He says he doesn't under-

stand this city ... it isn't what it used to be ... something's happened and he doesn't know what it is. He says once it was like a village, with its prostitutes and pimps and criminals, but now it's full of all kinds of stainless-steel lowlife.'

Stainless-steel lowlife, and probably connected up with a centralized data bank on stainless-steel lowlife, via tiny cybernetic wires made of nothingness spiked with cruelty. He too had felt fear recently, on several occasions, as if he had been forced finally to accept that he was no longer the measure of his external world, or even of his internal world, but just a precarious survivor.

'This food's delicious, Pepe. Isidro, my compliments to the *maître d'*.'

Carvalho was always intensely irritated by Charo's inability to distinguish between the cook and the *maître d'*, particularly when she started complimenting restaurateurs as if she was some Biscuter, talking man to man. Since Isidro was both the *maître* and the owner of the establishment, he bowed slightly and mentally complimented himself.

'But he *is* the *maître*, Charo.'

'I'll never learn. I always think that the *maître* is the one with the big white hat. Isn't the *maître* the one who counts?'

More than fifteen years spent absorbing gastronomic culture, and Charo still couldn't tell the difference between a *maître* and a cook.

'There's a call for you, sir.'

Carvalho seized this opportunity to beat a retreat. It was Biscuter. He had an urgent message for him. Camps O'Shea had called, and he was to contact him immediately.

'He was very insistent ... *immediately* ...'

Charo finished her profiteroles with vindictive slowness. She had been expecting that their after-dinner proceedings would take them to her flat, and she had put on the red underwear which Carvalho had absent-mindedly said that he liked during one of their happier encounters. And now, as Carvalho went off and abandoned her in the restaurant, she began to cry, with a serviette held to her eyes and a little white lie on the tip of her tongue. I'm crying for Bromide. Poor Bromide, she told herself, over and over again. But she knew that it wasn't true.

Camps O'Shea was pacing up and down his office, or rather bouncing, as if communicating to a spectacularly expensive carpet his happiness at suddenly finding himself centre-stage with an audience, on the basis of what was contained in the piece of paper that he had in his hand.

'Listen to this, Carvalho. Our man has excelled himself:

' "I shall open the cages where you keep your de luxe animals, and the sheen of their muscles will light up the evening more brightly that the moon of Samarkand.

' "But in its charge an animal will reveal its death wound, and it will not reach the gates of the city. There's the rub. The scapegoat which my theory of cruelty requires. The one who must die so that the majority can be free. And you, traders of muscle, are the guilty parties in this story.

' "He who must die will ascend to the heavens of innocence. His blood will cleanse my hands, because they will be the instruments of a new order on Earth. For all these reasons, and of this you can be sure, the centre forward will die at dusk." '

'What do you think of it?'

'Magnificent. It reads like it's written by a cop.'

'By a what . . . ?'

'By a cop. I'm not sure exactly what sort of cop, but

these days they're inventing new kinds of cops every day.
Just have a think about it — the man's obviously got an
obsession: opening cages, directing traffic . . .'

'I think it's rather beautiful.'

Camps O'Shea was so put out by Carvalho's lack of
poetic sensibility that he went quite red in the face as he
handed him the piece of paper as self-evident proof of the
magnificence of the writing.

'Whoever the author is, you can't deny there's a certain
lyrical content. Elegaic, even.'

'Come the day, we'll ask him to write our obituaries . . .'

'For God's sake, Carvalho, don't be so dismissive.'

'Do you know what I say? Our friend won't be killing
anybody. He's just a lousy poet, with a taste for floral
effects. I'd say he's going for a role in the next flower
carnival. That's what it is.'

'If there's one thing that this poetry doesn't have, it's
floralism. It is the most anti-floral thing I've ever read.
Come on, Carvalho, put yourself on the line. Why do you
say it's floral? Explain yourself.'

'I think we've got more important things to talk about.'

But Camps O'Shea had the bit between his teeth, and
he shook his head violently.

'No, no. I can't let you get away with that comment
about floralism. Let's be serious about it — this is a
serious piece of writing. What's more, a man's life could
be at stake.'

'I know, I know . . . The life of a Sunday hero, and the
literary career of a nutcase.'

Camps was furious, and Carvalho decided that he was
furious for two reasons: partly because of Carvalho's total
lack of interest, and partly because the arrival of the
third anonymous letter had fired his critical passions.

'It's important that we treat this seriously, because a
close analysis could lead us to discovering who the author

is. I'm not suggesting that we start doing content analysis, as Inspector Lifante would. However, even as an amateur I think I might venture an opinion. I think I'm a good reader, and I think I can guess at the kind of person that we're dealing with. "Open the cages . . ." — this suggests a familiarity with the spectacle that you see every week when the players come running out onto the pitch. Do you ever see it that way — it's as if they've just been let out of their cages? Anyway, let's carry on. The glistening of their muscles . . . Obviously he's referring to the fact that when they first arrive on the field a lot of them have come straight from the massage bench, and their muscles really do shine. That's something which a spectator probably wouldn't see from the stands . . . It indicates an immediacy. It's someone who is, or has been, close to footballers in his time — someone who might even be close to Mortimer. And what about Samarkand? What does Samarkand say to you?'

'Ann Blyth.'

'I beg your pardon?'

'I remember a film about the Mongols which I saw when I was a kid. It was called *The Princess of Samarkand*, and the lead role was played by Ann Blyth.'

'No, seriously, Carvalho . . . Samarkand has a certain semantic richness. As place-names go, it's very evocative. Like Asmara, or Córdoba. Some cities have names which evoke a whole history, a whole legend. Asmara, the lost city under the sands of the Sahara. Samarkand, Tamberlaine's capital, and the centre of life in an Asia that was brutal but at the same time fundamentally civilized. And what about the euphony, listen to the euphony: Samarkand.'

Carvalho switched off his hearing faculties in order to reflect on the surrealism of the situation. Camps was evidently suffering from something like Stockholm syndrome. He was the kind of person who would actually enjoy being kidnapped. So he decided to make a noise that would deflate this flow of poetical nonsense.

'What's more, I reckon he's queer.'

'Who's queer?'

'Whoever wrote the note. All those shiny muscles . . .'

'You disappoint me, Carvalho. And anyway, supposing he is "queer". So what?'

'So he's queer. There are people who come from Cuenca, and there are people who are queer. These are objective truths, or statistics, depending on your point of view.'

'No, Carvalho. You can't go ducking out of what you just said. You said: "What's more, I reckon he's queer." That implies a prejudice against our author's sexual preferences.'

'It might be a woman, and in that case I withdraw what I said.'

Camps O'Shea was either tired or put out. He retired to a defensive position behind his desk, which was also made of rosewood, although rather less ornately so than Basté de Linyola's, and he attempted to find some way of enabling himself to relax.

'This business is starting to get on my nerves.'

'I can understand that. However, I'm beginning to think there's really not much to worry about. Every time one of these letters arrives, I'm more and more convinced that we're dealing with an exhibitionist, somebody who's decided to play games with us, to prove to himself that he's cleverer than we are. Have you sent the police a copy of this latest one?'

'Yes. Of course.'

'And?'

'You know Contreras. He started making cheap cracks about you, and about intellectuals who like flirting with the underworld. I find his reaction grossly corporatist.

Don't get me wrong, Carvalho. I'm not trying to glorify our letter-writer. Absolutely not. I just think that there's a certain truth in what he writes, and what I read in it leads me to a different conclusion to yours. He could be dangerous. To have imagination is a dangerous thing in the times we live in. In among all this mediocrity, even if we are all accomplices in it, a man with imagination is dangerous.'

'What's a young man like you doing in a job like this?'

Camps shrugged his shoulders, but smiled a gratified smile. At last somebody had recognized the deep sense of unease that underpinned his life.

'A man has to do something. I studied art, and I was hoping to set up a gallery, or become an art consultant. I'd never have considered teaching. Teaching is a job for mediocrities, and sooner or later it ends up fossilizing you. But the trouble was, I had no money of my own, and my father is, as you might say, extremely down to earth. He wouldn't shell out a penny for anything to do with "spiritual matters", as he put it. My grandfather, on the other hand, was a very different sort of man. There wasn't a cultural initiative in Barcelona that he was not involved in. And he didn't just want to get rid of his money — he actually thought it was important. I follow in the footsteps of my grandfather. When Basté offered me this job, I thought that it might be interesting, and so it is. An organization like this has an important cultural side to it. It is something consciously created, an idea embodied in a mass of people, and the way in which it develops depends on who is there to mould it. The masses are basically stupid, and the footballing public is as neurotic and child-like as any collective subject you care to name. It was as if he was offering me something that I could mould and shape with my own bare hands.'

In general Carvalho didn't like confessions, but this

one was beginning to interest him. He observed the PR man as if he had only just discovered him. He, for his part, was ecstatic to note Carvalho's interest. He clearly felt the need to surprise, and was forever sending up little messages that said: Here I am! I'm not just the dogsbody that you saw at the press conference! I'm not just Mortimer's wet-nurse!

'Have you come up with anything?'

'Yes and no. I'm becoming more and more convinced that there isn't really a conspiracy to kill Mortimer. Nor can I see any logical reason why anyone would *want* to kill him. Basté has just taken over, the team's going well, and there's every reason to think they'll win the championship league. There's no opposition in sight. There are no petty feuds between Mortimer and the other players, because he's only just arrived and hasn't had time to create enemies, on the pitch or off. So we're dealing with a one-off situation. Too much of a one-off, for my taste. We might take these notes seriously if they were directed at a rock singer. Bad poets are capable of killing famous poets, but not of killing footballers. In these, what shall we call them, poems . . . there's something that doesn't ring true, and in my opinion that something is the word "death". If you ask me, he's just playing with words.'

'Let's hope so,' Camps sighed, and this sigh signalled an end to the audience. 'I'm sorry, but I've arranged to go shopping with Dorothy. We've managed to get rid of the aunt. She's busy packing her bags to return to England. She's now seen for herself that Barcelona isn't running alive with Aids, and Dorothy wants to shop and see the city without the old lady in tow.'

'Shopping?'

'Don't you like shopping?'

'To be honest, I'd prefer an intensive interrogation at

police headquarters to having to go shopping with a woman.'

'I find it both fascinating and delightful. I could write a guide-book on women's boutiques in this city. I have a sister, whom I get on with very well, and she always rings me to go shopping with her. She says I have excellent taste. Wouldn't you like to give it a try? Why don't you join us? Dorothy must be waiting downstairs by now.'

Carvalho accompanied him to his rendezvous, because he couldn't resist a second viewing of that creature with her air of future power, and the soft skin of the quint-essential Englishwoman. 'Voyeur,' he said to himself, as he discovered himself undressing the girl with his eyes. She was wearing a green woollen dress, close-fitting at the waist, which gave a good intimation of her well-proportioned rear. Then there was that fiery explosion of red hair. And that mouth like a carnivorous plant. And the eyes the colour of green peppers. He envied Camps O'Shea as he watched him drive off with the girl in his imported Alfa. But something told him that the girl was in no danger at all.

The collective brain of the city, of the whole country in fact, was savouring, as yet a further demonstration of its own intelligence, the fact that Mortimer and his team had won their match on the '. . . ever-dangerous Betis pitch'. On the other hand, for all that Centellas was supposed to be part of the city's collective memory, the fact that the team had managed a surprise home draw against a tough side from La Vidrera, achieved by another unexpected goal by Palacín, did not spark much interest. It merited a bare three lines in a summing-up of the day's results, about the 'Palacín effect' on the otherwise uninspiring Centellas team. Three lines, however, was better than no lines at all, and before the afternoooon training session at the Centellas ground the professionals and the amateurs alike eagerly devoured those three lines as a sign of identity justifying their existence. Palacín was crowned with an invisible halo: it was thanks to him that they were getting their name in the papers.

'You can count on me to pass you the goals, eh, maestro?'

'I don't know what we'd do without you, Confucius.'

'Come on, come on. Let's see some action! This is only the start. If I wasn't here to get you sweating, you wouldn't even have enough balls to tie your bootlaces.'

The players immersed themselves in the training session with an enjoyment that they hadn't felt in a long time. If Centellas created a stir, talent scouts would start arriving from the bigger clubs, and one day one of them might end up getting the phone call that changes a person's life — the call that gives meaning to what had previously been only a dream. Palacín, however, seemed unaffected by the euphoria of his fellow players, and as he ran and jumped and did his press-ups and dribbled a ball round oil drums that were strategically placed around the pitch, he did so with less than his usual enthusiasm — as if he had left his head somewhere and didn't know where. He was plucked out of his reverie by a couple of unpleasant fouls by Toté during the warm-up, and his anger got the better of him. He found himself caught up in a duel of pushing, kicking and elbowing which the manager had to stop.

'I've just about had it up to here with you two! What the hell do you think you're trying to prove?!'

He wasn't shouting at Toté, who was pawing the ground like an angry bull, but at Palacín.

'Why can't you just play football, and stop letting the goals go to your head?'

'The bastard tried to kill me.'

'Kill you . . . don't be so pathetic . . .! I've just about had e-fucking-nough of you. You, Toté, you go and do some circuits, and I hope they do you some good. As for you, Palacín, go practise a few penalty shots, so that next time the good Lord decides to grant a penalty in our favour, we'll give them something to remember us by.'

Palacín found the ritual of shooting penalties irritating. He never enjoyed the repeated exercise of gunning down a goalie, and only succeeded in getting twelve out of his twenty in.

He abandoned the penalties and stretched out on the ground for some leg exercises, raising first one leg and then the other skywards. It was getting late. Fluffy clouds were passing overhead, and passing flocks of birds gave an autumnal feel to the space that occupied his gaze. He abandoned the exercises and lay back, relaxed. He felt as if he was out in the country, lying under a tree, with the world feeling cool at his shoulders, and somewhere in his mind a notion that he could dive right deep into the universe, a notion which sometimes came to him in his dreams and made him wake up suddenly with a sensation that he was falling out of bed. His knee was hurting, and he had a feeling that he wouldn't be able to leave it many more days before he'd have to go looking for Marta again, to get his ration of cocaine and low-grade sex. He shut his eyes in an attempt to make himself disappear, but when he opened them again he was still there, lying on a small patch of grass that had somehow managed to survive in one corner of the Centellas pitch.

'Dreaming of the seaside, are you?'

'I'm not feeling well.'

'Is the knee hurting?'

'No. It's my guts.'

'It must be the salad they gave us at La Vidrera. You can bet your life they put rat poison in it to give us the shits.'

The manager sat next to him on the ground, and his voice was all of a sudden velvety-smooth.

'Don't get me wrong, Palacín. I know you're new to the club, but as far as I'm concerned you're not just anybody. I've always admired you, and I'm proud to have you with us. The trouble with Toté is that he's a nobody, but he's a particularly tough nobody, and he wants to prove that he's not scared of you just because you're famous. You follow? I have to do what I can to keep his morale up, because he's got no balls. Don't get me wrong.'

'Sure, sure . . .'

'He's still got a few years of footballing ahead of him, and he's like the others — worried that the club is going to fold. This is a very valuable piece of real estate. If the team goes down the pan, then Centellas disappears with it — and you probably haven't seen them, but every day there's a hundred vultures hanging around waiting for us to go under. You with me, Palacín?'

'I understand.'

'Right. On your way, now. If you're not feeling well, go home. We're going to carry on for another half hour. It'll be dark soon.'

But he didn't go straight away. He waited for a few more minutes, enjoying the illusion that he was a free man, communing with nature. As he lay back on the cool earth, he thought back to an old and favourite project of his, to buy a farm in Granada and to watch the plants and the hams grow. 'Hams don't grow,' had been Inma's only comment when he had invited her into his dream one day. This was at the time when she was carrying in her belly the other portion of his dreams, the son whom he already imagined wearing the club colours, taking the kick-off at the testimonial match when his father retired, with all the TV cameras there, and the boy suitably impressed by the sound of a whole stadium chanting his father's name. What was he going to do with himself when the season was over? Sánchez Zapico had promised him a well-paid job as a sales rep, but he couldn't really see himself representing anything other than his own deep-seated sense of fear and the memory of what he had once been. He felt a sudden pain in his kidneys and as he stood up he felt slightly dizzy, but after a few steps and a couple of deep breaths he felt better. He made his way over to the centre of the pitch where Mariscal, 'Confucius', was doing fancy tricks with the ball, apparently oblivious to the sarcastic comments coming from his manager on the other side of the pitch:

'Confucius, you should join a circus!'

'Did you hear that old creep? He doesn't like it, because

I know how to control a ball. He prefers gorillas and boneheads like Toté.'

'Ignore him. Just carry on with what you're doing. You're getting better.'

'Thanks, maestro. Remind me to send you a box of cigars for Christmas.'

He continued on his way to the dressing rooms, pleased at the prospect of being able to change in his own time and get a decent shower before the others. He stopped on his way for a few words with the young centre half, who had been sentenced by the manager to a session of kicking a medicine ball.

'He says I've got skinny legs.'

'Go easy with that, because you might very easily end up tearing a muscle. You're doing well, but take it easy. Try and kick with your instep and not with your toe.'

'My dad's always talking about you. The things he tells me, I sometimes think he must be making them up.'

'How old's your dad?'

'Um, I don't remember. About the same as you ... getting on a bit. About forty-something.'

'I'm not that far gone, son.'

'Well, you're fit, and he's not. He couldn't fight his way out of a paper bag.'

Palacín walked on to the open dressing-room door. He pushed the door. The sick hinges squeaked and the door opened to reveal a view of the corridor. The transition from light to shade meant that at first he wasn't aware of the sudden surprise on the faces of three men who were moving in the corridor. They froze. By the time he saw them he was already in the dressing room, and it took him several seconds before his senses associated their presence with danger. All the locker doors were hanging open, and the three reacted to his arrival by adopting automatic but differing bodily stances. One of them stepped back a few paces, as if to protect a sports bag which was sitting on the ground, and the other two came forward rapidly to within a few inches of him. He read in their eyes a fear at having been surprised, and they gave him no chance of backing off towards the door; one of them leapt round and put himself behind him. He heard the sound of a flick-knife clicking open. Seconds passed in concentrated panic and silence before he managed to stutter: 'Anything you'll find in here will hardly be worth the risk. Nobody's got any money here.'

'Shut up.'

The sound came from behind him.

'Shut up, or we'll break your legs.'

This time it was the one in front of him speaking, and in a flash he too pulled a flick-knife from his pocket, and opened it. Palacín's skin registered the sensation of the cold air moved by the knife by the simple fact of its flicking open.

'Who's he?'

'Can't you see? Maradona! It's Maradona, and he's very stupid, because he decided to go home early without anyone asking him to. Who asked you to come sticking your nose in where it's none of your business?'

Palacín sighed, tried to relax, and moved his arms as if in an attempt to distance himself from this nightmare. He was about to say: 'Go, just go, take what you've taken, and I won't say a word.' He wanted to tell them that he hadn't seen anything, and that even if he had, he wouldn't say anything because he recognized they were just poor bastards like himself. He needed them to go, to remove the weight of fear, both his and theirs, but most particularly theirs, which he could feel pressing against his back and his chest, extending in a direct line from the tips of their knives. However the sound that filled the room was not the sound of his voice, but the words of the man who had stayed in the background guarding the sports bag on the floor.

'He's seen us. The bastard's got a complete description of us.'

He felt the first knife-stab in his back, just below his shoulder blade and aiming for his heart. As he went to run forward, as if running from death, he ran right onto the knife that the other man was holding at just the right level. It was as if the knife was there to save him from falling, as if it was trying to hold him up. When the man pulled the knife out again, Palacín fell to the ground, his hands weak and trembling, uselessly trying to staunch the flow of blood. His eyes, at ground level, watched the movements of feet and he listened to the sound of voices which were showing no further interest in him.

'Have you done all the lockers?'

'Sure. You saw I did. Come on. Let's move. They'll be back in a minute.'

He felt as if he was floating in his own blood. He felt as if he had a fever. He didn't want to fall asleep, so he opened his eyes, looking to see as far as he could, and when a grey and increasingly opaque glass screen seemed to place itself between him and the damp-stained cobwebby ceiling, he engaged his brain in an effort to work out who was the owner of the woman's face which was leaning over and talking to him. No. It wasn't Inma. Nor was the voice that of his son. He tried to think what his son's voice would sound like. Anyway, it was a woman. Who was it?

'She's gone out.'

This was a statement of fact, but also an order and a justification addressed as much to herself as to her partner in crime.

'Now, we'd better think for a moment. Just think. We're

going to be depending on that car. Memorize the exact spot where it's parked. Don't forget the keys. We won't have a moment to lose. Everything's ready for the getaway, isn't it?'

'Sure.'

Her voice was filled with urgency, and she gave him a push to get him moving. She closed the window and went out onto the landing. He followed. She ran down the stairs and emerged hurriedly onto calle de San Rafael, where she started her reluctant streetwalker routine. He followed several paces behind her, allowing her to take up her position in the boarding-house doorway. Then he turned and looked from left to right. The street was deserted, as it usually was in the late afternoon, and the lottery ticket seller in pasaje de Martorell was just a distant shadow. Marta was ahead of him, up on the landing, and he called to her to slow down a bit. His legs were willing but he was panting a bit, and when they reached the front door of the boarding house she glared at him fiercely. The key trembled slightly in her hand, and it took two goes to get it into the lock, whereupon it gave out a pained metallic screech.

'Are you in, Doña Concha?'

The only sound of life in the building was a fridge loudly protesting its misfortunes, and its motor drowned the words of the old invalid at the end of the corridor, who had heard her, and had sought to make his presence known.

'There's somebody in.'

'It's the old man. Don't worry about him.'

Marta burst into the kitchen and started turning all the jars upside down, regardless of what they had in them. She pulled up the greasepaper linings in the cupboards, tipped out the drawers, and within minutes the kitchen read like a randomized inventory of its contents.

'Come on, the mattresses.'

She led the way by taking the largest knife she could find, ripping the mattress covers and probing their foam-rubber hearts. She searched under the carpets, emptied all the cupboards and left him the task of examining what she had tipped out. Room by room, there wasn't a single book that wasn't looked into, nor a window shutter, nor a piece of suspect wallpaper that wasn't ripped apart. But they found nothing. Her hands and face were sweating, as was his whole body, and he began to try to say that there was no point, because there was nothing there.

'The oven! We haven't looked in the oven!'

They ran to the kitchen and opened the oven door; he used the knife as a lever and lifted up the rusty bottom, only to reveal an empty space beneath.

Not a thing.

'Shit! Where's the old witch put it, then?'

All of a sudden the fridge found peace with itself, and in the silence they clearly heard the sound of the invalid trying to say something.

'The old man.'

'I heard it.'

'That's not what I meant. The old bitch has probably put her money in the old man's room.'

'But if we go into his room, he'll see us.'

'So? Who cares?'

'But supposing we don't find anything? What use will the car be then? We can't go anywhere without money.'

'We'll go anyway. I'm not turning back now. Let's go for the old man.'

They were momentarily stopped in their tracks by the look of terror that came from the sunken eye-sockets of that living skull, but they side-stepped it. The room was full of objects abjectly ashamed of their own wretchedness, and its windowless walls were illuminated by one bare lightbulb.

'The pot. Look in the pot.'

'What pot?'

'Where he pisses, idiot. It's under the bed.'

He pulled out the pot with a trembling hand, and part of the urine that was in it splashed onto his hand and spilled onto the floor. He managed to contain his desire to throw up, but not his desire to drop the vessel and its contents.

'Search his bedclothes!'

He pushed the invalid over to the other side of the mattress, and raised the sheet with one hand as he struggled with the old man's warm, stiff body. Then he reached under the mattress, searching around in the hopes of finding a promising lump.

'There's nothing here, Marta.'

'Shut up and keep looking. Search him.'

But his hands fluttered like paralysed crows over the frail little body that he couldn't bring himself to touch.

'What are you waiting for?'

'He's looking at me.'

'You're useless.'

And in the end she was the one who ripped open the buttons of the dirty flannel pyjamas covering his aged skeleton, and even reached down to his crutch in the hopes of finding what she was looking for.

'Shit! It must be here somewhere.'

She stared at the walls and the floor, looking for inspiration.

'But where? Let's check to see if we can find anywhere hollow. I'll try the floor, and you try along the walls.'

She went down the corridor, stamping up and down on the floor as she went. But her obsessive searching did not stop her hearing the clear sound of a key turning in the front-door lock, and in virtually a single movement the simultaneous apparition of Doña Concha, who was muttering to herself until the point where she registered Marta's presence and stared at her, dumbstruck and uncomprehending.

'What are you doing here?'

Her second question was answered even before she asked it. All it took was one look at the mess in the corridor, and down into the kitchen, where she could see the results of Marta's handiwork. But the 'how did you get in' continued as a silent logical link between the two women, the portly Doña Concha weighing up the evidence of her eyes as she tried to decide whether to hurl herself on to Marta or to retreat to the door and scream for help. But the sight of her there, at the end of the corridor, so thin and fragile and looking as guilty as a rat, gave her courage, and she advanced on her with an evil tongue at the ready.

'You've come to rob me! I'll scratch your eyes out!'

Marta backed off up the corridor, and tried to remember where she had left the knife. However the speed of her retreat was less than that of her advancing adversary. Doña Concha dived on her without giving her time to think, but in the blindness of her anger she didn't notice an apparition reaching up from behind her — the shadow of a young man with a bottle in his hand. Doña Concha had just succeeded in grabbing a handful of Marta's hair and digging the nails of her other hand into her face when the bottle smashed over her head, and water, glass and blood erupted into a kind of halo around her head. Her body leaned further and further forward until it finally collapsed and fell to the floor. Once there, she tried to protect her face with one hand while the other grabbed at the girl's frail legs. The man began mercilessly kicking at the mass of flesh, anger and fear, until Marta all of a sudden realized that she was out of her clutches, and leapt over her body. The pair of them ran to the door, and there they turned to see whether the woman was trying to follow.

'She's not moving. I must have killed her.'

'Don't be stupid. Come on, get the car.'

As they leapt down the stairs, he tried to get sufficient air into his lungs to be able to tell her that they had no money, and that there was hardly enough petrol in the car even to get them out of town. But as they arrived on the pavement down below she forced him to a walking pace, and told him that they should separate and go in the direction of pasaje de Martorell and the La Garduña parking lot. There was no sign of Doña Concha's feared presence on the balcony behind the pot of ivy which she tended with such loving care, and they reached calle de Hospital with a sense of having arrived at the frontiers of a country where, fortunately, nobody knew them. At this point they could no longer contain the urge to run, and they raced to the car park. He sat himself at the wheel of the car that he had stolen an hour previously in the upper part of the city — in paseo de la Bonanova, curiously close to the house where his parents lived. For a moment he had almost decided to call the whole thing off. He'd wanted to go and knock at their door, and let himself be treated once more as the returning prodigal son. But in the end he decided that their decision to leave made more sense, because Marta was the only thing in his life that had any meaning.

'Let's head for the South.'

'No. Take the coast road and turn off towards Pueblo Nuevo. Then we'll think what to do next.'

'What are we going to do there?'

'We're going to be leaving with money. I made you a promise, and I'm sticking to it.'

Then, as they drove along, he finally summoned up the courage to repeat that he was sure he'd killed the woman. He needed Marta to say that he hadn't, but she didn't oblige, either because she had her mind on something else, or because she was enjoying his suffering.

'Head towards the sea and pull up somewhere. I'll ask someone the way.'

Marta stuck her head out of the window to ask a couple of garage mechanics where the Centellas ground was. He tried to hide behind the wheel, because he was convinced that the fact of what he had done was written all over his face. They had to ask the way three times before they finally found themselves down backstreets that were as ruined as the abandoned factories that had been their *raison d'être*, and emerged into a wide panorama of newly constructed apartment blocks. There stood the perimeter wall that surrounded the Centellas ground. A huge ochre monstrosity of a wall, which had borne the indignities inflicted by the elements over many years.

'I killed her. They're going to be searching for us.'

'If you really did kill her, they won't be after us for a while. The real danger is if you *didn't* kill her. Leave the car parked so's we can make a quick getaway.'

It was as if somebody was trying to make things easy for them, because as they walked in they saw the faded lettering of a sign over one of the doors, which said: 'Dressing Rooms Only — No Entry'. Marta pushed the door, and it opened onto a small courtyard paved with weeds and broken bricks. On the other side was the door which led into the dressing rooms. From outside they heard the sound of somebody kicking a football, and voices, and a whistle, and people shouting to each other. The woman steeled herself and penetrated into the half light of the dressing room, where she was suddenly confronted with the sight of all the lockers hanging wide open. As her eyes got used to the dark, her gaze wandered downwards, and she saw a body lying on the floor, in a pool of dark blood. It was the body of a man. He was staring at the ceiling, and Marta leaned over him, and thought that she saw a glimmer of light in his eyes and his lips attempting to say something. Her companion just stood there, petrified, but she stretched out a hand to see whether Palacín was dead or alive. Then his lips stopped moving, and his eyes glazed over. It was at this point that they heard a screeching of car brakes outside and the opening and shutting of car doors. Before the pair of them had time to gather their wits, the dressing room door smashed back against the wall, threatening to demolish it on the spot, and a squad of policemen leapt at them, shouting, and with their guns raised and ready to strike. All the pair were aware of was a hail of blows raining down and a total internal silence.

The dressing gown was made of silk, and the tube of sleeping pills was innocent sky-blue in colour. This much registered on Carvalho as he toyed with the pills, while from the bathroom came the sound of Camps O'Shea spewing his guts up the sink. Basté de Linyola wrinkled his nose, as if his impatient pacing up and down the living room of his PR man's flat was not already a sufficient display of his disgust. The dressing gown looked like the best that money can buy, and it was awaiting the arrival of its owner once he had finished vomiting up the tube of pills that he had consumed shortly after having written notes to both Carvalho and Basté. Carvalho had not opened his. Since the attempted suicide had been a failure, he was waiting for Camps to give him permission before he read it. From the bathroom he heard the sound of a voice — that of the doctor who was directing the intestinal evacuation of the would-be suicide. The doctor was the first to appear, in shirtsleeves and looking as if he'd just supervised a particularly difficult birth. He was very young, too young in fact, and evidently felt it necessary to conceal his age: 'Everything's under control,' he said, with excessive rotundity, as if World War Two had just come to an end. Only when he had put his jacket on did he write out a prescription, which he left on top of the silk dressing gown.

'Do we owe you anything?'

'I'll see señor Dosrius about the bill.'

Just as he was about to beat a seemly but hasty retreat, Basté walked across and into his path.

'Just a moment. Is that all?'

'He was trying to tell someone something. The number of pills he took would only have been enough to put him to sleep for a day. I've made him vomit, but only as a precaution. He wanted to give you a fright. That's all.'

By now any residual sympathy in Basté had totally evaporated. He sat in an armchair facing the bathroom, and positioned himself into the stance of a father waiting to receive an ungrateful and inconsiderate son. There was no sound from the toilet, and when Camps finally appeared, he came in slow motion, as if willing himself forward. He stood before them, in his pyjamas, but obviously feeling naked. He had dark rings round his eyes, his lips were tinged with purple, and his face was hanging so low in shame that at any moment it looked like falling off. Basté allowed himself a dramatic pause so as to enable his first words to ring out more emphatically.

'So? You owe us an explanation, Sito. And particularly to me.'

'I'm sorry, Carlos.'

'Sito, you are a grown man, and I have helped you as much as I was able, out of the respect that I have for your father. But I cannot permit you to play stupid tricks, frightening your friends like this. I insist, you owe me an explanation.'

'It's in the letter . . .'

'Your letter is gibberish, Sito. I can't make head or tail of it. What are you supposed to be guilty of? Whom have you killed? In the name of all that's holy, who have you murdered, and what's all this about anonymous notes?'

Camps needed something to cover him, and he retrieved his silk dressing gown in order to don it as a protective armour. He thus regained sufficient stature to be able to lose it again in the depths of a leather armchair which enveloped him like a friendly glove.

'Well?'

'Stop it! I won't have you treating me like this! I'm not your slave, Carlos! For fuck's sake!'

It was probably the first time in his life that Camps had ever said 'fuck', and it was probably the first time in his life that anyone had said such a word to Basté de Linyola.

'Don't take it like that, Sito.'

'How am I supposed to take it? I am confused, humiliated, and angry with myself. Can't you see that? At least you understand, Carvalho, don't you . . . ?'

'I don't know anything about anything. I haven't opened my note, but I think I know what it says. You're the author of the anonymous letters, aren't you . . .'

'Yes. It's horrible.'

'Very good, Sito. So you're the author of the anonymous letters. But does that mean that you have to go round committing suicide and putting on this ridiculous performance? You have shown a degree of stupidity that I would not have expected from you. And that is that. Why do you have to complicate my life, and everybody else's?'

'I knew nothing about it until last night. I turned the radio on before I went to bed. That was when I found out about the murder.'

'What murder?'

'You mean you haven't heard? You neither, Carvalho?'

Carvalho admitted his ignorance. Basté also claimed ignorance, although he may only have been pretending, having by now recovered his bearings.

'You really haven't heard? It turns out that a footballer was killed last night. From one of the lesser clubs, but you'll know the name. Palacín. The centre forward who one time looked set to conquer the world. I remember him from when I was a kid. I used to think he was amazing. Do you remember Palacín, Carlos?'

Carlos remained silent.

'He signed a few weeks ago for Centellas, and yesterday the police found him dead. Apparently they also found the two people who killed him. And in four of the players' lockers they discovered drugs.'

'Well?'

'Is that all you can say?'

'No. The truth is, I'm going to get very annoyed in a minute. What exactly is the connection between this murder and your anonymous notes? Was it you who killed him?'

'No, for heaven's sake. What I was doing was a game, a dangerous game, maybe, but still a game. I didn't even know that Palacín was in Barcelona and that he was still playing. I swear it.'

'All right, you're going to have to explain, then. What on earth persuaded you to go and make yourself respons-ible for the murder, and drag us all out of bed at four o'clock in the morning?'

'Don't you remember, Carlos: "Because you have usur-ped the function of the gods who, in another age, guided the conduct of men, without bringing supernatural conso-lation, but simply the therapy of the most irrational of cries, the centre forward will be killed at dusk." He was killed at dusk! Don't you understand? I'm sure Carvalho understands, don't you?'

'I understand. You are a sensitive soul. A poet.'

'Stupid, more like.'

Basté got up and began buttoning his charcoal-grey velvet jacket. Its elegance was almost an affront at that hour of the morning.

'I am not concerned with the extreme stupidity of what you have done — both things — the anonymous letters, and then this ludicrous suicide attempt. The problem is that now you're going to have to be very careful, so that the police don't try and link your notes with the murder. They are two entirely separate issues, and I have no intention of letting the club's name get mixed up in this grubby little business. Not just for my sake, you understand. I'm concerned for the prestige of the club that I represent. You're going to have to get yourself sorted out with the police. I can cover for you as long as the situation gets no more complicated than it already is. That's as much as I have to say. When this has all blown over, I shall expect your resignation. As for you, Carvalho, you'll receive what's due to you, and I expect to hear no more of it. You haven't done a lot for your money. You'll get a cheque, and I won't require a receipt.'

'So at least I'll save on the VAT.'

'And the cheque will be sufficiently generous for you to keep your mouth shut. This whole business has been ridiculously childish. And before I go, Sito, I want to say something else. I realize that this job has been a bit restrictive for you, and you wanted to live it as a work of literature. That's a very dangerous exercise, of a kind which could destroy even the best of writers — which you, incidentally, are not. I am the president of a football club in the same sense that I could be president of the United Nations. I don't feel that I have been banished here from some higher destiny, probably because I have done things in my life. You, on the other hand, have acted like a spoilt child. You wouldn't even make an actor. And another thing: please, the next time you decide to try suicide, don't come bothering your friends.'

The noise of a closing door indicated that Basté was on his way out. Camps had a look of increasing incredulity on his face, and launched into a tirade against the cruelty of his departing employer, the cold-bloodedness of victors in their hour of triumph, and the even greater cold-bloodedness of victors who feel that their victory wasn't as great as they deserved.

'His only interest is in getting the shit buried.'

'I expect Contreras will be wanting to see us.'

'He's rung already. He's expecting us at ten this morning. He's of the opinion that the whole business has now been cleared up. Apparently the police found a couple of no-hopers standing next to the dead man's body. They had some kind of relationship with the man, although it's not entirely clear what. It appears it was a revenge killing, or a settling of accounts. The cocaine which turned up in the dressing rooms seems to have implicated other Centellas players too. It was a magical coincidence, Carvalho. Magic. Do you believe in magic? No. I thought as much. How else can we explain it, though?'

'Death is like fate. It comes to find you. But it has its own logic. Sometimes it's so complicated to unravel the threads that you end up getting lost. One centre forward was threatened, but another one ends up getting killed.'

'The similarities are entirely coincidental, Carvalho. That's the amazing thing about the whole business.'

'On this occasion everyone will agree that it was a coincidence. Contreras in particular, especially if he thinks he's already solved the case.'

'We'll have to let Contreras do the talking.'

Yes, they would have to let him do the talking. It was necessary that he made the final statement on the matter, and then signed it. The best statements are always the ones that the police write for you when they agree with you, or when you need to be in agreement with them. Carvalho turned into the street and went looking for a newspaper kiosk. There were few kiosks in the upper part of town, and this meant walking all the way to Plaza de Sarriá before he found one. The news was featured in a small item on the front pages: acting on information received, the police had shown up at the Centellas FC ground, which they suspected was being used as a base for drug dealing. The raid was mounted as a surprise operation, and as they broke into the dressing rooms of the historic football club they discovered a young couple and the body of a man who had been murdered. It appears that this was Alberto Palacín, a Centellas player. The couple were arrested, and their names have been given as Marta Becera Gozalo and M. Ll., both unemployed and of no fixed abode. It was subsequently revealed that the woman was a professional prostitute and drug dealer. After a thorough search of the dressing-room lockers, four other people were arrested — all of them Centellas players. They were found with quantities of cocaine in their lockers in excess of what could be expected for strictly personal use. It is still too early to formulate an overall view of the matter, but it has been suggested that Alberto Palacín was a linkman with the American Mafia, and that Marta Becera Gozalo and M. Ll. were drug distributors working for him. The evidence seems to indicate that the footballer was killed by the couple in the heat of the moment after an argument, and that Centellas FC was being used as a cover for drug-dealing operations whose ramifications the police are now investigating. The club's chairman, the industrialist Juan Sánchez Zapico, said that he was shocked to hear about these developments, because they threatened the very survival of this historic club, which has, he said, been under threat of closure after its financial troubles and its poor performance in recent years. Sánchez Zapico, who has fought hard for the club's survival, revealed his disappointment to us, and used a historic turn of phrase to indicate how depressed he was: 'I did not send my ships out to fight with elements such as these.'

Why did the girl have her full name printed, and her companion only his initials? Carvalho had only two possible answers: either his family had pulled a few strings, or he had been the one who had tipped off the police about the drugs. The news article said nothing about the weapon used or the circumstantial evidence of the killing. Carvalho browsed through the centre forward's brief CV with a degree of interest that surprised him. Some people are born lucky, and some are broken before they even start, he concluded as he read of the short life and the scant miracles of Alberto Palacín, and somewhere in the inner recesses of his brain there registered the fact that the authorities were seeking the footballer's ex-wife and son in order to inform them of his death. Carvalho had too much in front of him that day. Basté's phone call had caught him as he was getting over the effects of a bottle of red Cacavelos which he had drunk to his own health, toasting himself and wishing for the night to turn as quickly as possible into sleep and forgetfulness.

'They're putting Bromide into a home tomorrow. They've even found him a bed.' Biscuter and Charo had both phoned to pass on the news.

Having drunk the bottle he fell asleep. He dreamed of Camps O'Shea in the process of trying to commit suicide. He'd had to listen to the sound of his vomiting, spewing up everything, and now his consciousness was full of premonitions of death. The centre forward had been killed at dusk. If destiny exists, he thought, a person would have to commit suicide. Sooner rather than later.

'How many hours have you been on your feet, now?'

Marta shrugged her shoulders, but even this simple gesture sent a vibrating pain right through her body. She felt like a tensed steel hawser and she ached all over, from her swollen feet to her tired and drooping head. The weight of bewilderment in her brain was slowly turning into a tumour which was becoming increasingly malignant as she reviewed the absurd circumstances of her life.

'Do you want to sit down?'

What was the name of this unspeakable policeman, who was just as vile as the others, but who was offering friendliness in the manner of a gentleman offering a woman a seat on a bus?

'I'm going to tell you what happened, and then, if you care to repeat it the way I told you, you can sign the statement, and then we'll let you sleep for as long as you want, Marta. Look, kid, it'll be a weight off your mind. You had a relationship with the footballer. He was into big-time drug dealing, and you were just small fry. You got your boyfriend involved in the business as well. Palacín tried to pull a fast one on you. You went to see him for an explanation. When he refused to explain, you stabbed him.'

'What with? We weren't armed.'

'Your boyfriend had a knife on him.'

'For trimming his nails.'

It hurt when she tried to think. She was sore all over from the blows she had received at the hands of the police, and all her extremities were aching from the pain of not having been allowed to sit down, not even to go to the toilet. 'I want to piss.' 'Piss where you are, then.' And she had, and they had punched her in the back and threatened to make her drink it. 'Where's my friend?' 'He's said his piece. They'll be sorting out his bail soon, and then he can go home.'

'You did it because you were hooked on drugs. If you were hooked on drugs, the judges will count it as a mitigating factor. You know you're hooked. If you weren't hooked, you wouldn't have done what you did.'

'We only went there to steal money.'

'What about the stolen car?'

'Travel. We wanted to travel.'

'You know there's more to it than that, Marta. You can tell me — just think of me as your father. And just remember — I could always hand you over to some of our younger officers, and they're capable of just about anything. You know that there's a lot more to it than what you've told me. If you give me a way out, then I can sort things out for you. You with me? I can't go to my superiors, and those bastards from the press, without a result. You help me and I'll help you. I want a statement from you to the effect that Palacín was a drug dealer, and was also running you as a prostitute.'

'No. He wasn't a dealer. He was just a poor bastard like me.'

'Eighteen hours without sleep, kid. Eighteen hours without sitting down. And it can go on. Twenty, thirty, forty . . . I can use the anti-terrorist legislation in your case if I need to, because, in my opinion, you were preparing an armed hold-up. Are you with me, Marta? Now look, your boyfriend's been a bit cleverer than you. He's signed his statement, and let's say you don't come out of it too well.'

'Let him say it to my face.'

'You won't have a lot of face left, by the time the lads here have finished with you. Where did you get those scratches on your face? We don't scratch, that's for sure. Was it Palacín, before he died?'

'He was already dead when we got there.'

'I'm surprised at you, a well-educated girl like you, telling lies. We've talked with your sister and your brother-in-law. They appear to be respectable people. And your boyfriend, even more so. Now listen. His father has a lot of influence, and neither you nor I have a lot going for us. He's going to get an easy ride of it, because his family's got money. But as far as I can see yours hasn't. So let's be sensible, eh? How and when was Palacín getting the drugs to you? And what did he do that provoked you to stab him?'

She had lost her sense of time, and felt the need to find out where Marçal was.

'Where's Marçal? How is he?'

'A lot better off than you. He's signed already. We'll get him up before the judge shortly. He'll get bail, and he'll be off home in no time at all. Don't be stupid, girl. You'll end up signing what we want in the end. You'll end up signing even for things that you never did. It's just a matter of time and maybe a bit of rough handling. Nobody's going to tell you that they're going to jump you, because you'd probably like that. You're just a bit of shit, kid, why kid ourselves? But a couple of smacks in the mouth is the least that you're going to get from my boys . . . And I won't go into what the rough ones might do. Trust me. You won't hear a bad word against Contreras, Marta. I've been forty years in this job. A professional is a professional. Did you kill Palacín?'

'No.'

'You'll talk soon enough. Look at the state of your face. What's it going to look like after a good kicking? We've had guys in here who thought they were heroes, but they always end up singing like canaries, and I'm not going to have a dirty little bitch like you trying to bullshit me.'

A man who looked like he could handle himself and the world came into the office to tell Contreras that somebody was outside wanting to see him.

'Watch this girl. Make sure she doesn't move. Not even to lean her arse against the wall.'

On the other side of the opaque glass door he found Camps O'Shea and Carvalho waiting for him. He greeted

the detective with a grunt, and his companion with a
handshake that suggested they were both veterans of
a war that only the two of them remembered.

'You've come at an interesting moment. 'I hat's the way
it is in police stations. Days and days of routine, and then
all of a sudden a case that makes the headlines. It's a
shame that our man only played for a third-rate team,
because if he'd been a big-time player, then we'd have an
interesting case on our hands. I wanted to speak to you,
very seriously. As for you, Carvalho, I really don't care
one way or the other. I'll be happy as long as you just
listen and take note.'

Having ushered them into an office, he sat down and
waited for them to do the same. Carvalho did, but Camps
remained standing until Contreras offered him a seat.

'Right, now. I probably wouldn't have bothered you if
it wasn't for the fact that we've got a curious coincidence
here. We have a centre forward who was killed at dusk.
But the centre forward who was killed at dusk wasn't the
same centre forward as the one in the letters, was he? So
the question is, what is the connection here? Perhaps you
can supply an answer?'

Carvalho and Camps looked at each other, but
exchanged nothing more than the sense of expectation
that the inspector had succeeded in creating in them.
Thereupon Contreras resumed his role as the lead actor
in the proceedings.

'Do you see a connection?'

'The stars?' Carvalho ventured.

'What did you say?'

'The conjunction of the stars?'

'I don't know why I bother talking to you, and I find it
even harder to understand why anyone ever wastes their
money hiring you. The answer is, there *is* no connection.
There can't be. The purpose of the anonymous letters was

to generate confusion in a particular powerful club and
the cross-section of society that it represents. The actual
killing, on the other hand, was a gutter killing in which
the principal characters were not much better than sewer
rats. Coincidence required that the dead man in this
instance was a centre forward. But this was pre-destined.
Something guides the destiny of men, to be winners or
losers. And once that has been established, agreements
need to be arrived at. At this moment it is particularly
important that the business of the anonymous letters is
kept secret. Nobody must know, even if they continue
arriving. In my opinion they're being written by some
poor bastard who couldn't kill a fly. But imagine what
would happen if the news about the anonymous letters
got out, and the gentlemen of the press started weaving
fanciful notions around the fact that Palacín happened
to be a centre forward. This would be less than useful to
you, and less then useful to me too, because I have my
foot on the neck of the woman who killed him. She, incidentally, also managed to involve a young lad from a very
good family in her dirty dealings. Anyway, the anonymous
letters must continue to be precisely that — anonymous. All right?'

Camps nodded in agreement, and was about to accede
to the police chief's obvious intention of dissolving their
meeting.

'Who gave you the tip-off?'

'That's no business of yours, Carvalho. It's all sewn up
now. And the press has been informed.'

'Can I see your two prisoners?'

'Are they clients of yours? Is señor Camps paying you
to worry about them?'

'Maybe they're something to do with the anonymous
letters. Maybe I've seen them around the stadium.'

'Don't complicate our lives, Carvalho. What do you think, señor Camps?'

'Señor Carvalho is very professional.'

'I'm keeping the pair of them apart. For the moment I don't want to bring them face to face. You'll see the boyfriend first.'

The boy was sitting next to a lawyer who had been sent in by his family. He was in the process of dictating the statement which had earlier been dictated to him by the self-same inspector who was now taking it down on the typewriter. He was freshly shaved and looked more circumspect than evasive, although his eyes seemed to run a mile when you tried to read anything in them. The woman, on the other hand, was still on her feet. The huge weight of tiredness in her body proclaimed the way she had been mistreated for the whole of a lifetime. Carvalho recognized her as the young prostitute who had offered him a literary screw, but she didn't recognize him, and she gave him a desperate look full of fear and hatred.

'How have they been treating you, kid?'

Contreras leapt up behind him. 'Don't ask stupid questions, Carvalho,' he said.

'How do you expect them to treat me? Cops are shit.'

'I've got a good memory, girl. When these gentlemen have gone you won't be sitting down for a week. You hear?!'

Once they were out in the corridor again, Contreras exploded at Carvalho. He grabbed him by the lapels, and shook him so violently that it looked as if he was trying to shake his head off.

'You think you're pretty smart, eh, crutch-sniffer?'

Camps tried to intervene, but he received a verbal knockback: 'Who asked you to interfere?'

'What's this cocksucker trying to prove?'

The semiologist Lifante advanced on Carvalho, aggressively.

'He's trying to wind us up, sir. As per usual.'

'You've got what you wanted out of the boy. I doubt that the girl's going to come so cheap.'

'For your information, this young man has just signed a statement to the effect that she was the one who set it all up, and that the events in question didn't start at the football club, but with an earlier attack on a woman who owns a boarding house in the Barrio Chino, in calle de San Rafael. We know the kind of people we're dealing with here. They're garbage, and the best thing you can do for them, and for society, is to bury them as fast as possible. You're just here on a visit, Carvalho. We're the ones who have to clear up this shit every day. We're stuck with this garbage day after day, and we risk our lives, and we get small thanks from certain people who think that a policeman is as much shit as a criminal. Get out of here, before I stick your constitutional rights right up your arse.'

When Carvalho emerged onto the street in the company of a furious Camps O'Shea, he tried to rationalize his sudden intervention. He decided it was all to do with the morning's papers, and the separation between good and evil which had reduced the young man's name to his bare initials, while the girl's name had been proclaimed to the four corners of the earth. He explained all this to Camps, not expecting him to understand, but Camps was anyway in the midst of yet another obsessional, self-pitying dialogue with himself.

'It's just not right. It's fundamentally unfair.'

'It sounds like you've only just discovered that there's no justice in this world. What test-tube did you escape from, friend? Sooner or later that boy's going to be let out on bail. The girl, on the other hand, is in for a beating, although if you ask me the business in the dressing rooms sounds very much like a frame-up. They arrive at the club, murder the man, and they're immediately arrested. Reads more like a cheap thriller.'

'It's so unfair, what they're doing to me.'

So *he* was the victim of the injustice! Carvalho stopped in his tracks and waited for Camps to do the same so that he could look him in the eye, but Camps walked on, muttering to himself every variant on the word 'justice'.

'What are you talking about, "unfair"? Who's been unfair to you?'

'I created a little marvel there. An expectation. And now we have this grotesque denouement. It's sickening, and that disgusting police inspector just wants to sweep it all under the carpet. The whole business has ended up in the hands of sinister, sordid criminals ... It's so ... mean ...'

He spat out the word 'mean' as if it was stinging his lips.

'They seem incapable of seeing the difference between a work of art and a botch-up by a couple of no-hopers. For these idiot police it's all the same. It's all the same to Basté too. Did you see how he treated me this morning? Do you remember what he said? Carvalho, when you have a moment, take another look at the anonymous letters. I think the first one was the best. But the other two have their good points. They have a certain strength. And they should be seen as part of a crescendo. A poetic crescendo, I mean. I would say that the first one perhaps expressed me best, expressed what I'm all about. But the others are not bad. Did you notice the touch of Espriu in the first one, and the touch of Borges in the second?'

Finally Camps appeared in his true colours. He was not so much a frustrated poet as a literary critic without a writer to engage with.

*

He slept badly, and he had a nightmare. Bleda. Bleda, his puppy, had returned home. He kept telling himself that someone had killed his dog, and that he himself had buried her, but no, Bleda had returned home, as playful as she had been as a puppy but much more mannered, as if during the ten years of her absence somebody had been training her as a circus dog. A proper little lady, walking up on her hind legs, with a cover-girl smile, her ears pricked, and her tongue lapping up her audience's appreciation. When the show was over, the dog told him that she had wanted to come back earlier, but Amaro wouldn't let her. Amaro must have been her trainer, and it seems that they were in love, but Amaro must have been more in love with Bleda than she was with him, because when Carvalho asked if she would come home, she said yes, enthusiastically, and Amaro conceded defeat. Look, Biscuter, Bleda's back. She's got thinner, boss. Charo, Bleda's back! And Charo burst into tears — ten years' worth of tears, held back, waiting for Bleda to return. And when he woke up he reached out his hand in order to stroke her — a reflex action that had remained frozen for a whole decade since they'd killed her and he had buried her. But she wasn't there. Instead, reality stood at his bedside, an obscene reality which forced him repeatedly into the same pattern of life: paying his debts and burying his dead. But as he slowly resigned himself to accepting Bleda's second death he became aware of other faces and cases from those years popping up in the memory box of his imagination: the case of the *déclassé* entrepreneur, the builder of inner-city estates for immigrants. That sensation that everything had changed but had remained pretty much the same. Stuart Pedrell was whom he was thinking of — the rich man with the guilty conscience who, in 1978, had attempted to travel to the other side of the tracks, to what he saw as his 'Southern Seas'; with ten years' hindsight, he looked like not much more than a stupid, immature adolescent. Rich people with guilty consciences seemed to be a thing of the past now; perhaps the market had been cornered by those who have guilty consciences about not being rich. Basté de Linyola and Camps O'Shea were the most dangerous intelligent people he had ever known. They moved from the world of good into the world of evil, and back again, with no need to do anything other than change their language or their silence. Basté used philosophy and Camps used poetry, but the pair of them were none the less criminals — two quintessential Caucasian criminals, mixed in with all the rest of the quintessential Caucasian criminals, who stood out less in police line-ups than Arabs or blacks. So difficult, in fact, that nobody these days made the effort even to try. And on the marble morgue slab where once again he saw the body of Bleda with her throat cut he also saw the body of the dead centre forward. The body was wearing a football kit which was stitched together with knife-stabs — a visual contradiction which in no way suggested tragedy. It was the body of a puppet which owed its identity to the roar of the fans. Nobody seemed to claim possession of this body. It didn't belong to anyone, even though they were trying to stick it on a couple of junkies, and most particularly on the girl, because she didn't have a father who was one of those who were still a power in this city, or in any city, now, as it was in the beginning, and ever shall be ... For Carvalho, Palacín was just the shadow of a memory, but he was less concerned about the broken memory than about the fact that the broken toy was lying there in front of him, and as his mind returned unerringly to his latest obsession he tried to distance himself from it. I know you, Pepe, and nobody invited you to this funeral. Let them sort it out for themselves. However, when he emerged into the autumn light of his unkempt Vallvidrera garden, it took just one glance over to the corner where he had buried Bleda, for an image to stamp itself on his mind — of Palacín, dressed in blood-spattered football kit and apparently floating, weightless, in space. He began to dress more quickly, putting on something warm, and drove down to the main square in Vallvidrera to buy the morning papers. The Palacín case hadn't made the front pages, but it was in among the local news, and the young couple were named as the suspects. They were expected to be in court before too long, and speculation was tending to identify the woman as the instigator and material author of the crime and the young man as a helpless pawn in her hands. Sánchez Zapico had also contrived to put in an appearance, and his photograph appeared in the papers, over comments in which he reiterated his alarm at the serious threat to his club's survival.

'Maybe people are right when they say that Centellas has become an obsession with me. I'm going to throw in the towel. I want to spend more time with my business, and with my family. Being chairman of a football club is very time-consuming, especially in a small club where the chairman has to be all things to all people: the brains behind the scene, a father figure for the players, and an accountant into the bargain.'

As regards Palacín, he could only say that he had done all that was expected of him, and that he was well liked by his fellow players. As regards the cocaine that had been found in the players' lockers, Carvalho found his answer surprising: 'I can't be responsible for the private lives of my players. They are all grown men. This is a disastrous situation, but I shall have to accept it and act accordingly.'

It seemed to Carvalho that this was not an attitude to

be expected from a man eager to save his club at any cost. He was throwing in too many towels, and rather too eagerly, as if he was wanting to surrender before the fight had even started. In *El Periodico* there was an appreciation of Palacín, written by a certain Martí Gómez, who clearly had a soft spot for the player. 'He lost the last game of his life by three stabs to nil, and now the officials of the Spanish Football Federation are attempting to contact members of his family so that arrangements can be made for the funeral. In her modest boarding house in calle de San Rafael, señora Concha declined to make a statement — or rather, she had only one statement to make: "Palacín always seemed to smell of liniment." He had the smell of a beaten man. And Dóna Concha added: "Life is like the ladder of a chicken coop — short, and full of shit." '

He drove his car as far as the parking-lot on the Ramblas and allowed his legs to carry him up to calle de San Rafael; researching locations, he told himself, like a film director. He scarcely paused for thought when the cavernous porch of the Pension Conchi opened before him, and he went up until he found a sign on a door that looked almost new, although perhaps the impression of newness was due to the neglected decrepitude of the surrounding hallway. The door opened a fraction, to reveal a spider-like eye belonging to señora Concha. She blinked as she took in his severe look and his air of authority. The words 'private detective' prompted her to unhook the security chain on the door, and she patted her hair and smoothed her dress as if her hands were putting the finishing touches to a sculpture. Señora Concha was wearing a bandage on the top of her head, and she still had bruises on a face that was sporting more make-up than the statistical average would require, but the stranger had an air of authority about him, so she took on the smiling manner of a New Orleans brothel madam, as if between her and Carvalho there existed a degree of complicity that was as broad and deep but at the same time as narrow and shallow as the Mississippi river.

'You'll have to excuse the mess, but at this time of the morning, and with everything that's happened . . .'

Carvalho pointed to her face, as if requiring her to abandon her role as the exquisite host.

'Who did that?'

'That's a secret between Inspector Contreras and me. Who do you think did it? A bunch of bums. A little bitch.'

'Does this have anything to do with the Palacín case?'

She took a crumpled handkerchief from her pocket and raised it to her eyes. She really was crying.

'I have such a tender heart, you know . . . What a lovely man. And what criminals . . . They should do like the ayatollahs, and chop their hands off.'

'What do you know about Palacín? Did he have visitors? Did he like to talk? What did he tell you about his past, or what he was intending to do with his life?'

Like to talk? Doña Concha reacted to these words as if she was the soloist in a symphony and the conductor had just signalled her entrée. Talk? Murdered, he was, and may the poor man forgive me, because he's dead now, and may he rest in peace. She had given him a room here because he looked a decent sort of person, and he had no references, so he'd paid four months in advance, and as far as she was concerned football was boring, and in her opinion footballers were just little boys who had never grown up. As far as his relationships went, she had chosen to turn a blind eye, but she'd seen how that little whore had been hanging round the poor man, with that stupid nonsense about a literary screw, and her tongue hanging out, and her dirty little rat's eyes — just like a rat, yes — and I don't know why I didn't cotton on sooner.

I took pity on her because I felt sorry for her, and then she went and did what she did to me.

'What did she do to you?'

It was obvious. Her face bore eloquent witness, and she realized that without having actually said anything she'd given the game away. She raised her hand to her lips, but no, no words had come from her mouth. Carvalho's eyes had deduced the facts from reading the bruises on her face.

'When Inspector Contreras finds out, he'll kill me. He told me: "Señora Concha, this has to be a secret between the two of us."'

'In other words, you got those bruises from the girl and her boyfriend.'

'Contreras will kill me — although I don't know why he's being so secretive.'

'Well now there's a secret between you and me. You and I know that life is like the ladder of a chicken coop — short, and full of shit.'

'That's funny — that's just how I see life. That's what my father always used to say, and he was right. There's gratitude for you . . . ! I'd just been out for a walk, and I came home to find the litle bitch in my house, and everything turned upside down. Imagine it — I'd fed her, given her food, because I felt sorry for her, and then she comes to steal from me because she thinks that I'm stupid enough to leave my money where anyone can find it.'

'They came to rob you, but did they find anything?'

'Not a cent. And they even turned my poor invalid out of bed, in the room down the corridor, and we had to call an ambulance, and now he's in a hospice, because the poor soul isn't going to get over the shock. A hospice is one of those places where they take old people who haven't got long to live.'

'And they didn't find anything?'

A series of photographs flashed through Carvalho's head, showing a pair of clumsy burglars running breathlessly towards the edge of disaster and leaping over their failures with all the eagerness of determined suicides.

'It must have been after that that they went to break into the football club. There's no other possible explanation.'

'That's what I think too. But Inspector Contreras said it wasn't my job to do the thinking. He was doing the thinking, and the business about the drugs was obvious, even to a blind man, and he was going to teach them a lesson. He said that the girl and that miserable little rat she dragged round with her did it because they were hooked on drugs, and I can quite believe it, but as far as I'm concerned, it was the money they were after.'

'Did you ever see Palacín under the influence of drugs?'

'No. Mind you, it made me wonder sometimes, because there was always a strange smell in his room. A cross between Evostick and housepaint. But it turned out it was liniment. He used to take good care of himself. I never saw him under the influence of drugs. But as soon as I realized that the little bitch was chasing after him, and was taking him up to her flat, I told myself: "This is going to end up badly." I don't miss a lot from this balcony. This balcony is my life. That's the only enjoyment I have in life — this balcony, and my television. I always watch Professor Perich. I find him so amusing. Do you ever watch him?'

'I almost never watch television. It sends me to sleep.'

'Well, I don't know what I'd do without my balcony and my television.'

So saying, she suddenly turned stony-faced and studied Carvalho to see the effect of her words on him.

Carvalho avoided her gaze and began to take his leave, with a new secret under his hat. Namely that Doña

Concha kept her money either on her balcony, or in her television.

Doña Concha cursed herself. Several times over. Why do I have to be such a big-mouth?! She waited for Carvalho to disappear up calle de Robadors, and absent-mindedly caressed the big flowerpot in which she kept her money. A pot with a false bottom, from which grew the plastic ivy plant which the milk lady was always admiring.

'It looks so pretty from the street. So neat, you'd almost think it was plastic.'

But she didn't have time for self-flagellation now, and she rushed to her room in order to pretty herself. She needed to, she told herself, given the state of her face after those two bums had finished with her. You should look pretty if you're going to the police station. Pretty, but maybe a trifle war-like, because when all's said and done policemen like strong women. She was wearing a daisy-print dress, a pair of black stockings with seams, a belt with lashings of silver, and three rings on each hand, which looked expensive, as indeed they were. If you can't wear your rings to the police station, what's the point of having rings? And although she could easily have reached the police station on foot, by crossing calle del Hospital, the Ramblas and Puertaferrisa, with all this jewellery about her she didn't dare, so she took a taxi instead, like some queen who has been forbidden by her chamberlain to walk even half a step. Assuming a regal bearing, she asked for Inspector Contreras, and she was peeved when the inspector barely registered her existence and said: 'Would you mind waiting there.'

And there she had waited, sitting on a hard old chair in a corridor of the police HQ, surrounded on all sides by offices with opaque windows and people bustling about doing heaven knows what, or rather she knew what, because everyone was going about their business, and they couldn't care less if she rotted there. In the end, after she'd been waiting for at least half an hour, Contreras returned. He was obviously preoccupied and didn't even look at her.

'I wanted to have a word with you, Inspector.'

'I thought it was the other way round, actually — but go ahead — what's on your mind?'

'Well, it's just that a rather strange man came to see me this morning, at my boarding house. He said he was a private detective.'

'The repulsive Carvalho, as I live and breathe.'

'Yes, I think that was his name.'

'And did you tell him anything about our little secret?'

'Me? May I drop dead now, if I said so much as a word.'

'You shouldn't tell him anything, because he's poking his nose where it doesn't belong, and he's trying to make a name for himself. Right. That's enough on the subject of crutch-sniffers.'

Doña Concha burst out laughing.

'Crutch-sniffers — the things you say!'

'Anyway, down to business. I've called you in because the time has come to put you face to face with the girl. She doesn't know that I know that it all started with an attack on you. You follow? I want to surprise her.'

'I'm going to give her what she deserves.'

'You'll do no such thing. You hear?'

Doña Concha click-clacked along behind the inspector, and her heart almost leapt into her mouth when all of a sudden, on the other side of one of the glass doors, she saw Marta, standing by the wall, swaying on her feet, looking more bedraggled than usual, with her face puffed up and scratched, her clothes falling off her, her skin moist with sweat and her eyes bulging from lack of sleep. Doña Concha felt momentarily sorry for her, and didn't immediately reply when the inspector asked whether she recognized the girl.

'I said, do you recognize her? Are you deaf?'

'Of course I recognize her.'

'This girl tried to rob you. You used to invite her into your house, and you gave her food, and then she goes and tries to steal from you and leaves you half dead on the floor. Is that correct?'

'The truth, the whole truth, and nothing but the truth, Inspector.'

But her voice betrayed a tremor of pity, because she could see that the girl was falling apart.

'Are you prepared to sign a statement to that effect?'

'Of course, Inspector.'

'In that case, let's go.'

Doña Concha wanted to say something before she went, something which would express her bitterness but at the same time her generosity of spirit, and as she prepared to turn towards the door, she raised her head in Marta's direction and said: 'As far as I'm concerned, you're dead. But I forgive you.'

And off she went, with a paso doble sounding in her head which only she could hear, and hurried on by the inspector, who was clearly responding to the dictates of some secret urgency. He left her in the hands of a young officer seated at a typewriter, and went off to his office, where Lifante was waiting for him with two other young officers.

'Right. If that doesn't work, either we're going to have to blow her legs off, or we'll have to give her up as a bad job.'

'It's been almost seventy-two hours now; we ought to be thinking of using the anti-terrorist legislation.'

'How the hell are we going to be able to use anti-terrorist legislation, after all the fuss over El Nani? What on earth are you thinking, Lifante? Don't start with your contextual analyses now. Bring the boy in. Is he looking presentable?'

'He's just had a shower.'

'Just signed his statement and all ready to leave, I trust.'

While they went out to get the boy, he returned to the office where Marta was and, without looking at her, said: 'Sit down.'

She looked at him incredulously.

'Sit down, I said. Are you deaf? There's no point trying to be clever with me. I now know everything I need to know.'

Marta sat down, and felt a wave of relief, but at the same time a terrible pain between her shoulder blades. The door opened and in came Marçal, followed by two inspectors. He was carrying a plastic carrier bag in one hand. He looked fresh and wide awake for once.

'Well, here we all are. This boy is on his way home. He's signed his statement, and he's on his way. Give her the statement, Lifante. Take your friend's statement, and have a good read.'

She read it without reading it. He had admitted to everything that Contreras was wanting her to admit to. The deal was that he was to be the passive lamb who had followed her without realizing what they were getting into. She dropped the statement onto the table and tried to think, but she couldn't. All she felt was an enormous tiredness.

'Your friend is going to court now, and his daddy will be there to pay his bail. By tonight or tomorrow morning at the latest he'll be at home, safe and sound and right as rain . . . So there's no point in carrying on with this charade. We know everything that happened anyway.

Including what happened to the lady at the boarding house. Take him away.'

And they took him away. She waited for him to say something, something which might sum up their ten years together, ten years of rushing ever onwards. She savoured this phrase as if she was tasting the remnants of a meal which had been ejected half-digested into her mouth from a sick stomach. Rushing ever onwards. Contreras seemed relaxed.

'I didn't kill him,' she said.

Contreras waved Marçal's statement under her nose.

'The court will decide on that. Sign your statement and get out of here. You've done your bit. Me too. The lawyers and the judges will do the rest. You'll see, you'll come out of it OK. And when you get out of here, you'll feel better. Police stations are a lot more wearing than prisons. Take it from me, I know, because I spend all my days here. Are you going to sign?'

'Give it here.'

'What do you want? A coffee? Something to eat? Do you want a sandwich from the café? A roll?'

'A roll.'

Contreras placed a hand on her shoulder as he walked past on his way out. Now that she was alone, she savoured the chair as if it was a warm, soft bed that could counter the deep chill that she had in her bones. For ten long years she had not slept. She had been waiting, on her feet, unable to sleep, waiting for her own destruction, and now here it was, destruction itself, enveloping her, and Marçal had gone off, abandoned her for ever. He would go home for another attempt at rehabilitating himself, and maybe this time it would work, because this time he wouldn't be able to come running back to her. Miserable little shit that he was, growing under her skin like a parasite. And that fucking old woman had finished her

off. You should never trust anyone who feels sorry for
you. When she felt less tired, she would have a good cry,
but she would need a corner to do it in, even if it was
only the corner of a prison cell. Her sister would do what
she could to help her, and her mother, and that relation
who had always been a point of reference for her ever
since she was a little girl, a relation who had been a well-
respected figure both then and now. Captain Hook would
help too, at the price of a lecture. People like to be generous; it helps them hide the poverty of their own lives.
She was asleep when Contreras came back with the
papers, so he left her sleeping and put a guard on her:
'Wake her in half an hour.'

'But the coffee will go cold.'

'Well heat it up, then.'

Lifante took his shoes off, sat in his chair and leaned
back on its back legs so as to put his feet on the desk.
The girl was sleeping in a sitting position, strangely stiff,
and breathing gently. The effects of tiredness, Lifante
thought to himself, and he moved from dispassionate
examination to analysis. The girl was an interesting
study in bodily expressivity. If a reader had been ignorant
of the historical background — in other words had not
known the general and particular history of events that
had brought her to that chair, would he be able to deduce
it simply from examining her body and the way it was
positioned? He closed his eyes and tried to de-historicize
his own knowledge. Let's see. Let's suppose I don't know
that this girl has just spent almost three days on her feet
without sleeping, and that she is accused of attempted
robbery, assault, dealing drugs and murder. All I know is
that I have come into this room, and I see her as she
is now. Here I have a system of passive messages, so now
I have to apply the Moles and Zelteman principle: on top
of every particular piece of information is superimposed

a set of other pieces of information which are capable of being interpreted by the person receiving them. This body looks as if it's had a hard life. Resting, but tense; poorly dressed to start with, but the poor state of dress has probably been aggravated by a lack of care imposed by particular circumstances. An ill-treated body, the tell-tale signs of violence, a sleeping position which is tense and defensive, and a framing element (the chair) which is insufficient for the extreme tiredness which this body expresses. With all these elements I can arrive at a conclusion, but it will not be an innocent conclusion, given that my visual memory, that is to say, my visual culture, makes me associate this system of signs with similar scenes that I have seen in films or on television, or that I have read in books. That is to say, not only is there, as Moles and Zelteman would say, strict and objective information which is open to interpretation by me; there are also other reference points which help us to locate the meaning of this situation. There are only two possible interpretations: either this girl is in the hands of gangsters who have been mistreating her, or she is in a police station and is in the process of being interrogated. It's strange how everything tends to have a history, how all analysis seems to lead inexorably to the historic, even though this tends to diminish the pleasure of analysis.

'Lifante.'

'Yes, sir?'

'Wake her up.'

He put on his shoes and stood up to go over to the girl. He put his hand on her shoulder, and noted how insubstantial she felt. He found something repellent in this contact, but he couldn't decide whether it was her body as a material fact, or the historic context in which it was situated. The girl woke suddenly and tried to stand up.

'Relax. Do you want a coffee? It's gone cold because we let you sleep for a bit.'

She shrugged her shoulders and drank the milky coffee, sipping it first, and then drinking greedily. Why drink a coffee like that? Is it a cultural norm? A 'manner', as Princeton would say? Or is it not a 'manner' but a simple response reflecting an elementary need made urgent by force of circumstance? And she was devouring the roll. When all's said and done, the girl's got a good appetite, Lifante thought, and he was glad for her.

Sánchez Zapico let it be known that an insuperable wall of obstacles stood between him and Carvalho, but when his secretary filtered to him two of the words which had emerged from the lips of his visitor, he gave them some thought, and finally decided to see him: the words were 'Contreras' and 'investigation'. Most particularly 'Contreras'. However, he prepared himself to receive him in the manner of a man who was extremely busy, looking as if he was expecting simultaneous telephone calls from Tokyo, Singapore and San Francisco, whereas in fact he was overseeing his plurality of interests in scrap iron, sugared almonds and building sites, which were manifested in a series of phone calls that bounced around the walls of a cheap office, and orders shouted to a pair of hapless secretaries. He explained that Carvalho would have to keep it brief, and so would he. He had needed a player who was good, but cheap. Centellas couldn't run to the luxury of big names, so he had approached a middleman who had once had something of a reputation: Raurell. Did he remember the name? Well, never mind, because in the 1960s, when it seemed that the only footballers you could sign up were Latin Americans, Raurell had filled Spain with self-styled sons of Spanish fathers, who in fact had been nothing of the sort. Now he had run into hard times, was more or less retired, and his list of footballers ditto. When Carvalho asked him what references he had had for Palacín, he replied that he had relied on his own memories of the man. Palacín had no current form as a footballer, and Centellas hadn't even had enough money to buy a video of his past performances. He had seen some photos, and a few newspaper cuttings from the Mexican press, which said that Palacín had won himself a reputation as a gentleman with the Oaxaca fans — 'I repeat, a gentleman!'

'Did you really think you would be able to solve your team's crisis by hiring a player who's basically clapped out?'

'I didn't know that the man was finished. He was a name. A ground like Centellas could very easily be filled by the likes of Palacín, and in fact he played some very good games. He still had something of his old self.'

'How do you explain the business of the drugs, and the involvement of the four other players?'

'I can't explain it. Can you? No, I can't explain it at all. I'm going to have to pack it in. We were already on the verge of shutting up shop under the previous management, when the players decided to go on strike. Ever since I became chairman of this club, we have paid our players on the dot... Sometimes I might be a couple of weeks behind, but the professionals always get their money.'

'I find it odd that the three players who've been implicated in the drugs business are your amateurs, not the older professionals, who might have needed the money.'

'All this is extremely delicate, if you know what I mean. The investigations are under way, and if you want you can wait around to see what comes out. As for me, I've had enough. I'm going home, I'm going to revoke the club's contracts, and we're going to have to sell the ground. The days of Don Quixote are past and gone; I'm tired of being a Quixote.'

This would not have been the first case of a man deceiving himself by his own rhetoric, and as far as Carvalho was concerned Sánchez Zapico was more a Phantom of the Opera or a Napoleon Bonaparte than Don Quixote. There was too much bitterness in what he was saying, as if not only had life not been what he had hoped, but it hadn't even been what he deserved.

'The hours and hours that I've spent on this club are hours that I could have spent on my family.'

Carvalho imagined the man's family being horrified at the prospect of having the old grouser around the house all day.

'Every Sunday I'm a slave to the game, and my poor wife doesn't even get to go out like a normal couple for a trip to the country or something.'

He spoke the Castilian of a comic opera villager, from some village which could have been anywhere in the Spanish interior, but spattered with phrases in colloquial Catalan. He sounded like a latterday propagandist for bilingualism, an interesting case for Contreras's 'polysemic' inspector. The more he protested the impossibility of maintaining his loyalty to the club he so loved, the less credible he became.

'I owe everything to this barrio, and to Barcelona, and to Catalonia. It was here that I made myself what I am, and for me Centellas was the heart and soul of the barrio. But today the barrios have lost their soul, you know what I mean? People no longer live in the streets. They drive everywhere these days. Home . . . work . . . home . . . work. Then every weekend they take off for a drive in the country, and the only football they ever watch is on telly, with the likes of Maradona. What can you do with a modest little club like ours? I've had it up to here.'

Carvalho tried to convince him not to give up his presidency of Centellas, saying that he couldn't desert all those fans, after they had put such trust in the spirit of sacrifice of a grateful immigrant.

'They're going to miss you.'

'Well, they're going to have to sort themselves out. Like they say, nobody is indispensible. Mind you, it's only people who are useless who say that, the kind of people who are no good for anything. Of course they're going to miss me, of course.'

'It'll be an irreparable loss.'

'Well, we're going to have to do it. All things have a beginning and an end. That's what my wife tells me: "You always get yourself too tied up in things, and one day you're going to come unstuck." '

'But you can't just leave. I can't imagine this city without you as chairman of Centellas.'

'Nobody will even notice!' Sánchez Zapico complained, with more than a hint of bitterness, but at the same time slightly intrigued by Carvalho's evident interest in the matter.

'I didn't realize that Barcelona was so dependent on me.'

'This morning nobody's talking about anything else.'

'Where?'

'All over the place. In fact, Inspector Contreras is particularly concerned.'

'Contreras? What's my resignation got to do with the police?'

'It might turn into a public order problem. Can you imagine how the people of Barcelona are going to react when they hear that Centellas is about to disappear from the scene?'

He wrinkled his nose. There was a definite hint of sarcasm buried somewhere in the conversation, but Zapico couldn't fathom out quite where, and before he had time to work it out, Carvalho was on his feet and preparing to leave.

'Why did you say that about Contreras?'

'Don't worry about it. It was a comment of no importance.'

'No, no. I want to know. Why am I being talked about at the police station?'

'You're going to have to ask Contreras. He's worried. That's all.'

Carvalho left Sánchez Zapico annoyed with himself, with Carvalho, and with the situation as a whole, and as he left via the reception desk, he recognized the man who was waiting there. He smelt of something very expensive, and was sufficiently well dressed to clash seriously with the mediocre decor of this second-rate office. Carvalho sensed a certain interest in the sideways glance that the dandy gave him, and as he emerged from Sánchez Zapico's office he remembered where he had seen him before. He was the man who had introduced Basté de Linyola at the conference on the future of urban planning in Barcelona.

'Who's the gentleman who's just gone in to see your boss?'

'The lawyer, Dosrius.'

'Is he Sánchez Zapico's lawyer?'

'Sometimes.'

'Señor Zapico told me to ask you for the address of the gentleman who supplied players for Centellas. Raurell, that's the name, Raurell.'

Carvalho imagined her turning to a tattered old book containing the entire affairs of the Centellas club, but instead she spun round in her seat and switched on a computer, which she proceeded to interrogate. The screen went blue and provided implacably linear answers in strings of letters which the woman scrutinized attentively, as if she didn't trust the truth of anything that might emerge from the magic box. When she was finally satisfied with its replies she pressed a button. Then the secretary tore off the piece of paper which had come out of the printer and handed it to Carvalho. There, in letter-quality print, he read: 'Frederic Raurell Casasola. Mare de Déu de Núria Geriatric Residence'.

'Will he still be alive when I get there?'

Either the secretary was in no mood for irony, or she didn't know what a geriatric residence was, and anyway she was more interested in a half-eaten tuna sandwich in the drawer where she kept her diskettes. Carvalho emerged onto the street and set off in search of a phone box. The first one he found was occupied by a fat women who was ringing her mother and was having to shout because her mother lived in a small village somewhere in Andalucia. In the second box somebody had removed the entire contents of the earpiece. The third box seemed to be suffering from terminal depression and suicidal tendencies. It wouldn't accept his money, not even hundred-peseta pieces, and not even if they were new. Finally, at the fourth box, Carvalho was able to ring Fuster.

'Don't tell me — you've decided to pay!'

'I haven't been to ask for a loan yet.'

'What are you waiting for?'

'Someone told me that if you go to borrow money from a bank these days, not only do you get the loan, but they also give you a free trip to the Caribbean.'

'You must think that bankers are stupid. Anyway, you don't have any collateral.'

'Do you know a lawyer called Dosrius? He appears to be a man of many parts. I've seen him around with Basté de Linyola, and I've just seen him with one of the city's nouveau riche. He's his lawyer.'

'If we're talking about the same Dosrius, he's a bit of a go-getter. About the same age as me. Started life as a socialist and now he's earning loads of money. Very good connections. He's got an open door to all the left-wing councils, and the right wing are happy to roll out the red carpet too. You'll find he does a lot of work for the large building contractors.'

'What do you make of him?'

'There's a lot to the man. But if you want more detailed information, I'll have to drop it through your letterbox tonight.'

'Just by way of back-up.'

The Mare de Déu de Núria Geriatric Residence was over by San José de la Montaña, and from the outside it looked like a hotel that had been converted into a boarding house for old people with money. It had two palm trees in the garden and a fountain in the shape of a Hercules who would once have been pissing but now appeared to be afflicted with incurable prostate problems. However, once you crossed the threshold the place was lit like a dingy basement and smelt of stew and the leftovers of the previous day's supper. The residents were mostly engaged in playing cards or reading newspapers, and seemed to be waiting for no visitor other than Death himself. The matron was equally short on humour, and her sense of humour evaporated still further when she learnt that Carvalho was wanting to see Raurell.

'Have you asked for an audience? You should always ask for an audience to see important people, you know.'

'We important people never ask for an audience.'

She was about forty-nine, but looked fifty. Carvalho had often observed that people who looked a year older than they really were were very bitter people.

'Has anyone seen Raurell?'

Answer came there none.

'Even if they had seen him, they wouldn't tell me. Look, go try your luck. If he's in, you'll find him in his room.

It's room twenty-two, on the first floor. Knock before you go in. Señor Raurell is a stickler for protocol.'

Carvalho's nose followed the smell of the stew, and as he passed by the kitchen door he couldn't resist taking a look. There he found an old man with his hand in the stewpot, in the process of lifting out a piece of meat and wrapping it in silver foil. He had a shifty air, as if in fear of being discovered, and when he saw Carvalho he froze.

'It's not for me. It's for a dog that waits for me outside every morning.'

'Take another piece. I'm sure the dog deserves it.'

'I don't think I should.'

'I'll keep an eye out. Take another piece.'

By now he'd half emptied the stewpot, and the greasy package would no longer fit into his jacket pocket. He was cursing the fact that he was going to end up with grease spots all down him, but he clung onto the package and passed in front of Carvalho on his way out into the street, without so much as a thank you. The detective continued on his way, up a marble staircase with a wrought-iron banister, topped by a modernist angel, and at the end of the corridor on the first floor he saw a door which sported the number twenty-two on a porcelain plaque which was chipped and half hanging off. He knocked on the door, and from the other side came the voice of a man with a sense of his own self-importance: 'Who is it?'

'Raurell? Is that señor Raurell?'

The door remained firmly closed, and a slightly irritated voice from behind it said: 'I'm very busy. What do you want?'

'Sánchez Zapico sent me.'

'Come in.'

Raurell was wearing a dirty felt hat, over a face that could have been the face of an Indian chief. He was in a double-breasted blue suit, a tie with a gold tie-pin, a silk handkerchief in his top jacket pocket and two-colour spats, and he had a cane walking stick between his bony hands. He was listening to the radio, and on an old office desk he had a cardboard file-box and an Underwood typewriter which looked as if it had been stolen from some museum specializing in artefacts of the Industrial Revolution.

'I'll make an exception for you. I don't usually do business in the mornings. Mornings are reserved for thinking.'

Carvalho looked in vain for a chair on which to sit. The only chair in the room was occupied by Raurell.

'The woman downstairs, who I presume tried to stop you seeing me, has removed the other chair. She says that she's already doing me a big favour by allowing me to have a desk. I try to avoid talking to her. Nor have I given her the good slap that she undoubtedly deserves.' Here the old Indian paused for a moment, before spitting out: 'My doctor has told me that I should keep away from shit.'

'Palacín was one of my latest successes. Not the only one, by any means, I should add. I've got some important deals under way at the moment, and don't be surprised if one of these days the sporting press starts talking about Raurell again. There was a time when there was not a single club in Spain that didn't have at least one of my players. I used to travel over to America, and whenever I saw a young player — white, of course — who showed a bit of promise, I sorted out his papers, and off he went to Spain, claiming a father or a grandfather from the Estremadura. They make their damn silly laws, and then they have to live with the consequences. They decided to get all nationalist about their football, and as a result teams were dying for lack of players. You can't fill football stadiums with local players. Only the Northern clubs can, because they have large enough catchment areas. From this room I pull the strings in clubs all over Spain, and at this precise moment more than one club manager is thinking of getting in touch with me. "I must have a word with Raurell. He's bound to have what we need." And I do. I have a complete collection of all of Spain's best older players. They come in all sizes and at all prices. In the old days I used to deal in imported cars, nowadays I deal in second-hand footballers. Life rolls on, and it's not my fault if club directors shit in their pants when the public remembers the promises made to them. It's also not my fault if players aren't capable of hanging on to what they earn, or if they don't earn as much as people think they do. People only talk about the millionaire contracts, and they either don't know or don't want to know about what happens to the majority of players. Some of the first division clubs owe their players up to six months' wages, and there are second division teams owing as much as a year, and who pay when they can. These days players are more protected, and better prepared, but twenty or thirty years ago footballers were just cannon fodder who had no way of defending their rights. What's more, they all thought that as soon as they got a couple of pesetas in their pocket, the thing to do was to open a bar and live off the proceeds. I have known, personally, more than a hundred first division players, and out of those only twenty have enjoyed any kind of prosperity. The others live off what they used to be, and that's not much of a living. They take the first job they can get their hands on, and more or less live for their photo albums and newspaper cuttings. If I had wanted to, I could have squeezed them like lemons, and I would have made a lot of money, but I've always treated them like my own children, and if you ask me it's not surprising that every day it costs more and more to find Spaniards who are prepared to take up football professionally. Do you remember Vic Buckingham? He was a manager with Barcelona in the old days. He said something that was very true: as time goes by, you're going to get fewer and fewer players coming into the game, because young lads these days prefer to study economics, and good luck to them. Once upon a time every town had a thousand bits of wasteland, and kids kicking balls around. Nowadays there's no wasteland, and people have their heads screwed on better. A career in football can last ten or fifteen years, always assuming that you don't get injured. But what then? Palacín was a typical case, and I had him on my files because one day he was bound to end up

coming to me. He had made a name for himself, then he'd
been forgotten, but it would be easy for him to make a
comeback. He'd done his time playing soccer in the Ameri-
cas, and people here are so provincial: when they know
that somebody's played abroad, they treat him like God.
If you looked through my files, you'd see that I keep them
up to date, and that I'm building for the future. At the
moment I'm preparing files on the country's best players
between the ages of twenty-five and thirty. I can guarantee that within five to ten years a lot of them will end up
knocking at my door. I'm a patient man. I sit here and
wait. Raurell's job will be to find them a team, just as I
did for Palacín. They're my boys — all the more so since
my wife died and my own sons kicked me out. I'm prepared to make you a bet. When you leave here, buy one
of the sports papers. Write down the names of the players
that they're writing about — I don't mean the super-
millionaires, of course, because their futures are assured.
I mean the middle-of-the-road players. Write down their
names, and I bet you anything you like that in the next
five to ten years they will be clients of Raurell. I've earned
a lot of money in my time, but I've spent it as fast as I
got it, and now I know that when some club manager
turns up on my doorstep, it's a bad sign. He's coming to
suggest that I split my commission, or that I get them
out of a tight spot. Sánchez Zapico, for example. Can you
believe that he came asking me for a second-rate player?
No, it wasn't quite like that, but almost. He came and
said: "Raurell, I need a player who's cheap, with a bit of
a name, but not too good." I was amazed. It was the first
time that anyone's ever asked me for a turkey and so I
said: "Raurell doesn't deal in turkeys. He deals in wrecks,
but not in turkeys." Zapico told me I had a suspicious
mind, and he told me that the reason why he didn't want
anyone too good was because he didn't want to give the

rest of his team inferiority complexes. Sometimes a top-
notch player can stimulate a side, but sometimes he just
makes them nervous. As it happened, while Zapico was
saying his piece, I already had Palacín in mind. Wait a
moment, I'll show you the file. Here it is. Newspaper
cuttings. I didn't miss a thing that was written about
Palacín, even though, mark you, there wasn't a lot after
he left for Los Angeles. But here it all is. Take a look,
have a read ... I knew the point that he had reached,
and he was at just the right point for what Sánchez
Zapico was looking for. Palacín is your man, I said, and I
had to remind him who Palacín was. We paid his flight
over, and he arrived in Spain in the middle of July. He
surprised me, because he was in better condition than I
had expected, so I tried to put the price up, but Sánchez
Zapico is stingier than my eldest son, who even grudges
passing you the salt at mealtimes. Mind you, even though
Palacín was physically fit and healthy, he had problems
up here, in the head. He's the kind of player who can't
face getting old, and what's more he was in a bit of a
family mess. His wife had left him, and they had a kid
between them, and I reckoned he was probably heading
for a fall. I warned Sánchez Zapico. I said, "This kid might
crack if he doesn't get psychological help, because it's
obvious, his head's somewhere else." But Centellas
weren't worried, and they signed him anyway. I pocketed
half my commission, and on to other things. These days
it doesn't do to worry over other people's problems.
Palacín was like a country boy lost in the big city, even
though he had lived in Barcelona when the city was at its
best. He didn't even have a place to stay. I recommended a
boarding house run by an old girlfriend of mine, a lovely
lady who was a chorus girl in Gemma del Rio's troupe at
the Moulin in the 1940s and early 1950s. I haven't seen
her for years, but we're still good friends, because we first

met in those difficult years when she was an artiste down on her luck and I was working on remaking my life. And look where it's got me. Football has made me rich a thousand times over, and a thousand times over I've lost it all, and do you know what I'm living on now? I tell people, and they don't believe me. I've worked for a good thirty years as an agent supplying footballers, and before that I worked the markets, and for a while I was even a crockery salesman, selling door to door. But you can't live on that. No, what was my bad luck during the post-war years was the fact that I had been a policeman under the Republic. But that's exactly what provides me with a living now. They give me a pension which is sufficient for me to pay for this asylum — I call it an asylum because it is an asylum, even though the sign outside says that it's an old people's home. Fifty years doing every job under the sun, and not a penny to show for it. But three years in the Republican police, and your old age is assured. Of course, being with the Republic meant that I ended up in prison after the Civil War, but I made some handy contacts there who turned out to be useful over the years, particularly the black-marketeers — the few that actually ever ended up in prison. I live like a king here, and I expect people to show respect, and when that creepy woman comes up here whingeing and moaning, I show her my files, I show her all this, and I send her off with her tail between her legs. You are not talking to some useless old fogey, señora. I am a professional man, very active, and my visiting card opens just about every door on the Spanish football scene. What's more, I am writing my memoirs, which are going to stir up a juicy scandal in some quarters. Do you listen to José María García's programme on Radio 3? I recommend it. It's like a circus! García interviews club directors, referees, managers and so on, and they let him say what he likes, because they're

scared of him — he knows his stuff, and he's got them by
the balls. Well anyway, when I start talking, García's
programme is going to look like chickenfeed. "Super-
garcía", I think they call it. I've written to him a couple
of times, offering my services as a collaborator. I suggested that we did a section of a programme called: "Look
Back in Humour". I know them, you see. I know the
football world inside out, and take it from me, the best
people in it are still the players, and the biggest rogues
are the club directors, closely followed by the middlemen,
because most of them aren't as considerate as me. You
know, it makes me cry sometimes, because you see these
lads out on the pitch, and they look like hard men. But
they're made of clay, and they're easily broken. All it
needs is for a few fans to start booing them, or a bit of
an injury, or a row with the wife or the mother-in-law. Do
you remember the case of Pérez? You don't? Well, his
mother-in-law ran off with the team's assistant trainer,
and his wife got so depressed that she ended up crying
all night. As a result, he never got any sleep, and was
always half asleep out on the pitch. Nobody ever knew
why it was that Pérez was so dozy, even when he was
taking a corner, but Raurell knows, because I was his
agent, and I had to sell him off cheap at the end of the
season to a second division team. A couple of kicks in
the wrong place, and a flighty mother-in-law — that's
what ruined Pérez. I tell you, when I talk, the shit will
really hit the fan. And I'm still in time to bring down a
good few reputations, because I know the truth behind
a lot of the characters you see in the news these days.
Mind you, five years from now it'll be another story,
because I'll be eighty by then, and a lot of the people I've
known will be out of it. Do you know how old I'll be in
1992? Eighty years old. And what about the year 2000 —
I don't even want to think about it, with the amount of

business there's going to be in the football game in the
next fifteen years. The future for a middleman is in indoor
football. Do you think that indoor football is going to take
off in the same way that basketball, hockey and volleyball
did? Where are the players going to come from? Very
simple — from the second- and third-ranking players in
league football. And that's where I come in — that's the
area I've been specializing in over the last while. One day
I said to myself: Raurell, these days there are middlemen
who work with computers and fly private jets. You're not
up to that. You know your limits, but you know that
you're the best in your field. And so I am. Look at this pile
of envelopes. I keep them because I collect the stamps, but
these letters come from all over Spain, and they all know
that they can rely on Raurell, whether it's for a bit of
advice, or for a player like Palacín. And I know it's not
good to speak ill of the dead, but after everything I did
for him he never even came to visit me, never told me
how it was going at the boarding house ... Mind you,
maybe that's because I advised him not to mention my
name in front of Conchita, because she's still a little bit
annoyed with me about the pension I told you about.
When she decided to give up her trade, if you know what
I mean, she went round all her regular clients, and asked
us to make a little contribution so that she could set
herself up as a landlady. But she caught me at a bad
time. My wife was very ill, which involved me in spending
a lot of money, and at the time I wasn't getting the kind
of contracts that I used to have, and I was frank with
her: "Look, Conchita, I like you now, and I've always liked
you, and if you were ten years younger, and I was twenty
years younger, then maybe I would have taken out a loan
for you so that you could start your business. But you
aren't ten years younger, and I'm not twenty years
younger, and I'm not taking out a loan. Why kid

ourselves?" She wanted to scratch my eyes out, because that's the sort of lady she is, but when all's said and done, she's got a kind heart, and when I told Palacín about her boarding house I knew I was putting him in good hands. She would treat him like a mother. Poor Palacín. What bad luck. Conchita's a darling, you know, and Sánchez Zapico is the exact opposite, because he still hasn't paid me the balance of my commission, and I'm having to ring him day after day in case he thinks he can try and get off the hook now that Palacín's kicked the bucket. It's hardly my fault if things turned out the way they did. I put the boy in a position where he could earn good money in the last years of his footballing life. That's my job. In the old days I always used to tell my lads: I'll get you the contracts, but when they hire you you're going to have to use your heads and look out for yourselves. Watch out, and don't any of you kid yourselves. I'll put myself in the front line as often as I'm needed, but never my arse, eh? Never my arse.'

Biscuter was not in the office, but his absence was more than sufficiently made up for by the presence of three North Africans, one of whom was Mohammed. This would not have been the first beating Carvalho had taken in his life, and he sounded out his body, asking it for some small sign of solidarity. His body made no answer. It wasn't looking for a fight. When he tried to estimate the distance between himself and the door, with the idea of making a run for it, and as he looked over at the drawer where he kept his gun, he deduced that his fate was more or less sealed, and that he wouldn't achieve a lot by attempting elaborate conversation with a man of as few words as Mohammed. What's more, the three men were rapidly forming up in a triangle around him, and Carvalho stood at the centre, trying to relax his body so that the blows would hurt less when they came. But nobody hit him, and nobody said a word. Mohammed's face showed a degree of inscrutability more appropriate to an Asian than to an African, and when he finally spoke his tone struck Carvalho as alarmingly normal.

'Relax. We've come to talk with you.'

Carvalho moved across to his chair and sat down. The triangle reformed. Two of them stood behind him, and Mohammed had only to turn round in order to continue his role as the apex.

'You know too much, but you probably don't know everything. When somebody knows some things, but doesn't know everything, he ends up saying a lot of stupid things.'

There he went again, with his 'stupid this' and 'stupid that'.

'You don't worry us, but go easy with what you tell people, and just so that you don't go saying stupid things, we want to tell you something. What did you think when you saw me near the stadium?'

'I thought we'd already discussed that.'

'I was "discussing", as you put it. You were acting cocky. And that was stupid, because now we could give you a bit of what you deserve. You deserve a good kicking. But a year has many days, and a day has many hours. For the time being it's more important that you listen. Somebody killed a football player, and you were telling me that a football player had been threatened. Now I know it wasn't the same football player, but a football player was still killed. We want you to know that it wasn't us who did it.'

'Who are "you"?'

'We are we. You know perfectly well what I mean. Stupid. You're all racists, and you know perfectly well what I mean when I say "we". We know that somebody has hired certain people to organize a frame-up and to get certain other people to admit to a crime. The people they hired were stupid people, not very professional, the kind of people who use drugs, and who'd do anything for a dose. They did it very badly, and someone got killed, but we had nothing to do with it; and we want you to know it, and we want your tongue to know it. Watch out what your tongue goes round saying, because otherwise we might just have to cut it out.'

Just behind the nape of his neck Carvalho heard the click of a flick-knife opening.

'Show him.'

A dark-skinned hand appeared before Carvalho's eyes, offering him the image of a splendid flick-knife, capable of cutting out his tongue with one flick of the man's wrist.

'Only stupid people go outside their limits. For us, survival means not going outside our territory. Here, inside, everything's easy, but outside we'd be like fish out of water, or like you with a lump of concrete tied to your feet at the bottom of Barcelona harbour. One of these days, they're going to dredge that harbour, and they're going to find a lot of stupid people just like you.'

'Who set up this whole shebang?'

'This what?'

'This stupid thing. The business about the murder and the "confession".'

'I don't know. Nor do we want to know. Those kinds of decisions are made outside our territory. You might find out, and I don't envy you. There's nothing so stupid as knowing things for no reason, because it doesn't get you anywhere. We come from a poor country, where we have learned to live on very little, and by knowing only what it is necessary to know. You Spaniards have too much of everything, and you also know too much. Knowing too much is for stupid people. We can't waste any more time now, but don't forget, watch your tongue.'

'At least you must know who actually did it.'

'There's no point your knowing it, because they're not here any more. You'd have to hunt them on rubbish tips all over Europe and North America. Who's going to go looking for them?'

He gave a nod of his head, and the triangle broke up. The three North Africans made for the door without taking their eyes off him, and before they left Mohammed pointed to something on the desk.

'Your servant has left you a note. The shoeshine man is very ill.'

They hadn't even left yet, and the room was already filling up with deferred responsibilities: Charo, Bromide, Biscuter ... Biscuter had written in his childish hand: 'Bromide is very poorly and Charo and I have gone to see him. He is in the El Amparo clinic, on calle Ponterolas. Come quickly, boss.'

But the necessity of exorcizing the omen obliged Carvalho to remain in his chair, with a painful pressure in his chest, as if his lungs had been filled with rotten air. Eventually he opened a drawer and pulled out his map of Barcelona. He managed to locate calle Ponterolas in a remote corner of Barcelona, a forgotten street for a clinic that was probably equally forgettable. From the open drawer an alarm signal registered in his head. His gun. His gun was missing. The Africans had taken it. He went down the outside stairs two at a time, and was in such a hurry to get his car started that he put it into the wrong gear and crunched into the car in front as he tried to get out. As he drove down the street his thoughts were getting too painful for him, so he turned on the radio. The speaker was announcing that a press conference was about to begin, which would be addressed by Basté de Linyola, and he emphasized that something important was probably in the air, because this time it would be the club's chairman appearing before the press, and not the club's spokesman, Camps O'Shea, who was apparently away on business that morning. Another indication of the importance of the press conference was the fact that Basté was accompanied by the club's vice-chairman, along with Mortimer, and the team captain. The radio announcer found the absence of Camps O'Shea surprising, seeing that he was usually the medium for the club's official pronouncements.

'I can now see Basté de Linyola coming into the main hall, together with Riutort, Mortimer, and the club captain, Palacios. The press conference is about to begin.

There was the sound of camera flashguns going off; then the room quietened to let Basté de Linyola begin.

'Ladies and gentlemen, friends . . . In the past few days the citizens of Barcelona have been distressed to hear of the events surrounding the death of Alberto Palacín, who, a few years ago, was an outstanding player with this club, and was once one of Spain's most promising footballers. Even though the facts of what has happened are quite unconnected to the life of our glorious club, we cannot remain unmoved at the death of someone who has been part of our history. A great Catalan singer, Raimon, says that those who lose their origins lose their identity. Well, paraphrasing him I could say that those who lose their history also lose their identity. We would like to do something to show that this club does not forget, all the more so because this unfortunate case has cost the life of one of us. The club wants to do something for Alberto Palacín and his family, and when I say "the club" I'm not just referring to the board, but to the team as well, and our fans. We are organizing a testimonial match for Alberto Palacín, between a club side and a selection of overseas players who are playing for other clubs in the Spanish League. At the same time I can tell you that we have got in touch with Palacín's family, and at this very moment Palacín's wife Immaculada, and his son, are on their way to Spain from Bogotá. We hope that in this moment of grief our great family — among which, of course, we include all of you — will show itself capable of sharing this grief, of making it our own, and we hope that Palacín, wherever he is now, will be able to give that final sigh of relief which heroes, whether fallen or not, give after a decisive victory. Thank you.'

A salvo of applause rose above the insistent noise of camera flashguns, and the radio announcer's voice rose above both combined.

'An emotional moment like this leaves you with a lump in your throat, but news is news and unfortunately we now have to interrupt this relay to go across to the airport, where any moment now we're expecting the arrival of two people who meant the world to Alberto Palacín. While we share the emotion of the words just spoken by Basté de Linyola, we're going to have to interrupt this transmission so that we can get over to the airport. I now return you to the studio.'

Carvalho suddenly changed his mind, gave a turn of the steering wheel, and pointed the car in the opposite direction to the hospital where Bromide was, with the instinct of one who goes looking for inconclusive endings. He mentally asked Bromide's forgiveness, and told himself that the man was in the company of better people than himself. The city seemed to be trying to escape from itself even more than usual, and the armada of cars driving out to the airport seemed unusually dense. As he arrived, Carvalho saw a crowd in the international arrivals lounge that was probably bigger than any Centellas gate. He had only to merge with the throng to hear the glories of Palacín being sung on all sides, in varying conversational styles and richnesses of vocabulary.

'There's been nobody like him for using his head — not since the days of César.' It sounded like a bit of Shakespeare, but it was a comparative exercise in footballing reminiscence. The general opinion was that somebody had had it in for Palacín and had destroyed a man who could have been the best Spanish footballer of all time. By the time he got to the sliding door that led into the customs area, Palacín had been transformed into the best player in the world, and everyone had seen him play, regardless of the fact that some of them were too young to have been around at the time. Press photographers and TV cameramen were hovering about with the light of obsession in their eyes, and the *guardia civil* had to force a way through so that the reception committee headed by Basté could take up position near the customs exit. There was still no sign of Camps O'Shea, and Mortimer seemed incapable of stopping smiling, despite the fact that he was effectively attending Palacín's second funeral. His head was probably occupied with thoughts of the following Sunday's goals, or maybe he was remembering goals from the past, and this whole performance must have looked like an anthropological ritual. Anthropological in the sense of national characteristics. The Latin temperament, and all that . . . Flashing green letters announced the arrival of the flight, and everybody struggled to get a better position for the moment when the doors would open and the last remains of the life and works of Alberto Palacín would slide into view, like an appetizing morsel of collective spirituality. And while the more enthusiastic were trying to involve the rest in singing the club's theme song, without much sign of anybody being able to remember the words, all of a sudden the doors opened, and behind one pair of *guardia civil* appeared another pair of *guardia civil*, and then another, and the crowd and the cameras swayed and moved with the pushing and shoving of the police as they tried to clear a path to the centre of the celebration. Basté de Linyola was propelling a woman through the crowd, his arm around her shoulder. She was in mourning. Her whole body was in mourning, as were her eyes behind her dark glasses. The splendid flower of her big pink mouth seemed to be the only live thing in her thin, bony frame. And at her side came a boy, who was tall for his age in the opinion of various experts in heights and ages of boys, and he stared at the ground, partly because he was confused by the triumphant smile that he was incapable of repressing, and partly because his father was posthumously bestowing on him the role of hero. The applause seemed to legitimate the sadness of his family and the triumphal death of a footballer who had been killed under a cloud of suspicion. A sense of the ridiculous defeated various attempts to shout 'Long live Palacín!' but when the more eager among them resorted to chanting the club's name, the effect was more rousing than their singing. Carvalho pushed his way through to the line of *guardia civil*, because he wanted to see if he could read anything in Basté de Linyola's face which would betray his real state of mind, given that Basté de Linyola was very busy being Basté de Linyola at that moment. Several hours previously he had turned the appropriate phrases . . . 'our great family . . . will show itself capable of sharing this grief, of making it our own, and we hope that Palacín, wherever he is now, will be able to give that final sigh of relief which heroes, whether fallen or not, give after a decisive victory . . .' — a complex sentence, which he had thought up over breakfast. Basté actually seemed to have tears in his eyes, and while the boy continued smiling the woman was tearful behind her dark glasses. When it was all over, Carvalho followed the caravan of cars returning to the city, and on the way he tuned in to pick up the last few crumbs of the radio news. The testimonial match would take place in a fortnight, and the kick-off would be given by Palacín's son. In a separate development, the police had announced that Palacín's presumed killer had now confessed and would be appearing in court in a few hours. The caravan of cars had the feel of a collective subject returning from a funeral. It was as if they had all just attended a cannibal banquet. The fans were drunk with emotion, and the cars seemed to share a certain complicity. And what was he going to do about Bromide? Bromide, who now stood at night's distant horizon.

When he got to the clinic, there was no one in reception and the whole place smelt of disinfectant. Somebody had recently applied a coat of grey long-life paint, one of those long-lasting paints which wash their hands of whatever it is they're covering. His attempt to locate Bromide involved him in opening and shutting the doors of various rooms that had four beds apiece, separated by folding screens which hid some of the most ancient old men imaginable. It was like a beehive of old people, a beehive full of dribbling skulls with eyes that were terrified, or resigned, or simply shut. He saw Charo first, sitting on a chair, with her skirt neatly arranged on her knees and her handbag in her lap; then, at her side, he saw Biscuter, leaning back against a wall that was painted with the same long-life paint, a wise investment, designed to be stared at, year after year, by each incoming batch of terminal invalids. In order to reach Bromide's bed, Carvalho had to pick his way round three beds, three old men, three greedy gazes, three chamber pots placed next to metal bedside tables which were also painted with grey long-life paint. And there lay Bromide, snoring, with his eyes shut and his toothless mouth open, and each tuft of his grey hair pointing in a different direction, like rays radiating from his bald head, with its blackheads and wrinkles. Carvalho leaned against the wall next to Biscuter and tried to avoid his eyes, because Biscuter was crying. And just as the chill of the wall began to register between his shoulder blades, Charo slipped the warmth of one of her hands into his. It wasn't clear whether the hand was seeking comfort or offering it. They weren't talking. The three of them said nothing until Bromide tilted his head slightly, opened his eyes to see who was there, and after a great effort worked out that it was Carvalho he was seeing.

'Jesus, Pepe.'

Charo got up and went to see what she could do for the shoeshine. She arranged his pillow, gave him a drop of water to drink, and mopped his face with a damp towel.

'They didn't even have any towels here, boss. I had to go and get one from the office. No toilet paper, either. Charo had to go down to the shops to buy some. And if you want mineral water, you have to bring it yourself. This place is disgusting.'

Bromide made an effort to focus on Carvalho, and when Charo left off straightening him up, he looked him in the eye and repeated: 'Jesus, Pepe.'

Something was obviously hurting him, because he grimaced and pointed under the bedclothes.

'I want to piss.'

So Charo passed a plastic bottle under the sheets, and put his penis into the opening, and held it up for him while Bromide made a great effort, with the few muscles he could still mobilize, to get a few drops out.

'He's up to his ears with uraemia, boss,' Biscuter whispered in Carvalho's ear.

Charo gestured to Carvalho to follow her out into the

corridor, whereupon she burst into tears, crying to herself at first, and then flinging herself round his neck.

'He's not going to last out the night. That's all they can say. And if he was their father, they'd let him die where he is, because there's no point, Pepe, there's no point. But this place is so disgusting, Pepe . . . it would be better to take him home.'

'What do you mean, home? That revolting lodging house of his?'

'You don't have to tell me . . . When I went to get his things, I had a row with his landlady. He owes her months of back rent, and she said she wouldn't let me take so much as a handkerchief away. As if Bromide had handkerchiefs! I had to pay his back rent. Let's get him out of here. It's like a morgue!'

'At least they have doctors here.'

'Doctors can't do anything for him now. They can give us prescriptions for anything he needs. Why don't I take him back to my place?'

Carvalho found the duty doctor. He was the only young person in the whole building, and he listened to Carvalho's request for removing Bromide, with an air of scientific-biological perplexity.

'He's going to die. He might as well die here as anywhere else. I have to say, we can't do anything for him, and the main thing is to keep giving him the painkillers. He could carry on in this condition for quite a while. Hours. Even a couple of days, although I doubt it, but then he does have a strong heart.'

'I want to take him with me.'

'I have to tell you that I won't be held responsible for anything that happens. And the lady who brought him in is going to have to sign the form authorizing his removal. I hope you realize what a lot it takes to get a bed in a place like this.'

'I'm sure.'

'Anyway, how are you going to take him? We have no ambulances available at the moment.'

'Would he be able to sit up in a car, or will he fall over?'

'He can sit up, but you're going to have to support him between two of you. He hasn't eaten for several hours, and I've not tried to give him anything. It's not worth it.'

'Do you at least have a stretcher, so that we can get him down to the street?'

'A stretcher, yes, but I'm not sure about someone to carry it.'

'We can carry him down ourselves.'

When he got back to the room, Charo was trying to get a jumper over Bromide's drooping head while Biscuter tried to hold him up.

'We're going home, Bromide.'

The shoeshine's eyes asked 'What home?'

'My house. Vallvidrera.'

Bromide gave Charo and Biscuter a disconcerted look, as if to say that Pepe had gone crazy.

'Jesus, Pepe.'

As they drove in the car, he alternated between dozing and suddenly waking up and trying to recognize the streets as they passed.

'Avenida Virgen de Montserrat. . . . Plaza de Sanllehy.'

'Right every time, Bromide,' Biscuter said, encouragingly.

As they were halfway up Tibidabo he vomited, and a deep well-like smell engulfed the car. By the time they reached the house he had lost consciousness, but he was still breathing calmly. Carvalho picked him up in his arms and laid him on his bed. Charo arranged around him the requisite equipment — urinal bottles, towels, hypodermics — and out of her handbag she produced a medallion of the Virgin of the Miracles, which she sewed onto Bromide's underpants without Carvalho raising so much as an eyebrow in protest. Biscuter was the first to fall asleep, in an armchair in the living room. Then Charo followed suit, dozing off, having first given Carvalho a whispered account of some of the events of the previous two days, in which she had had to hump Bromide here and there, from one diagnosis to another, from one disaster to another, until, through someone she knew, she had managed to get a place in the clinic.

'Apparently all the other clinics are just as bad. I was talking with some of the relations of the other old people there, and they said that they're the same. No sooner do you put an old person in than they die.'

After Charo had fallen asleep on the sofa, Carvalho went to watch over the sleeping Bromide, and he had to put a hand on his chest in order to be sure that he was still breathing. Bromide began to snore gently, and gradually his sleeping bulk under the blankets began to be illuminated by the light of a new day, and birds began to sing, and Carvalho stretched a bit to restore the life to his muscles. Then he went out into the garden to watch the dawn rising over the city. He cast his eyes over the warren of Barcelona Vieja, that labyrinth to which Bromide would probably never return. No. Would definitely never return. By the time Carvalho returned to the room, Bromide's tattooed chest had been transformed into something else, a pitiful box of cold bones and icy skin. He closed the shoeshine's eyes, and with the same hand grazed the lips through which Bromide's last breath had escaped. He felt an urge to murmur Bromide's name, his real name, but he couldn't, because he didn't know it. He wanted to make some symbolic gesture that would have pleased the old man, so he went down into the garden with the idea of finding five roses, those five roses of which Bromide had sung so often in his Falangist youth.

You fucking fascist, Bromide, you fucking fascist . . . But there were no roses in the garden, and he suddenly felt an urge to get out of the house, head into town, and get the florist to open his shop. He passed the first cars of the morning as they struggled over the obstacle of Tibidabo on their way to a new day's work, and a motor-cyclist who was tossing newspapers over people's garden gates. Then he remembered that there was probably a letter waiting for him in his mailbox — Fuster's report on Dosrius — and something approaching a smile revealed to himself the extent of his own scepticism. When he arrived at the main square of Vallvidrera, everything was shut save for a single bar and the newspaper shop which was in the process of sending out its delivery men. His eyes were aching, and he began to reflect on the scene that he'd just left, and the state that Biscuter and Charo would be in when they woke and discovered simultaneously his absence and Bromide's death. And there were no flowers, nor would there be any till hours later. But there were newspapers, yes, and a headline in *El Periodico* caught his eye, with its gigantic letters and a shock of the unexpected: 'New Development in the Palacín Case. Anonymous Death Threats to Centre Forward'. He bought the paper and returned home, going up the hill with all the tiredness of a night without sleep. The journalist had tried to be concise, and to convey the news in a manner that allowed the facts to speak for themselves. Just as the Palacín case seemed all sewn up, the main Barcelona newspapers had all received copies of an anonymous letter, a strange letter, which announced the forthcoming death of a centre forward. The note was not written in the normal style of death threats:

'Because you constitute transparent pyramids for your ego-worship as failed gods, and because eunuch societies and plastic warriors are thronging at the gates, I warned you that the centre forward would be killed at dusk.

'And he was killed at dusk.

'Because you contented yourselves with placing crêpe on the pyramids, and you continue from within calling the attention of the eunuchs, leaving the warriors to offer you the leisure of gods, while poets turn away from the evening and commit suicide with elixirs of perplexity.

'I summon you.

'Because you are the usurpers of liberty and hope, of poetry and victory, and for that reason the centre forward will be killed at dusk.'

Was this a polysemic message? Carvalho made a mental note to ask Inspector Lifante's opinion, the next time they met.

Also by Manuel Vázquez Montalbán
and published by Serpent's Tail

Murder in the Central Committee

Translated by Patrick Camiller

'A sharp wit and a knowing eye' *Sunday Times*

'I cannot wait for other Pepe Carvalho titles to be published
here. Meanwhile, make the most of *Murder in the Central
Committee*' *New Statesman*

'Montalbán writes with authority and compassion –
a Le Carré-like sorrow' *Publishers Weekly*

'A thriller worthy of the name: a taut, intelligent tour de force
set in the shadowy minefield of post-Franco Spanish politics'
Julie Burchill

'Splendid flavour of life in Barcelona and Madrid, a memorable
hero in Pepe and one of the most startling love scenes you'll
ever come across' *Scotsman*

The lights go out during a meeting of the Central Committee
of the Spanish Communist Party – Fernando Garrido, the
general secretary, has been murdered.

Pepe Carvalho, who has worked for both the Party and the
CIA, is well suited to track down Garrido's murderer.
Unfortunately, the job requires a trip to Madrid – an
inhospitable city where food and sex is heavier than in Pepe's
beloved Barcelona.

Southern Seas

Translated by Patrick Camiller

'Pepe Carvalho is a phlegmatic investigator. His greatest concern is with his stomach, but when not pursuing delicacies, he can unravel the most tangled of mysteries' *Sunday Times*

'Montalbán is a writer who is caustic about the powerful and tender towards the oppressed' *TLS*

The body of Stuart Pedrell, a powerful businessman, is found in a Barcelona suburb. He had disappeared on his way to Polynesia in search of the visionary spirit of Paul Gauguin.

Who better to find the killer of a dead dreamer than Pepe Carvalho, overweight bon viveur and ex-communist? The trail for Pedrell's killer unearths a world of disillusioned lefties, graphic sex and nouvelle cuisine – major ingredients of post-Franco Spain. A tautly-written mystery with an unforgettable – and highly unusual – protagonist.

An Olympic Death

Translated by Ed Emery

'Montalbán's Barcelona has a truly great sense of place'
Northern Echo

As Barcelona prepares for the Olympics, the city is turned
over to make way for new roads, new stadia and the giant
prawns of Mariscal.

Pepe Carvalho who remembers the good old days when a
hammer was always to be found with a sickle is forced to
work for Olympic entrepreneurs whose only game plan is
to make a fast buck.

As Carvalho tries to come to terms with the new values of the
present, his life – gastronomic, amatory and professional –
confronts the disillusion of middle age.

The Angst-Ridden Executive

Translated by Ed Emery

'More Montalbán please!' *City Limits*

Antonio Jauma, an old acquaintance, dies desperately wanting
to get in touch with Pepe Carvalho. Jauma's widow has good
reason to believe that her husband's death is not what it
seems. And who better to investigate than Carvalho, a
private eye with a CIA past and contacts with the Communist
Party.